CW00520349

WICKED WAYS

THE WITCHES OF HOLLOW COVE
BOOK SIX

KIM RICHARDSON

FABLEPRINT

This book is a work of fiction. Any references to historical events, real people, or real locales are used fictitiously. Other names, characters, places, and incidents are the product of the author's imagination, and any resemblance to actual events or locales or persons, living or dead, is entirely coincidental.

FablePrint

Wicked Ways, The Witches of Hollow Cove, Book Six
Copyright © 2021 by Kim Richardson
All rights reserved, including the right of reproduction
in whole or in any form.
Cover by Kim Richardson
Printed in the United States of America

ISBN-13: 9798539160173
[1. Supernatural—Fiction. 2. Demonology—Fiction. 3. Magic—Fiction].

BOOKS BY KIM RICHARDSON

THE WITCHES OF HOLLOW COVE
Shadow Witch
Midnight Spells
Charmed Nights

THE DARK FILES
Spells & Ashes
Charms & Demons
Hexes & Flames
Curses & Blood

SHADOW AND LIGHT
Dark Hunt
Dark Bound
Dark Rise
Dark Gift
Dark Curse
Dark Angel
Dark Strike

TEEN AND YOUNG ADULT

SOUL GUARDIANS
Marked
Elemental
Horizon
Netherworld
Seirs
Mortal

Reapers
Seals

THE HORIZON CHRONICLES
The Soul Thief
The Helm of Darkness
The City of Flame and Shadow
The Lord of Darkness

MYSTICS SERIES
The Seventh Sense
The Alpha Nation
The Nexus

DIVIDED REALMS
Steel Maiden
Witch Queen
Blood Magic

WICKED
WAYS

THE WITCHES OF HOLLOW COVE
BOOK SIX

KIM RICHARDSON

CHAPTER
1

We killed someone.

Okay, not exactly the words I was expecting to spew out of my Aunt Dolores's mouth, but here they were. And here we were. Now, what the hell was I supposed to do with them?

Just when I thought I could finally get a well-deserved break from the shit show I'd been living for the past months, my aunts dropped a bomb.

I rubbed my temples with my fingers. "Who? Who did you kill?" The words sounded dark and foreign on my lips.

My aunts all shared a look. Beverly's features scrunched up for a moment, but then she smoothed them, her small nose and perfect lips easing into a pleasant expression.

"His name was Nathaniel Vandenberg," answered Beverly, her beautiful voice showing a hint of distress. "He was the most eligible bachelor in the witch community. Tall. Dark. Handsome. Powerful. Rich. He had the whole package."

"More like the *crazy* package," prompted Ruth, tension carrying through her words.

"Why's that?"

Again, the aunts shared a look, but none of them answered. Instead, Dolores pushed back her chair and stood. She moved to the kitchen and grabbed a wine bottle from the wine cabinet along with four glasses. She set a glass in front of each of us, twisted the cork with a corkscrew, lifted it out, and poured a generous amount of red wine in each glass.

Living with my aunts over these past few months, I came to understand that the more wine they poured, the bigger the problem. Judging by the volume of red sloshing in those glasses, we were facing a crisis of gargantuan witchy proportions.

Beverly grabbed her wineglass first, titled her head back, and downed the entire contents. She smacked her glass on the table. "Hit me again."

Yup. This was going to be a big one.

"You gonna eat that?" Hildo, the black cat familiar I'd rescued from the in-between and revived, eyed the cheese on the table. On my lap, he turned his yellow eyes on me and gave me an eager look. More like a starving-kitty look he'd mastered over the last few hours. I broke the cheese in half and gave him a piece. He'd barely been here twenty-four hours, and he already had me wrapped around his little fingers.

Beverly took a big gulp of her freshly poured wine. "I met Nathaniel about a year ago at the Winter Solstice Ball in Providence. That's in Rhode Island." She sighed dramatically. "Ugh, he was so handsome. Fit as a shifter in his prime. And as hard—"

"We get it, thanks," I said, raising my hands. Yeah, not going there.

Hildo snorted, and I caught a glimpse of him expertly swiping his paw over the cheese platter and snatching up a piece in his claw. Clever little bugger.

"Which was very unusual for a witch in his late fifties," continued Beverly, her red manicured fingernails wrapped around the base of her wineglass. "Rare stock. He reminded me of Sean Connery in the James Bond movies. He had skills. With just one look… he made you want to rip your clothes off. So, when he asked me for a date, well, I didn't see why I should refuse. I was—"

"Thrilled," said Dolores, her eyebrows high on her long face. "You wouldn't shut up about it. I remember quite well you saying that only the *devastatingly* beautiful and voluptuous would catch the eye of Nathaniel Vandenberg."

Beverly shrugged and threw her blonde hair over her shoulder as a tiny smile pulled the corners of her lips. "That's true. I can't help it if I was blessed by the goddess with a body that is *every* man's desire…" Her green eyes filled with sudden terror, and whatever she was going to say next vanished.

I wasn't surprised if such a handsome man would want to date my Aunt Beverly. She was gorgeous with a small, but voluptuous body, perfectly proportioned and fit. Any man would be lucky to have her on his arm. So why did they kill him?

I took a sip of my wine. "So, what happened? I get the feeling he was no Prince Charming, this Nathaniel character."

Ruth made a face as she peeled the label off the wine bottle. "He wasn't. I still have the pins in my voodoo doll to prove it."

My lips parted. I stared at my sweet Aunt Ruth—the tiny witch with the large, innocent blue eyes and her white hair piled on the top of her head in a messy bun held by two pencils, who always saved the spiders and beetles found in the house and let them out in the backyard—wondering who this new witch was.

"You made a voodoo doll of this guy?"

Ruth looked smug. "I made thirteen. You want to see them?"

"Maybe later." Not really. Voodoo dolls gave me the creeps. But if I ever needed to make one, I knew who to ask.

Again, the kitchen went to silent mode, the hum of the refrigerator and dishwasher cutting into the silence. Though no words were needed to see the gravity of this situation, if the tight expressions on each aunt's face were any indication.

My shoulders stiffened with tension in the new silence until Beverly broke it.

She lifted her head and said, "It started about a month after we were dating." Her face twisted in a memory that would haunt her for the rest of her life. "There were little signs, you know, at the beginning. But I ignored them. I thought I was overreacting." She gave a forced laugh. "How could Nathaniel Vandenberg be anything other than a perfect gentleman? It was absurd."

Fury seemed to stop my heart. I frowned, knowing what she was trying to articulate without having to say the words. "He hit you?" I loathed nothing more than an abusive man. It got me all worked up, and not in a good way.

"Worse. Much worse," informed Dolores, her voice strained. "When she came home with bruises around her neck one morning, I knew precisely what *kind* of man he was."

"The kind you push down the basement and forget about," growled Ruth, rolling a torn piece of the wine bottle's label between her fingers, a crazed look in her eyes.

Grief and anger slammed into me at the thought of anyone hurting my Aunt Beverly. And bruises around her neck could only be one thing. He'd tried to strangle her.

Fury gripped me. "Son of a bitch bastard."

Beverly wiped at her eyes. "He did things to me… he… he…" She swallowed hard, her face pale, and my gut twisted, that piece of cheese threatening to say hello again. She shifted on her chair and said, "We all know there's not a prude bone in this exquisite body. I'm the first one to try new things in the bedroom. Hell, I *invent* things in the bedroom. The Kama Sutra's got nothing on me. I'm the Beverly Sutra of my generation." Again, that forced smile hidden behind a mask of horror. "But…" Tear-framed green eyes met mine, and a terrible fear lay in her gaze. "But the things he did to me were… unnatural."

I stiffened in my seat, my imagination running wild, afraid to ask what kinds of things she meant because I had a pretty good idea what they were.

Beverly took a sip of her wine and let out a shaky breath. "He promised he would stop. He booked a suite at the Harbor Inn Hotel in Cape Elizabeth for the weekend. We were going to spend a romantic weekend, just the two of us." She brushed another tear away. "He could be persuasive, and I believed him." She shook her head as angry tears spilled down her pretty face. "I was so stupid."

Dolores reached out and tapped her sister's hand. "Stop. This isn't your fault. You didn't ask for this to happen. The witch was crazy."

"He was a psychopath," blurted Ruth. She twisted her face. "Or is it sociopath? I always get these two confused. Oh, I know. He's a psyciopath," she added happily.

Now, I was really interested. "And? What happened?"

"Well." Dolores leaned back in her chair, her face hard and her lips pressed together. Her gaze flicked to Beverly before she spoke. "When she didn't come home after the weekend—"

"We went looking for her at the Harbor Inn Hotel," interjected Ruth, her eyes on Beverly and looking like she was about to burst into tears.

Dolores cleared her throat. "When we found her room, she was …" Her expression darkened with horror. "She was on the floor. Bleeding, broken, barely alive. He'd performed the magicae effusio spell on her."

"What's that?" It sounded familiar, like I'd read about it or heard of it, but I couldn't remember.

"An illegal spell," answered Ruth flatly. She looked over at Beverly. I could see that my aunt was still struggling to keep it together.

"It's a magic absorption spell. It's when a witch taps into another witch's power to drain them of it." Dolores's expression was laced with a threatening warning. "The way a vampire might drain the blood from its victim. Only this spell kills the witch in question and absorbs her power inside the other witch, making them stronger."

My jaw clenched. "Like the immortals in *Highlander*."

Dolores raised a questioning brow. "I've never heard of the *Highlander* immortals? Are they some kind of demon?"

Hildo chuckled, and I shook my head. "Eighties movie. Never mind." Though it was cult classic and one of my favs. Christopher Lambert in a kilt? Need I say more?"

Beverly began to sob silently in her chair. The sound tore some holes in my heart until I could practically feel it leaking. I strained to keep my damn waterworks from spilling all over my face. I hated seeing her like that—frail, defeated, beaten. If this Nathaniel character wasn't already dead, I would have killed him myself, and then I would have raised him from the dead, only to kill him again.

"Nathaniel was in the shower when we got there, so he didn't hear us come in," continued Dolores. Brow pinched, she inched forward in her chair, the emotion in her voice raw, and she blinked fast. "We were doing everything we could to revive her."

"And then he came out," said Ruth. Her shoulders stiffened. "And he tried to do to us what he did to Beverly."

Hildo whistled. "Looking at your expression, that was a mistake. Am I right?" said the cat, and Ruth squared her shoulders proudly.

I leaned forward. "And?" I asked, though I already knew the answer. I caught a glimpse of Ruth sneaking a piece of cheese in Hildo's direction.

"And…" Dolores let out a sigh. "We fought. We won. End of story."

I cocked a brow. "I seriously doubt the story ends there."

"We tried to make him stop," said Ruth. "We begged him, but he wouldn't. And then… and then we might have *accidentally* killed him."

"How so?"

"He was going to kill us too. We pushed back… maybe a little too hard… and he died. It was an accident. I never meant to kill him —"

"I did." Dolores's scowl was fierce, and she reminded me of Gran. "It was self-defense. We were within our rights to fight back. To make him stop. To do whatever it took to save ourselves."

My gaze fell on Beverly. Her eyes were red, but she'd stopped crying. "You saved Beverly."

9

KIM RICHARDSON

Dolores's lips twisted in thought. "Having him in the same room saved her. We had minutes to work. Maybe less. We pulled Nathaniel's body next to Beverly's, and we were able to reverse the magicae effusio spell."

My gaze roved around my aunts. A new appreciation blossomed for them, how they saved their sister from this psychotic freak. They were badasses. This sisterhood was tight. Every family had its share of dark secrets. This was theirs. But I was also touched that they trusted me enough to share their secret with me.

A pair of black ears rose from Ruth's lap, followed by a head and a pair of yellow eyes. Hildo. I glanced down at my now-empty lap. How the hell did he manage that? Sneaky little furball.

My eyes fell on Beverly. "I'm sorry. I'm sorry this happened to you." My throat tightened. I didn't know what else to say for fear of bringing more pain to her by reliving the experience. She'd been traumatized enough tonight.

Beverly said nothing as she took another sip of wine, blinking fast.

"Okay, I get it." I leaned back in my chair and eyed that letter on the table. "I would have killed the bastard too. The creep deserved to die, and it was self-defense. But… what does the letter have to do with anything?"

"Everything." After a moment, Dolores emptied the last of the wine in her glass.

Beverly stood. "I'll get another bottle."

Uh-oh.

"You see, Tessa. Nathaniel comes from a line of one of the oldest and most prominent and powerful White witch families," Dolores explained just as Beverly came back with another opened bottle of the same wine and poured some in Dolores's glass.

Beverly set the bottle on the table and took her seat, her shoulders and face tight with an old fear.

"His family's loaded," said Ruth and spread her hands wide to show me just how big of an amount.

"Thanks for that visual, Ruth," snapped Dolores, pulling her gaze from her sister back to the letter. She looked up at me and said, "This letter is from MIAD." At my questioning frown, she added, "Merlin Internal Affairs Division. Think of them as the internal affairs within the Merlins. An internal investigative division. The group examines incidents, possible suspicions of lawbreaking, and professional misconduct attributed to Merlins—a police force policing itself."

"They can take our Merlin licenses away." Ruth snapped a cracker in half. She gave one piece to Hildo and popped the other into her mouth.

Dolores interlaced her fingers on the table. "You see, Nathaniel's family is looking for him.

They filed a missing person's report. The letter states his last whereabouts were here in Hollow Cove. Beverly is mentioned." Dolores sighed through her nose. "They're coming here. To investigate us."

"What happens if they find out you had something to do with his *disappearance*?"

"They'll take our licenses and make sure the Davenport name goes down hard," said Dolores.

I edged closer in my chair. "My license as well?"

"Maybe not yours," said Beverly. "But our reputation as Davenport Merlins will be finished."

Great. Just when I just was finally starting to like my Merlin status.

Dolores tapped a finger on the table. "But I'm worried about his *family*. If they find out... their enemies have a way of disappearing... never to be seen or heard from again."

"Poof," said Ruth, making hand gestures. She was on fire tonight.

"Then..." I said, leaning back, "we make sure they don't find anything that'll lead them back to you." I didn't like the way the three sisters glanced at each other again after I'd said that, like there was a giant piece of the puzzle they still hadn't told me. And I had a feeling I knew what that was.

I cast my gaze to each aunt in turn, my heart leaping in my chest. "Where's the body?"

Dolores gave me a nonchalant shrug and said, "We buried him in the backyard."

Of course they did.

CHAPTER
2

My boots crunched on the snow as I followed Dolores and Beverly across the backyard to the left of Davenport House, past Ruth's vegetable garden (which was immersed under two feet of snow) to a line of leafless oak trees. The sky above us was black with not a single star or the moon in sight.

Dolores's witch light was our only source of light, and it followed us like a well-trained pixie, hovering three feet above our heads and showering the ground in yellow light.

"What happened to Ruth?" She'd disappeared, she and Hildo both, while we were putting on our coats and boots.

"Probably got lost in the house again." Beverly swung her red feather boa around her neck, over her red wool, mid-length coat that she'd paired with red leather knee-high boots. "It happens when she drinks too much wine. Opens the wrong door, falls asleep. We lost her in the basement once for an entire night."

I laughed. "I'm not surprised."

Dolores gave her sister a contemptuous look. "You look ridiculous with that around your neck."

Beverly gave a puff. "It's called having style. Not that you would know."

Dolores made a sound of disbelief in her throat. "It's called looking like a five-dollar hooker."

I was just about to open my mouth to tell them this wasn't the time to start arguing about five-dollar hookers when I heard the sound of someone approaching.

The height and build matched that of Ruth, but I couldn't see her clearly in the darkness. But when she stepped into the light…

"Uh… Ruth?"

A black hoodie covered her head, hiding most of her white hair. She had on a pair of black pants and finished the look with black leather gloves. On her face, she wore a smile, but the rest was covered in black war paint.

"Ruth? What the hell are you wearing? And what's that on your face?" growled Dolores.

Ruth beamed. "I'm incognito," she whispered. "I'm wearing a disguise."

I bit my tongue to stop from laughing, but I couldn't help the smile that marked my face. God, I loved my Aunt Ruth. There was never a dull moment with her in my life.

Beverly rolled her eyes and smacked her forehead. "I need another drink."

"Who are you in disguise from? The snow?" Dolores raised her hands. "We're standing on our property in the middle of winter in the middle of the night. Who do you think is watching us? Frosty the Snowman? There's nothing here but trees and snow."

"And a dead body, apparently," I muttered, to which Dolores shot me a glare.

Ruth shrugged. "I like to be prepared. That's all. No need to be rude."

Dolores shook her head. "And you wonder why the MIAD are coming to investigate us." She raised her voice and said, "Because we're all mad!"

Ruth in disguise was a riot. But the real ticket was when I spotted Hildo.

The cat, well, looks could be deceiving, stepped forward from behind Ruth's legs, the snow coming up to his knees.

On his head was a headband with large, floppy, light-brown puppy ears attached. A long muzzle with a large brown plastic nose covered his mouth and was attached at the back of his head with string.

Hildo was disguised as a dog.

This night was just getting better and better.

Beverly pressed a hand on her hip. "Make that two more drinks."

Hildo was a cute cat, but he was *adorable* as a puppy.

"Perfect," growled Dolores. "It's the Scooby-Doo gang." She marched away, her hands clenched into fists with her witch light following above her.

"You guys look great," I said, making Ruth smile, her teeth brilliant in the witch light.

"I look ridiculous," muttered Hildo, though I couldn't see his mouth move behind the mask.

"Here," came Dolores's irritated voice. "This is the place."

We all rushed forward to the spot where Dolores was pointing, a long patch of grass under a birdbath, which made no sense considering all the snow we'd gotten over the past week.

It was as though someone had poured a bucket of hot water over the snow, leaving a six-foot strip of grass, the size of a single mattress. A soft humming came from the birdbath. No, not the birdbath, but from the body six feet under. Magic.

It didn't take an expert in magic to recognize the power the dead witch still held. It was making the freaking snow melt. And it wouldn't

17

take a genius to find the spot where they'd buried him either. It was like a giant sign claiming, "The asshole's right here."

I looked at my aunts. "Who else knows about this? Does Marcus know?"

"Cauldron, no." Dolores's eyebrows shot to her hairline. "Just us. And now you and Hildo."

I stepped on the patch of grass, and my leg reverberated with power. This was not good. "Why didn't you tell anyone? It was self-defense. They can't hang you for trying to protect yourselves."

"Witches have been hung for much less," expressed Dolores. "And burned."

The thrumming of power was starting to make me anxious. "This is bad. You have to come clean."

"What!" Dolores threw up her hands, her face incredulous. "And end up in Grimway Citadel? The witch prison? Is that what you want for us?"

"No, of course not. But… what about Marcus? I'm sure he'll understand. He loves all of you. You're like family to him."

"We can't tell him." The witch light cast dark shadows over Beverly, making her look years older. "We buried the body about a year ago. It makes us look guilty."

She had a point.

Dolores rubbed her temples. She looked at me and said, "Marcus is a man of principle and honor. He'll be forced to tell the Gray Council and the White witch council. There'll be an investigation, and we'll be found guilty. Simple as that."

I stared at the patch of green grass. Forget about going to see Marcus later. I'd text him that I needed to stay with my aunts. Family business. He'd understand.

Ruth moved next to me with Hildo perched on her shoulder. She wrapped her arms around herself and said, "We panicked. Beverly was injured. She was close to death. We put all our efforts into saving her. We didn't think someone would ever come looking for him. Being the way he was."

"But someone is." I exhaled, thoughts swirling. I knew what I had to do, knew what I had to say now, and I braced myself. "When will the MIAD be here?"

"Tomorrow afternoon," answered Dolores.

"Ladies." I flicked my gaze to each aunt. I swallowed hard and said, "We need to move the body."

My aunts all looked at me like I was about to jump off the roof of Davenport House to see if I could fly.

Dolores was the first one to break the spell of silence. "You cannot be serious?"

"We have to," I pressed. I pointed to the grass below the birdbath. "X marks the spot. And in this case, it's that strip of grass. It's the first place they're going to look. You know I'm right."

I could tell they knew what I was saying was right. They just didn't like it.

Dolores let out a long sigh. "I'll get the shovels." I watched as her tall frame moved toward the white garden shed, which was a miniature version of Davenport House. She came back moments later with two shovels and a rope. "There're only two. We'll have to take turns."

Dolores dropped the rope on the ground and pushed one of the shovels at me. "Me?" I said, surprised, though I knew I shouldn't be.

"Yeah, you," said Dolores. "This is your bright idea. Start digging."

I grabbed the shovel, slightly irritated because one, I hadn't buried the guy in the first place, and two, Beverly was staring at me with a satisfied smile on her face, which didn't help.

I leaned on the handle. "Isn't there a spell that can dig for us?"

"There isn't," said Beverly quickly, and by her tone, I knew it was likely something they'd looked into a year ago.

Ruth moved in and quickly removed the birdbath for us. When she caught me looking, she gave me a thumbs-up.

"All clear," she said.

Okay then.

Seeing that Dolores had picked the front of the grave (I called it like it was) I moved to the other edge. With my shovel firmly in my grip, I pushed the blade into the soil, and I was surprised at how easily it went in. The ground wasn't frozen at all. Pressing my right boot on the shovel's step, I used my weight and pushed down, getting the shovel in the earth, and began to dig.

Even taking turns every half hour, it still took us about three hours of constant digging before we finally saw progress—or rather *felt* progress, all the while Hildo giving us some encouragement.

"You've got this," he said. "Lift with your legs. Not your back. That's it."

When the edge of my shovel hit something hard, I flinched, feeling both disgusted and excited. "I've got something," I said, panting.

"Thank the cauldron." Beverly tossed her shovel away, her face red and sweaty from all the digging. She'd removed her feather boa and her coat hours ago. "The last time I was this sweaty, I was naked in a sauna, with Jason Lang between my thighs," she said with a smile and cocked her hip.

A few specks of dirt covered the left side of her face, but I wasn't about to tell her. It was hard to imagine that only a year ago, the three of them had sneaked the dead witch into the Volvo (so they'd told me), dragged him all the way out here, and dug this grave in the middle of February. I was pretty certain the ground had been frozen then.

I set my shovel down and knelt. A tangle of dark cloth poked through the earth. Without the witch light casting down illumination as a spotlight, I would have thought it was just dirt. Using my gloved hands, I leaned forward and began to remove some of the earth, trying not to think about what I was actually doing, that my fingers—though gloved, thank the cauldron—were touching a dead witch.

A dead witch who'd tried to kill my aunts, no less.

The thrum of magic was even more intense now, sliding over my skin like tiny electrical currents and making me shiver. Jaw clenched, I picked up clumps and pushed them to the side until I found what I believed were legs and a torso. I kept going, moving the earth off the body and noticing that Beverly was just standing there watching. Finally, I wiped the earth from around the shoulders to the head.

"Holy crap," I said, wiping the last earth away from his face.

There, resting at the foot of the hole we'd just dug, were the remains of the witch Nathaniel Vandenberg.

I'd seen my share of dead bodies before, just a few weeks ago when the town's dead rose from the cemetery to say hello, but that's not what had me staring in utter shock for a few seconds.

I blinked at a handsome face with a strong, clean-shaven jaw and a straight nose. Hints of gray graced his otherwise immaculate raven-black hair. Even covered in dirt and earth I could see that his dark clothes were the expensive kind, possibly a silk shirt. He looked to be in his fifties and in excellent shape. It was no wonder Beverly had fallen for him. Alive, he must have been quite the catch.

And the eyes? Well, they were dark and staring right at me. Weird.

He was holding up pretty well for a man who'd been dead for over a year. There were no signs of decomposition. Weirder. For whatever reasons, I was expecting to see discolored skin, a sunken face with chunks of missing flesh like the dead that had risen from the cemetery a few weeks back, some pale bone, and possibly worms, or other squiggly critters.

This, well, this was nothing like it.

And then it hit me that I should be smelling the stench of rot and other unmentionables of a decomposing body. Yet all I smelled was the scent of earth and leaves.

"Do all witches preserve like this?" I asked, thinking of Gran. "It's like he's made of wax or something?"

"No." Dolores leaned over the edge of the six-foot hole we'd dug and looked down at me.

"No. We cast a conserving spell before we covered him up. To keep the coyotes away and the smell from alerting the neighbors."

Smart. If it weren't for the visit from the MIAD, Nathaniel could have been buried here forever.

"His eyes are open?" Ruth's face appeared next to Dolores. "He's alive!" shrilled Ruth.

Dolores slapped her sister on the arm. "Quiet, you idiot. Do you want to wake up the whole town? He's been in the ground for over a year. How can he be alive?"

"I know that." A frown lined Ruth's face. "But why are his eyes like that? Should they be like that? I don't like the way he's staring at me."

Ruth had a point. Nathaniel's eyes looked... *alive.*

Movement caught my eye. Beverly stepped forward and gave Nathaniel's body a hard kick in the nads.

"There," she said, a satisfied smile on her face as she pressed her hands on her hips. "The bastard's dead."

This was a strange night. One to go down in my strangest-nights-ever book of records.

A heap of rope fell next to me. "Here," said Dolores. "Wrap the rope around his armpits and we'll pull the bastard out."

Like I said. Strange night.

After I'd done what I was instructed, I climbed out of the hole, and the four of us, Hildo cheering us on, pulled on the rope until finally, we'd hauled Nathaniel's body out and onto the snow.

I let go of the rope and bent over panting. "Heavy sonofabitch."

"The dead always are," commented Hildo, back perched on Ruth's left shoulder.

"What do we do now?" Ruth kept giving the dead witch covert glances, as though if she stared at him long enough, he'd come back to life.

"Good question," said Beverly. "Now that we've done all this work, what do we do with him? Where do we put him?" Her face twisted in a mix of disgust and anger as she eyed Nathaniel's body as though she was contemplating kicking him again.

"The town's cemetery," I answered, knowing it was the right place. "No one would think to look there. It's the perfect place to hide a dead body, with the rest of the dead bodies," I said, remembering Sam the witch who'd been murdered and hidden there as well.

Beverly wiped her gloved hand across her brow, leaving a long brown mark. "Well. It's too late for that now, and I'm too exhausted to dig up another grave."

"Me too," said Ruth, waving her arms up and down. "I can't feel my arms."

Dolores exhaled heavily. "And the ground'll be frozen. It'll be like trying to dig through cement. It took about an hour of spellwork just to thaw the ground here last year. I don't think I have the energy to do that tonight. I'm not thirty anymore."

"More like seventy," muttered Beverly.

"Okay." I had to agree with them. Even at my age, I was in no shape to dig up another grave for Nathaniel here. They made it look so easy in movies. "You said they're coming over tomorrow afternoon. Right?"

"That's right," answered Dolores.

"So, let's get some sleep, and then at dawn tomorrow, before the town is up, we'll sneak in and dig up another grave for Nathaniel in the town's cemetery. Should be enough time before the MIAD shows up."

"That's fine, darling," said Beverly. "In the meantime. Where do we put him?"

I looked at them and said, "Tonight, he's sleeping with us."

CHAPTER

3

I woke the next morning with my lower back, thighs, and triceps searing in pain. That'll teach me to think I can dig up a grave and assume my body was prepared for that kind of assault. It wasn't. Especially since those muscle groups weren't in my daily workout routine, which consisted of me going from my desk to the bathroom and back again.

I should have stretched. You should always stretch before performing a new exercise. Isn't that what they say? Using a shovel and hauling up earth for three hours had been exactly that. I was going to add gravedigger to my list of accomplishments for the new year.

Gravedigger.

Shit. Heart thrashing, I jerked up, looking around my room and finding it way too bright to be 5:00 a.m., which was precisely the time I'd set my phone alarm to ring. Pulling off my sheets, I swung my legs over my bed and leaned over to grab my phone. The clock on my phone read 7:13 a.m. I'd never set the alarm.

"Damn it."

Hildo was supposed to wake me up too. Where the hell was this cat?

Muscles groaning, I rushed to the bathroom, feeling like I was in my eighty-year-old body again. I took a shower while brushing my teeth and towel-dried my hair. If I was late and my aunts hadn't woken me, that meant we'd all slept in.

I yanked up a pair of clean jeans and pulled on a gray T-shirt before rushing out of my bedroom and hitting the stairs.

Skipping Iris's bedroom door, since her late-night text mentioned that she was sleeping over at Ronin's, I made for Ruth's bedroom door.

"Up! Wake up! We slept in!" I howled, banging on her door. Using the same momentum, I reached Beverly's door, raised my fist—and the door swung open.

"I'm going to kill you," snapped Beverly. A sexy, black nightie hung over her feminine frame, just above her knees. Her face was fresh and makeup perfect. Not a bag under her eye, no puffiness, nothing. There was no way any regular woman or witch could look *this* good in the morning without a little magical help. But right now, Beverly's morning routine was the least of our problems.

"You howl like the banshee of Vanleek Hill," growled Dolores, stepping out of her bedroom. She flipped her long gray braid over one shoulder, her periwinkle nightgown brushing her ankles.

"We're late. We slept in." I brushed past Dolores and rushed to the staircase. When I hit the bottom of the stairs and smelled the coffee and butter sizzling in a pan, I realized Ruth wasn't in her bedroom.

"Wakey, wakey, sleepyhead." Ruth's blue eyes widened, and she smiled at me as I rushed into the kitchen. Her green apron over her white blouse read, JUST WITCH IT. "I'm making Dolores's favorite—coconut-cream strawberry pancakes. I know, I know, it's not your usual buttermilks. But she's been so grumpy lately. I thought this would cheer her up."

I stared at her openmouthed. "Ruth? How long have you been up?"

"Oh, I've been up for *hours*." She spun around, beaming, a stainless-steel bowl pressed against her chest, her right hand whisking away at some light-pink mixture. "You know how Dolores gets if she doesn't get any carbs." She laughed. "Dolores-Zilla." She laughed harder.

Hildo sat on the counter next to the stove. A finger from his front paw swiped the edge of one of the two other mixing bowls and brought it to his mouth. He caught me staring and froze.

I pointed a finger at him. "I'll *deal* with you later."

I yanked my attention back to my aunt. "Why didn't you wake us up?"

Ruth shook her head. "I wouldn't dare wake you when you were so sound asleep, silly." A faintly troubled expression screwed up her face. "I've learned my lesson. I'll never go in Beverly's room again to wake her. I've seen her naked plenty of times, but penises from strange men? It kind of puts me off before my morning coffee."

I let out a breath and rubbed my eyes. "Ruth. We were supposed to go to the cemetery this morning? Remember?"

Her mouth parted. "Oh. I forgot."

"It's fine," I reassured her, regretting my irritation and raised voice. "We've still got time. I doubt anyone will be visiting the cemetery this early. We should be fine." I had no idea if this was true. But what choice did we have?

Ruth pushed her mixing bowl forward at me. "Do you still want some pancakes? I make grumpy faces on them." She laughed.

I didn't think we had time. "Sure." I grabbed a seat at the kitchen island. A moment later, Ruth plopped a plate in front of me with a pink pancake and a grumpy face made up of a string of strawberries for their eyes and mouth, dripping in maple syrup, that strangely resembled Dolores's face. My mouth watered just from the smell. With my fork, I cut a piece and took a bite.

"Oh, my, God," I moaned, my mouth full. "It's like a taste-bud dance-a-thon in my mouth. These are spectacular. I think these are my new favorites too."

Ruth beamed proudly. "Told you." She moved to the stove and high-fived Hildo.

I laughed and stuffed another piece of my coconut-cream strawberry pancake into my mouth.

"Ruth! What the hell is this? We don't have time to play kitchen witch." Dolores stormed into the kitchen. She wore jeans and a loose burgundy wool turtleneck sweater. Her eyes narrowed in anger. "You featherbrained, white-haired ninny! We've got a grave to dig. Remember? You know, I wonder where your mind is sometimes…" Her dark eyes landed on my plate and then flicked to the fork I'd packed with as much pancake as I could. "Is that… coconut-cream strawberry pancakes?"

"Yup." Ruth gave me a knowing look.

"Well. Maybe just five minutes. Then we have to go." Dolores took the seat next to me just as Ruth set a plate with two pink pancakes with the semblance of her grumpy face on them, which she didn't seem to mind.

31

I took the last bite of my pancake and washed it down with a gulp of coffee Ruth had just given me. "Is there a spot in the cemetery you'd prefer we put Nathaniel?"

"Yeah, six feet underground," said Dolores between chews.

"I get that," I told her. "But it would be better if we picked a spot now before we got there. You know. Being prepared is going to save us lots of time and trouble." We still needed to grab the shovels from the backyard where we'd left them last night. "What about the spell to thaw the ground? Do you have it ready? If not, you should go get it ready now."

Dolores set her fork down and turned her dark eyes very slowly on me. "Who do you think you're talking to? Of course the spell is ready. It was ready last night before I went to bed."

Ruth ducked her head and spun around to the stove.

Pissed, I opened my mouth to tell her off but then stopped at the last moment. I got they were all stressed out. I was too, and I never even killed the bastard. Emotions were high, and if I opened my big mouth, I would just make matters worse and possibly ruin the relationship I had with my aunt. I wasn't willing to risk it.

"Seeing as you've already eaten," said Dolores, turning back to her pancakes. "Why don't you get the car ready instead of barking out orders like a sergeant major."

Maybe I was willing to risk it. "Sergeant major? Why you—"

The doorbell rang.

I jerked. My heart pounded as adrenaline surged. "Are you expecting anyone?" I looked at Dolores, who'd stiffened like a statue as though she'd performed the "stone curse" on herself by accident. The only things that moved were her eyes; they just kept getting wider and wider.

I checked the clock on my phone. The screen read 7:31 a.m. It wasn't Iris. She had a key. So, who was here this early in the morning?

"That's Marcus," said Ruth, her back to us. "He's here to pick up the echinacea tea I made for Grace. Poor thing, she's fighting off a terrible cold."

"You called him!" Dolores shouted as I let out a breath. "What's the matter with you?"

Ruth turned around, looking warily between us and knowing something was wrong but not what exactly. Her brow pinched. "What? It's Marcus. You love Marcus. We all do."

"He's *the chief*, you half-wit!" she hissed. "You know what we have to do this morning. We can't have him here snooping around. He'll know something's not right. You know what's *hidden* in this house at this very moment!"

"Oh." Ruth made a face. "Guess I messed up again."

"You guess?" Dolores stood and placed her hands flat on the kitchen island. "We have to make him leave. He *can't* come in."

"I'll do it." I jumped off my stool, feeling both excited at the prospect of seeing my hot wereape yet dreading the fact that I had to make him leave somehow. I had a few seconds before I reached the door to come up with a good enough lie that he wouldn't see through.

I'd texted him last night, saying I couldn't come over like we'd planned, but rather I had to stay with my aunts to smooth things over with them now that I was back in my thirty-year-old body. We needed some "family time," which wasn't a total lie. It was family time. Family-planting-a-body time.

Feeling jumpy, I reached the front door. After twisting my face into what I hoped was a neutral mask, I grabbed the door handle and yanked the door open.

"Hi, Marcus—"

The man who stood on the threshold was not my uber-hot wereape. Not even close.

He was tall and lanky, maybe six three, with dark hair pulled back in a low ponytail and matching goatee. Tattoos of magical runes and sigils covered most of his brutish features, and I could see glimpses of more tattoos around his neck. He was dressed in all black, under a leather coat that brushed his heels.

He smiled nastily at the reaction he was getting from me, and anger trickled in my gut.

I hadn't seen him in months. But I'd recognize that goatee and smug smile anywhere.

He was one of the witch arbitrators from the Merlin trials, the ones I had to complete and pass in order to get my Merlin license. And he was the one who repeatedly called me a loser.

Silas.

CHAPTER

4

My face was probably a mix of utter shock and constipation. "You? What the hell are you doing here? I passed my trials. I did everything right. You're not taking it from me."

My pulse hammered as I stood there. A cool morning breeze wafted through the open door, the icy air soothing my hot face. I was about to punch that smug smile off his face. Maybe I'd kick it. Whichever came to me first. One thing was for sure. He wasn't going to take my license from me.

Doubt soared. Had I done something wrong? Had they changed their minds after all this time? Had using the ley lines been a mistake?

My mind swirled, and I felt Ruth's pancakes rising in my throat.

A sliver of fear tried to rise but I quashed it. His cool dispassion had my blood boil. "You can try to take it from me, but that would be stupid," I challenged him, my thoughts circling and finding the perfect power word to use on his tattooed ass. "And if you try, I'm going to fight you."

"Tessa? Don't be rude. Invite your friend to come in," Beverly purred, appearing next to me, her smile dazzling as she sized up Silas. She looked, well, she looked sexy as hell with her tight black pants and fitted low-cut cashmere sweater. She looked and radiated confidence and sex.

Beverly batted her eyelashes at Silas, twining a finger through a lock of blonde hair. I could see her appreciation for his physique and the tatts. Silas was so in love with himself, he probably never even noticed when a beautiful woman was right in front of him. Even if she were naked.

Silas still hadn't said a word.

"He's no friend of mine," I corrected. *More like an enemy, really.* Maybe we could fry his ass and bury him alongside Nathaniel in the cemetery. That was a great visual.

Silas smiled, showing some disturbingly white teeth. "That's right. We're not friends," he said, his voice rough with the same lilt of an accent I remembered. "I was one of her arbitrators in the Merlin trials." I didn't like the way he kept staring at me like he knew something I didn't.

"Oh?" said Beverly, her sexy smile widening as she inched closer to the male witch. "If my arbitrators looked like *you* when I was doing my trials, I would have performed them naked."

Oh, boy.

Eyeing Beverly with open annoyance, he turned to me and said, "If it were up to me, I would never have given you a Merlin license." He met my gaze, frightening savagery in his eyes. "You cheated. Like I said. You're a loser. Losers always cheat."

My lips parted as anger pounded through me. "I didn't cheat. I completed each trial. I passed them. Greta gave me my license herself. She's the boss of those trials. Isn't she? Well, she wouldn't have if she felt that something was off, or that I cheated."

Silas's eyes traveled to my hands and up to my face again. "You're just lucky ley lines are not recognized as a magical enhancer, yet. Not enough witches know how to use them. And there isn't enough information on them at this time. But we're working at making sure no new witches can use them to cheat again. Like an athlete using steroids. You had an edge over the others that you shouldn't have been allowed.

The other Merlins got their licenses on pure merit. You didn't."

I stared at him, feeling my face going through the different stages of red. I hated that he'd started to make me doubt myself. Though he was right about one thing. Without the ley lines, I would have never been able to pass the trials.

"Tessa didn't cheat," said Beverly, her hands on her hips and her smile replaced by a frown. "She's an extremely capable witch for someone her age and who's only recently come back to her magical roots. We'd given her the license without the trials, as is in our right. Greta was just bitter because she wasn't informed. It was the only reason why Tessa was forced to do those stupid trials in the first place."

"You're wasting your time, Beverly," I said. "Nothing you say'll change his mind."

A tattooed rune on his neck glowed red. I knew the guy drew his power from the runes and sigils tattooed on his skin. His ink was his magic. It gave him power. The guy was a walking spellbook. It was kind of cool. Too bad he was an ass.

He watched me with an intense gaze, and I felt a hum of power lift around me like he was trying to see through me to see what made me tick on the inside.

"That tickles," I laughed. "You better stop that. It's pretty pervy to look inside a woman without her permission. Look, if you wanted to ask me out"—I smiled a smile reminiscent of one of Beverly's—"this isn't how to do it."

Silas's face hardened, but the hum of power lifted. "There's something different about you," he said, making my heart race faster. "You're not like the other witches. I'm going to find out what."

If the Merlin Group was acting this way because of a little ley line power, I didn't want to know what they'd do if they found out my father was a demon. And I was going to keep it that way.

"If you could have taken away my Merlin license, you would have done it by now. So what the hell are you doing here?"

Silas pulled a card from inside his leather coat and handed it to me.

I glanced down at the card, and my face fell as I read the inscription:

Merlin Internal Affairs Division
SILAS CARDINAL
MIAD agent
North American Board of Merlin Division, USA

I stared at Silas hard, my heart lurching with shock. "Is this a joke?" The utter disbelief was that I was staring at his stupid face when I'd hoped to never see it again. This couldn't be true. Could it?

"It's no joke," answered Silas, his posture unable to hide his annoyance at my disbelief. "I work for the Merlin Internal Affairs Division. I'm here investigating the disappearance of Nathaniel Vandenberg. You wouldn't happen to know anything about that. Would you?" He smiled.

The sound of plates crashing on the floor from the kitchen made me jerk. Beverly's face blanched as she took a careful step back from the witch until she stood behind me.

I slipped his card in my pocket so he wouldn't see my hand trembling. "You're early. The letter said you wouldn't be arriving until this afternoon."

Oh. Shit. Oh. Shit. Oh. Shit.

Silas flicked his dark eyes at something behind me. "I find that being spontaneous, arriving precisely when not expected, keeps the guilty from hiding anything."

I really hated this guy. "Who says we're hiding anything?" I crossed my arms over my chest before I realized that was *exactly* the body language I was giving off. Crap. I dropped my arms, feeling like a fool.

A cruel smile curled his lips at what he saw on my face, and a chill spiraled up my spine.

"That's not how it looks to me," said Silas flatly.

A hysterical laugh slipped out of my mouth. "Well. I don't care who you are. You can't come in yet," I told him.

"What are you trying to hide?" Silas slipped his hands in his coat pockets, and I caught a glimpse of the runes and sigils that marred his skin.

"Nothing." I took that moment to press my hands on my hips. "But you can't come in yet. My aunts are naked." When his eyes shot to Beverly, I added, "My *other* aunts."

Silas's intense gaze never left my aunt. "Are you Beverly Davenport?" he inquired, shifting slightly forward. "If you are, I have questions for you."

I moved to the side to hide Beverly with my body. "Like I said. Your questions will have to wait."

Silas looked at me, the tattoos on his neck glowing brighter. "You know," he said, "interfering with the Merlin Internal Affairs Division will land you a cozy room in Grimway Citadel. But it wouldn't be the first time a Merlin went… bad."

Bad? I cocked my head to the side. "You mean like sometimes the urges are too strong to hurt a few dicks?" I told him, watching as his neck rune faded from red to a dull black.

Silas looked behind me again as another crash of pots sounded in the kitchen. His eyes went patronizing. "Why is there a freshly dug hole in your backyard? Gardening in the middle of winter?"

Oh… shit!

We forgot to fill in the hole. We'd even left the shovels out, thinking we'd have plenty enough time to fill it in before the MIAD showed up. Boy. When Davenport witches screwed up, we screwed up big.

Adrenaline soared as my heart went into overdrive. My emotions warred between panic that we'd been caught and anger that we hadn't had the time to fill up the damn hole.

My jaw gritted as I steeled myself in the most relaxed and unassuming posture I could. "We're thinking of putting in a pool. There's no crime in that. Is there? It's our property. If we want to put in ten pools, we can."

Silas gave a mock laugh. "A pool? In the middle of winter? Do I look stupid to you?"

"Do you really want me to answer that?"

Silas blew out his breath through his nose in a long exhalation. The runes on his neck began to glow again. Oops.

The witch made to move past me, and I jumped to stand in his way. "Don't you need a warrant or something? You can't just come in here?" I had no idea if that was true, but it was worth a try.

"I can go anywhere I want," answered the witch with that pompous, irritating smile again. "I'm the warrant. I go where I want and when I want. I don't need your permission. MIAD gives me that authority. I'm like a god."

Cauldron help me, I was going to kick him in the balls.

Eyes narrowing, I glanced over at Beverly. Seeing the open fear all over her face told me what he said was true. Damn.

"Out of my way." Silas brushed past me, hitting me hard in the shoulder in the process. Bastard.

"Hey! Boots!" I yelled, closing the front door, but the witch ignored me as he walked into the living room, leaving a trail of wet prints from the snow.

So, of course, I followed him.

He walked with a kind of arrogant confidence, like he knew he was going to find what he was looking for. He wandered into the living room, going from the sofas to the fireplace, pausing for a few seconds each time. His arms were up all the while his tatts glowed brightly as though they were some sort of a magical detector.

I spotted Dolores and Ruth staring at him from the kitchen, their faces pale, though Dolores managed to look annoyed, while Ruth showed a barely controlled panic. Hildo, sitting on the kitchen counter, flattened his ears, curled back his lips, and hissed at Silas from afar. Good kitty.

"So, what exactly are you looking for? If you tell me, maybe I can help you." I decided to play dumb. When in doubt, go for dumb.

I knew he was looking for traces of Nathaniel, more specifically his aura.

And if he continued this way throughout the house, he'd find him.

CHAPTER

5

"There's nothing here." I stood next to the tattooed witch as he waved his arms over one of
the bookcases. "We lead a very boring life by
witch standards. You know, some spells, hexes,
throw in a few curses from time to time. Nobody's perfect, right? It's all very rudimentary."

I glanced at my aunts again, worried about
the way Ruth's face was turning red. I knew that
face. She was either going to run away scared,
or she was going to blab. The longer Silas was
snooping around in here, the worse it was going
to get.

Just when I thought Silas was about to go
through to the dining room next, he stepped

back into the hallway and made for the stair-case.

Again, I was right behind him.

Beverly's eyes were wide as I passed her in the hallway, following Silas as he climbed the staircase with ease like he'd done it a thousand times. I hated this guy. And the fact that he was in my home, trespassing because of some stupid card that said he could, going up to our bed-rooms to look through our private belongings, was more than an invasion of our privacy. It felt wrong.

Once he reached the platform, Silas made for Ruth's bedroom.

"Like I said, you're not going to find any-thing." My voice was harsh in the confines of the hallway. I couldn't help the tremor of anger in it. Part of me wanted to throw him over the railing to see if his ego could fly.

But then Silas did something that surprised me. He stopped just beyond the threshold of Ruth's bedroom, tilted his head like he was lis-tening for something, and stepped out.

Weird.

Next, he did the same to Iris's room and Dolores's. He just stood there, hands up, the runes on his hands gleaming red, and then stepped out.

The last bedroom was Beverly's. Just like he did with the previous rooms, he stopped at the threshold and raised his hands. Only this time, Silas walked in.

I hurried to catch up.

My heart raced. I knew what he was doing. He'd traced Nathaniel's witch energy to Beverly's room. No doubt they'd shared some *intimate* moments in here. My chest tightened as I stood in the middle of Beverly's room. I didn't know if something in here would incriminate her. It's not like we'd had the time to go through the house and get rid of all those things.

Silas moved to her closet, opened the door, and peered inside.

"He's not in there," I told him with a laugh. "You're wasting your time. That guy Nathaniel is not here. We don't know where he is."

Silas didn't even look at me as he moved over to Beverly's distressed pine double dresser with a matching mirror.

That's it. "If you're going to go through her underwear drawer, I'm cutting off your balls."

This time the witch gave me a magnificent glare. "You've got a mouth on you."

I beamed. "Aww, thanks. That's the nicest thing you've ever said to me."

The witch moved away from the dresser and stood over Beverly's bed, his hands hovering just above it as his runes blazed a hot red, the brightest yet. Yup, Nathaniel had been in her bed. I didn't need Silas's glowing runes to tell me that.

Without a word, the witch spun around and walked out.

"That's it?" I ran to follow him as he headed down the stairs, finding it strange that he didn't even bother to go up to the attic to my room. "See, I told you there's nothing here." *All I need now is for you to get the hell out of my house, you jackass.*

He was leaving. Thank the cauldron. We'd been lucky. I climbed down the staircase behind him, feeling my tension ease. But when Silas reached the bottom of the stairs and proceeded toward the kitchen, my heart was jackhammering against my rib cage.

Uh-oh.

I followed him, seeing my three aunts sitting at the kitchen table. Hildo sat on Ruth's lap as she stroked his head a little too roughly. The poor cat's head kept bobbing up and down.

Silas popped his head into the potions room and kept going. My aunts all looked up as he entered the kitchen. If death-by-stare was a thing, Dolores would have killed Silas by now. Beverly let go of the coffee mug she'd been holding, like doing that was against some witch law or something. I'd never seen Ruth so pale before. Well, she actually looked a little green.

Silas's dark eyes glanced around at the kitchen cabinets and island to finally settle on my aunts, Beverly specifically.

His thin shoulders swung as he moved to stand next to the table. He pulled out his cell phone and swiped the screen before placing it on the table. I spied the red microphone icon on the screen. He was going to record this.

"When was the last time you saw Nathaniel Vandenberg?" he questioned Beverly with his arms crossed over his chest.

"Well," said Beverly, her motions stiff as she folded her hands in her lap. "It was last year. On Valentine's Day. We were on a date. We went out for dinner at La Bella Vita, the Italian restaurant in Cape Elizabeth."

I smiled inwardly at the calmness of her voice. I couldn't detect any nerves, nothing. She was good.

"And then?" asked Nathaniel.

Beverly pulled her face into one of her famous sultry looks. "And then, I'm afraid that's a little X-rated, darling. Can you handle that? I'm not sure you can."

I choked on a nervous laugh as I bent over. When Silas scowled at me I said, "Sorry. Gas pains."

Silas's gaze was unwavering as he continued. "Where did you go after your date?" he demanded of Beverly. "Did you come back here?" His tone was expectant, like he was trying to catch her in a lie.

"No," said Beverly, seemingly to have caught on to his scheme. "Back to his place for some…

alone time," she added, her smile widening. "Would you like to hear about which positions we performed? Or how long it took me to climax? The first time or the last time? How about how many different types of lubes we used?"

Silas's jaw clenched in annoyance as his face grew a shade darker. "How long were you and Nathaniel in a relationship?"

"I wouldn't call it a relationship," corrected Beverly. "We went on a few dates over the course of a year. He was good company. And I was always happy to see him. We had lots of fun together. But we weren't exclusive, if that's what you're asking."

"So, the fact that he saw other women didn't bother you?"

Beverly leaned forward on the table, her ample cleavage exposed, and I knew she was trying to distract him. "Darling. Why would it? When *I* was seeing other men too." If I could have, I would have given Beverly an Oscar for that performance.

Silas hesitated a moment. "Why didn't you alert the authorities when you didn't hear back from him? Didn't you think it strange?"

Beverly shrugged. "No. Why should I? As I said, we weren't exclusive. I just thought he didn't want to see me anymore. I hate to admit it, but it does happen. It's hard to believe. Isn't it?"

Silas's dark eyes were fixed on Beverly, evaluating. "What is?"

She dipped her head and said, "That I'm not *every* man's desire." She licked her lips, very, very slowly, tracing her eyes down his body to his groin.

God, I loved my aunt.

"So, you're telling me," continued Silas as the muscles in his jaw jumped several times, "that a witch like Nathaniel dating *several* women at the same time didn't affect you in any way?"

I saw the twitch on Beverly's face at the mention of several, but I doubted Silas saw it.

"It didn't," she answered, leaning back a little. "Just like it didn't bother Nathaniel that I was seeing other men. I'm a woman who's extremely comfortable with herself."

"We've noticed," mumbled Dolores.

"It didn't make you jealous?" pressed Silas, frowning pensively. "Enough to get back at him in some way? Enough to hurt him?"

Ah, I saw where he was going with that. "My aunt didn't kill him if that's what you mean."

Silas turned to look at me. "Who said anything about *killing* him?"

Oh crap. "I just assumed," I said, my pulse racing worse when I caught Dolores's glare. "You said he's been missing a long time. And if he hasn't contacted his family, as per the letter we got, it's normal that I'd assumed the worst." *Damn. Nice going, Tessa.*

"I'm not the jealous type," announced Beverly, and Silas pulled his attention back to her. "Besides, I'm too young to settle." She smiled and batted her eyelashes at him. "So many more eligible, sexy fish in the sea who'll scream my name when I'm done with them."

"Weren't you married before?" he inquired.

"Yes."

"And he died suddenly? Isn't that right? Under strange circumstances?"

Beverly's pretty mouth fell open in shock, clearly taken aback by this line of questioning.

Anger surged, and I pulled on the elements around me before I could stop myself. "My aunt's not some black widow, you creep." Wisps of my hair rose off my shoulders, moving freely in the breeze of elemental energy and feeding off my hatred of this guy. "This interrogation is over. I think you should leave before I smash your man berries into jam."

Silas turned, the tatts on his neck and hands blazing a fiery red. We stared at each other for what felt like minutes.

Oh goodie. We were going to fight.

But then the witch pulled his gaze from me, picked up his phone, and dropped it in his pocket. "I'll have some more questions for all of you later as I continue my investigation."

"You do that," I grumbled. I let out a long breath as I let go of some of the elemental energy but kept some at the tips of my fingers in case I needed to throw this bastard out.

He hesitated a moment before he began to leave. I could see a visible tension lessen around my aunts. He was leaving, finally. We were going to get away with this. We were home free.

However, sometimes my life is all about bad timing.

As he turned, Silas's eyes flicked over Ruth's face. She looked even greener than before, and her eyes kept darting nervously to the basement door and back, like a cartoon character.

She looked like, well, she looked guilty, like she was hiding something or someone.

And Silas saw that.

My heart seemed to stop. And before I could do anything, he was standing in front of the basement door.

Silas reached out and pulled on the handle. "Why is this door locked?" His dark eyes found mine. "Open it."

His ordering everyone around was starting to really piss me off. I gave him a smile with some teeth. "You didn't say the magic word." Seething anger warmed my face.

I shared a look with my aunts, and their panic and fear mirrored my own. We all knew if he opened that door, we were screwed.

"Open it," repeated Silas, his low resonating voice making me want to kick him in the throat.

I had two options. I could tell him to go screw himself, which only made us look guilty. He would then probably go and get reinforcements and force us to open the door, or I could open the door, and we'd all be on our way to the witch prison by tonight.

Dolores reached out and took Beverly's and Ruth's hands in hers, her face grim. They knew what was coming. There was no stopping it now.

Pulse pounding and knowing that I had no other choice, I moved next to him and pulled open the basement door.

Silas pushed me out of the way and hurried down the steps.

"I really hate this guy," I growled, following behind him.

I didn't rush. There was no reason to.

It was all over.

As I made my way down, my eyes found Nathaniel, or the carpet rather. Just like in the movies, we'd rolled him up really good in one of my aunts' old carpets. Kind of cliché. He was in the exact same spot we'd left him last night, just off to the right of the stairs, too tired to put him in the cemetery. Our exhaustion was going to cost us our freedom.

I never thought my life would end up this way. Sure, I didn't kill the bastard, but I'd just helped my aunts cover it up. It was a punishable offense. I just didn't know to what extreme.

I thought of Marcus. What would he say when he found out what my aunts had done? And me, the accomplice?

One thing was for sure. We needed a good lawyer, or some sort of advocate to help us plead our case before the courts.

Wire tight, I hit the bottom of the stairs, feeling this pain, this tightness in my gut that I might lose my aunts forever. "What's going to happen to us?" I asked, my heart thrashing so hard it was difficult to concentrate. I stood next to the body, staring down at it and wishing this had never happened.

I looked up to find Silas crossing the basement floor, his tatts glowing. "Nothing, for the moment." He moved in the *opposite* direction of Nathaniel's body, his hands out in front of him like he was following a trail of invisible magic. He'd missed the body completely.

What the hell?

"This basement is filled with energy," said the witch. "Many different kinds of energies." He turned toward me, his face hard. "What is this place?"

"A basement," I answered, knowing full well that wasn't what he was asking.

How could he not see the body? It was right there. Nothing else was in the basement apart from white walls, a staircase, and a dead guy rolled up in a carpet at my feet. It was almost as though… almost as though House was hiding the body from Silas.

And I'd almost screwed us up with my big mouth.

"You're feeling the ley lines," I told him, which was partly true. Davenport House did sit on one, but it was also a very powerful magical house with its basement being some kind of magical portal. But he didn't have to know.

Silas paced around the basement, frustration written all over his face. He could probably feel Nathaniel's energies but couldn't *see* him. Even though the witch was dead, I could feel the soft pulsing of his magic while standing right next to the dead witch. I just hoped House was smart enough to hide some of that too.

"There's nothing here," said Silas, releasing an exasperated breath.

Thank you, House.

"Told you." Though my heart was still racing, I felt a hell of a lot better than before. Even more so when Silas started to climb the steps back up.

When I reached the top, all three aunts were standing up, eyebrows high in confusion as they watched the witch march out of the kitchen and out into the hallway.

I raised a hand and gave them an "I'll tell you later" look with my eyes as I hurried after the witch down the hallway to the front door.

Silas showed himself out, opening the front door and stepping out onto the porch.

"Well, that was exciting," I told him as I stood in the doorway. "All that fuss for nothing. We must do this again sometime."

Silas paused and turned around. His dark eyes narrowed, and I wasn't sure what that expression was on his face. It had my pulse quickening and not in a good way. "Whatever you do," said the witch, the tatts around his hands and neck fading back to a dull black. "Don't leave town." He watched me for a moment, almost as if he were daring me to skip town so he could catch me. "I'll be back."

"We'll be here," I answered, a smile curving over my face.

Silas watched me for another moment before turning around and stepping off the snow-covered porch.

I watched him get behind the wheel of a black Escalade SUV and drive off.

We'd been lucky this time. But it had been a close call. Too close. He'd be back, and it was going to get a lot worse before it got any better.

I steeled myself. I was a Davenport witch, and we didn't fly away scared on our brooms at the hint of danger. No. We met it head-on.

And that's exactly what we did.

CHAPTER
6

As soon as Silas had left, we'd dragged rug-Nathaniel out of the basement (none too gently as I made sure his head hit every step) and all piled into the Volvo with the dead guy in the trunk.

We'd picked up Iris along the way to Hollow Cove's cemetery from Ronin's place. I didn't feel great about adding Iris to all our mess, but she'd agreed, and we needed all the help we could get. Besides, I trusted Iris with my life. She had my back, just like I had hers. She was part of the Davenport family now, and my aunts all adored her. The fact that she'd been thrilled at the idea of burying the witch who had tried to kill my aunts, how could I possibly say no to that?

Though Hildo had whined at first at being left behind, one gust of cold air from the opened kitchen back door, and the cat was visibly delighted at being left in the house. He hated the cold and the snow. Just like most cats.

"I need you to stay here in case Silas comes back," I'd told the cat, rubbing under his chin and smiling as he started purring.

Hildo's yellow eyes gleamed up at me. "What do you want me to do if he comes back?"

I grinned. "Pee on him."

The cat showed me his teeth. "Consider it done."

And while under Dolores's invisibility bubble, which was a semitransparent, purple half sphere the size of about three cars, the aunts managed to finish their thawing earth spell within an hour so we could start digging.

We'd picked a spot on the south side, near a line of trees with fewer graves, which was considerably harder to get through, trekking through the heaps of snow. We figured there'd be fewer visitors as we started digging. Despite my body still being in some serious pain and digging withdrawal from only last night, I found my second wind and dug like a seasoned grave robber. Fear of being caught combined with a healthy mix of adrenaline would do that to a person—at least to a witch.

And between Dolores, Beverly, Ruth, Iris, and me, after two hours of digging, we'd finally dumped Nathaniel's rug-rolled body into the grave we'd just dug for him.

"Let's not *murder* anyone else for a while. Shall we?" panted Dolores, leaning heavily on her shovel. "It'll take weeks to heal the blisters on my hands."

Beverly stretched and then winced. "I haven't had this kind of back pain since I fell out of Stewart's hot tub." She smiled and added, "Stewart fell out too, of course. On top of me."

Ruth's face was red and blotchy as she moved forward and stared down into the hole. Then she made a face, leaned over the edge, and spat. So did Dolores. So did Beverly.

Ruth saw my confused expression and said, "It's to keep his spirit from haunting us. To keep it here, like glue." And then she spat again for good measure.

Okay then.

Iris and I exchanged looks, and then we both took turns spitting. Hey? Might as well, right? Wouldn't want Nathaniel's ghost haunting me or my aunts. He was a creep, alive. I didn't even want to think about how creepy he would be as a ghost.

"Okay, Tessa. You're up," commanded Dolores as she stepped away from the grave and leaned on her shovel, giving me room to work.

Once Iris, Ruth, and Beverly joined Dolores, I tapped into my will and pulled on the elements around me, feeling the tug on my will and my aura as they answered. Then I raised my right hand, focusing on the mound of earth next to Nathaniel's grave. In a sweeping motion, I voiced, "Inflitus!"

A blast of kinetic force hit the heap of dark soil. It pushed the earth like an invisible snow-plow, driving it forward and down into the six-foot-deep hole until it covered it completely.

But I wasn't done yet.

Focusing my will, I drew forth the elements again and uttered, "Ventum!"

A gust of wind rushed out from my out-stretched hands channeled from the power word's magic. The wind I called up wasn't my usual kick-ass outburst. It was more toned down and refined, and it poured steadily out of my hands. It soared through me and dragged the snow next to the grave, gently brushing it over until the dark earth disappeared and only a white blanket of snow remained. The snow lifted like a white wave and settled over the dark earth until we couldn't see any traces of disturbed earth and couldn't tell that only a few hours ago, there'd been a six-foot-deep hole in the ground.

I let out a breath. "Well. That should do it. No one will ever suspect a thing," I said proudly. I wasn't proud that I'd just become an accomplice to hiding a dead body but rather at how I was getting better at manipulating the power words. I hadn't just blasted the snow. I'd controlled it, weaved it like it was an extension of my arms, of me.

A ripple of nausea hit as the magic took its payment. Always did. Always would. But I steadied myself, pushing the feeling away. We'd gotten a lot done today, and it was just a few minutes past two o'clock in the afternoon.

My shoulders slumped in relief and I exhaled. It worked. No one would ever find him now. Hopefully, Silas would give up and leave once he realized nothing was here, no incriminating evidence against Beverly. Maybe it was wishful thinking, but we'd gotten lucky this far. Maybe we still had luck on our side.

"Time to go, ladies." Dolores stood with her arms outstretched and clapped. A wash of energy fell on us, my skin erupting in goose bumps as it dropped down back into the ground like rain. The invisibility bubble was gone.

"I need a drink." Beverly waltzed away and clambered over a heap of snow into a recently plowed path that led out of the cemetery to the front gate.

"I need to pee," said Ruth. She gave me a tight smile and followed her sister.

Iris came to stand next to me. "This was great." The Dark witch smiled, looking delighted. "If there're more dead bodies to hide, count me in."

I laughed. "God, I hope not. One dead, murderous witch is enough for my lifetime." Cauldron help us if more skeletons were in my aunts' closets. Knowing them, there probably were.

I felt the weight of someone's eye on me, and I stared out in the cemetery, sweeping my gaze around. A shape moved between a heap of snow and two gravestones. I blinked and it was gone. It was dark, but I hadn't seen it clearly enough to differentiate what it was. I stared at the spot where I'd last seen it, hoping I'd see it again, but I didn't. Probably just a squirrel.

Feeling more relaxed than I had since last night, we followed the aunts down the path and headed toward the front metal gate at the entrance where the Volvo was waiting for us.

Trouble was, it wasn't the only thing waiting.

A familiar, sexy-as-sin male came into view as he stepped around the front of his burgundy Jeep Cherokee and headed straight for us.

Crap on French toast.

My heart thudded as Iris shot me a worried look. Could wereapes see through my aunt's invisibility bubble? If so, we were in all kinds of trouble.

Marcus walked up to me and gave me a peck on the cheek. Okay, it was *just* a peck, but it still had my heart going.

"What are you guys doing here?" he asked, his expression one of wondering curiosity. "And why are you carrying shovels? You're not digging up graves, are you?"

Uh-oh.

The five of us froze, which really didn't help our situation. The guilt shared between us was almost palpable.

"Uh…" I stammered. "Our brooms were in the shop." *Our brooms were in the shop?* Here I go again with the word vomit. I needed some serious help.

Marcus laughed, his gaze shifting between us. "Were you visiting your grandmother's grave?" he asked me, seemingly having dismissed our carrying shovels as a subject of interest.

"Yes. Yes. Absolutely," I blurted, looking at my aunts. "That's exactly what we were doing. Just saying hi to Gran." I gave a little wave. "Hey, Gran."

"Dear old Mum," said Dolores, a false smile on her serious face. "How we miss that miserable old lady."

Okay, that was a bit much coming from her, but Marcus didn't seem to catch that either.

"We always visit on her birthday," commented Ruth, nodding her head like she was trying to convince herself. "It's tradition."

"And sometimes we run around naked under the full moon howling like desperate, hungry animals. That's also a tradition," said Beverly, her green eyes brightening as she added, "Maybe next time you can come too."

Dolores rolled her eyes. "I don't think Marcus wants to hear about old sluts running around in their birthday suits."

Marcus was nodding his head like he approved, clearly unsure how to respond to that offer.

"Umm. Marcus. What are you doing here?" I asked, wanting to change the subject, but I also wanted to know what he was doing at the cemetery and why he'd seemed to be waiting for us.

The chief's gray eyes found mine. "Looking for you. All of you."

Damn.

I gave a mock laugh. "Why's that?" I felt Iris's eyes on me, but I wouldn't look at her for fear my face would betray me.

"There's a MIAD agent in my office claiming he's here because he's investigating you." Marcus swept his gaze again over my aunts. "He was very vague on the details because of my history with all of you. Is there anything I should know?"

"Like what?" I answered, a little too quickly. Here I go again playing dumb. Lying to Marcus was like stabbing myself in the heart repeatedly with a sharp knife. The last thing we needed was for Marcus to get involved in our dirt.

Because, let's face it, this was getting dirtier and dirtier every second.

Dolores put her hand on her hip. "The Merlins have always been at each other's throats throughout the years. One group always hates the Davenport witches and wants to bring us down because, well, we're better. This is just another ruse to try and diminish us. Our name. It's nothing new. And it won't be the last time."

Marcus's posture shifted to something like protective aggression. "So, this Silas guy is here to find dirt on you?"

"I'm afraid so," answered Dolores, which was true in a way. "But don't worry. We can take care of him."

I wasn't sure I liked the way she said that, like we were going to take care of him permanently, the kind of permanence that didn't require a beating heart, like Nathaniel's.

"I could take care of him for you." Marcus had a smug smile on his face. "Just say the word. If he's harassing you, I can *escort* him out of this town. No problem."

Beverly laughed and squeezed the chief's arm. "You are such a sweetheart, Marcus. Just like your father, you are. All overly protective. But it's like Dolores said; this is nothing we can't handle ourselves." She let go of his arm and said, her voice hard, "He'll be gone before you know it."

Again, I wasn't sure I liked the innuendo behind her words. Was something going on? Were they planning to eliminate Silas and didn't inform me? I was going to have to have a little chat with my aunts once Marcus was gone.

I wasn't sure why Silas hadn't come clean about his investigation into Beverly and about the missing witch Nathaniel. Maybe these MIAD agents were secretive that way. Maybe they didn't want outsiders messing up their investigations. Maybe he was just a douchebag.

Still, if Marcus threatened Silas, I was positive the witch would then spill the beans about Beverly. So far, Marcus was ignorant about the situation, and I wanted to keep it that way. For all our sakes.

Marcus's eyes swept over me and dipped to my lips. "Dinner at my place tonight?"

My mouth opened to say yes, but I knew there was just too much crap going on with my aunts right now. I had to stay and keep my eyes on them. "I have a book cover to finish. I promised the client she'd have it tonight." Total lie. "Rain check? How about tomorrow night?" I was fully aware I might need tomorrow night as well.

The chief watched me for a moment, his eyes squinting ever so lightly like he knew I was lying about something. "You sure there's nothing you want to tell me?"

I shook my head. "No. Nothing at all." I felt like a fraud. Here we were, supposed to be trusting each other, and here I was messing it up.

Either he knew I was lying and didn't push it, or he thought he'd get it out of me later.

Marcus smiled then, his face resplendent. I could get used to looking at that face forever. "Sounds good. I'll call you later."

"Okay."

"Goodbye, ladies," said the chief as he waved at my aunts and Iris before turning around and heading toward his Jeep.

"It's getting cold," said Ruth. "We should go." Without waiting, Ruth made a beeline for the Volvo.

"Right behind you," commented Dolores, her long legs propelling her fast with Beverly behind her.

If I didn't know any better, it seemed as though they wanted to get away from me and Iris. Yeah, they were definitely planning something.

Iris stepped beside me. "That was close."

I let out a long breath. "Too close."

"Well, at least it's over now," said the Dark witch. "You can all relax and breathe easier."

It was done. But I wasn't that naïve to think this was over. Not until Silas was out of our town. And not until I figured out what the aunts were planning. Because, well, the one thing I knew for sure was they were most definitely planning something.

And nothing good.

CHAPTER
7

Exhausted and feeling like I slipped and fell in a meat grinder, I took Iris's offer for a late lunch at Wicked Witch & Handsome Devil Pub, which, after two glasses of wine and three hours later, turned out to be an early dinner.

My aunts had refused. No surprise there.

"I need a nap," Dolores had said as she'd parked the Volvo at the curb of the restaurant. "I barely slept last night. You know how I get when I don't get a full night's rest."

"Dolores-Zilla," whispered Ruth, in my ear where she was squeezed in between me and Iris.

Dolores turned in her seat and glared at Ruth before turning on me. "I'm tired. Okay? Is that a crime?"

"No," I replied. "No need to bite my head off."

"You should know, Tessa," offered Beverly, sitting in the front passenger seat, checking herself in the sun visor vanity mirror. "You've been *much* older than us. I don't know how you managed *not* to take naps every ten minutes. You looked like you were just about to keel over and die."

I narrowed my eyes. "I'm not buying it."

Dolores cocked a brow. "Excuse me? What are you *not* buying?"

"I know you're planning something," I told them. "Out with it."

Dolores watched me. "What are you talking about?"

"You *know* what I'm talking about."

Beverly pushed the sun visor back up. "I think she's just horny."

Heat rushed to my face as Iris laughed. "What? I'm not horny?" I can't believe those words came flying out of my mouth. Okay, so maybe I was, just a little.

Dolores pointed a finger at me. "Don't be difficult with the older gals. We've spent a lifetime learning that skill."

I crossed my arms over my chest. "I know you're planning something. What is it?"

Dolores let out a sound between a snort and a laugh. "I think you need a nap too. You sound crazy." She turned back around.

I could tell by her tone that whatever they were planning, they wouldn't tell me. "Fine. Keep your secrets," I said, my hand on the door. "But I'm going to find out." I clambered out of the car with Iris.

And though I was having a great time with Iris, I couldn't shake off that foreboding feeling that my aunts were in over their heads. They were scared. And most of the time when people were scared and desperate, they used shaky logic. Their reasoning went up in smoke.

"I better get home," I told Iris once outside the restaurant, glancing at my phone as the clock hit 4:56 p.m. "My aunts are up to something."

Iris was texting on her phone. She looked up at me, a frown wrinkling her pretty features. "What makes you say that?"

"Call it Davenport intuition. I just know. I can feel it. It has something to do with Silas."

Iris's eyes widened. "You don't think... noooo... you think they're going to do something to him?"

I nodded. "Knowing them, that's a definite yes. From what I know of Silas, he's not going to give up until he finds something to use against Beverly. My aunts felt this too. I'm sure of it."

73

Iris laughed. "Well. Tell me all about it later. Okay? I'm off to see Ronin before the poor half-vampire throws a fit. He can't stand to be away from me for more than an hour at a time." She rolled her eyes, but I could tell she was thrilled. She stepped forward and then turned around. "But call me if you need reinforcements."

"I will."

I watched Iris walk down Shifter Lane for a moment, and then she turned and hurried in the opposite direction. From here, Davenport House was a ten-minute walk at a leisurely pace. Seven minutes at a brisk walk.

Guess which one I chose?

It wasn't just the idea of my aunts planning something that had my thighs working over-time. I looked like a complete fool, half walking, half jogging. To anyone watching, I looked like my bladder was about to explode. Except that my speed-walking performance wasn't just for the aunts. It was also because Marcus finished work in less than four minutes. I didn't want him to see me and have to lie to him again. I'd done enough lying to him for the day.

I needed to get my butt back at Davenport House.

And my butt and I got there in less than seven minutes.

I strode up the snow-covered driveway, and seeing the old Volvo parked, I smiled. Not because I liked the old car, even though I did, but because I was going to catch them in the act. Whatever *that* was.

Feeling confident in my scheme, I pushed the door open as silently as I could and stepped in.

Two things hit me at once. The first thing was how silent the house was. The second thing was how silent the house was.

Not wanting to spoil my entrance, I slipped off my boots and tiptoed along the hallway to the kitchen. The thought of Dolores's scowl at my surprising them had a smile plastered across my face. Holding my breath, I crept into the kitchen. Gleaming white cabinets and white subway-tiled backsplash stared at me. It was completely deserted.

Hmm. Where were they?

They had declined to come to the restaurant with me and Iris because they didn't want me to know or get involved with whatever scheme they had going—a scheme that was no doubt orchestrated right here, in Davenport House. So where were they? And why couldn't I see any traces of their plans?

At that moment, a hint of candle smoke tickled my nose. Following my witchy instincts and my nose, I stepped into the potions room just to the left of the kitchen.

Flicking on the light switch, I moved inside. Shelves and racks lined the walls, packed with an assortment of jars along with unidentifiable objects, books, containers, and pouches full of all sorts of herbs, roots, candles, pendulums, and boxes of chalks. Piled on the tables sat a vast collection of cauldrons, shiny copper pots, ceramic spoons, and bowls that were perfect for mixing potions.

I loved visiting the potions room. But I didn't have time to marvel at all the magical stuff in here. I needed to find my aunts and what they were up to. I knew my answers were in this room.

A rack of drying herbs and flowers hung over a center island. In the middle of the island lay a large, leather-bound tome.

I made for the book. I didn't recognize it as one from Dolores's collection. Its yellowing pages and worn cover and spine were a testament to its age. Old as dirt, it seemed to be. The older the book, the more magic could be drawn from the spells. Isn't that what they say? Nah. I just made that up.

It was open, daring me to read it, and so I obliged.

Some parts were written in Latin, which I was still struggling with even with my own spells, so that didn't help.

But when my eyes settled on a familiar word, familiar *words*, rather, my heart stopped.

It was a curse. And I recognized it.

I moved my fingers over the words and read, "Osculum est mortis." Translation. *The kiss of death.*

"Holy shit. Beverly was going to seduce Silas, pucker up, and then kill the bastard."

I didn't like the guy. Hell, one could say that I even despised him, but he was just doing his job. He didn't deserve to die for following orders. Maybe just a little.

Didn't they realize that if they killed Silas, *another* MIAD agent would take his place and show up? Didn't they realize how this made them look? Guilty. And then some.

It was worse than I thought.

I placed a hand on either side of the book. And where was Hildo? If my familiar companion was in the house, he would have shown himself by now, which only meant they took him with them. I knew familiars could be used to amplify a witch's power or as a conduit, depending on the familiar in question. Some were more powerful than others, just like witches.

Damn. They'd taken my cat. I frowned, not appreciating the cat-napping. But from what little I knew of the cat, he was probably loving it.

I let out a long breath. "Why me?"

I had no time to debate that. I had to stop them before they made a huge mistake and made a bad situation a hell of a lot worse.

To do that, I needed to find them.

"Well, you can't be that far," I muttered to myself. "You left the Volvo, and Beverly hates walking." Which meant, wherever they were, they went on foot. It had to be near, walking distance…

The garden shed.

It fit. I knew Ruth stored some of her potions and mixes in there when she ran out of space in the potions room. It was also the perfect place to perform illegal spells without being seen.

I darted for the front door. A shiver of excitement mixed with dread sifted through me. Once I had my boots back on, I rushed out into the night.

I hit the bottom porch steps, ran across the driveway, and made a right turn toward the back of the house.

Only someone was blocking my way.

Someone? A figure in a heavy black cloak faced me.

The figure was a tad taller than me. Its face was hidden under the cover of the cloak. I say figure because it could have been male just as it could have been female.

I laughed. "Allison? Is this you? Are you trying to scare me?" She'd told me that she'd hired a witch to help her get back at me for Iris's curses. "Sorry about your eyebrows." Not really. "You know, now's really not the time for payback. I need to find my aunts. It's an emergency. They're in trouble. You can curse me all you want tomorrow. Okay? I'll even let you get the first hit."

I felt a sudden pulse of power stir the air, and a string of black energy lashed out from the figure's fingertips. Allison was a wereape. The only magic she possessed was the ability to dislocate her jaw to fit as many bananas as she could in her mouth at once.

"Okay, not Allison."

The figure reached up and removed the cowl.

"Definitely not Allison."

His features were gaunt and weathered, and I say *he* because he was undeniably male. He had oily black hair that fell to his shoulders, the type that hadn't been washed in weeks. He had one red eye, which sparkled with something like humor and excitement. The other eye was pale with a white scar running through it, from his hairline down to his jaw. That eye looked ruined, completely blind. Another wave of energy stirred the air, cold as a thread of it brushed against my skin.

Nope. This was not the tall, gorgeous blonde wereape, though she did have wide manly shoulders. The scent of sulfur made my eyes water.

And if I had to guess, I'd say this was a demon.

Yay me.

CHAPTER
8

The demon on the sidewalk stared at me for what felt like minutes, an unwavering creepy glare that could only be described as "serial killer" type. Not speaking from experience, of course, but I've seen the movies. It was obvious he was here for me. Only, I wasn't exactly sure why.

"Huh." I stared at the demon. "Are you *the others* my mother was talking about?"

From what I understood, my mother's referral to "the others" was a group or a faction of demons who opposed the relationship my mother, a mortal witch, had with my father—a demon. She had pushed me away from using magic for my own good, to keep me safe from the likes of this guy right here. My ley line tampering had landed my father's attention, and it looked like it had also attracted the wrong kind of attention.

The demon said nothing. Just kept staring at me. That red eye of his rolled over me and not in a sexual way, more like he was contemplating which part he was going to hurt first.

"Your timing couldn't have been worse," I told him. It occurred to me that I wasn't as afraid as I should have been. Which was probably a mistake, come to think about it. But there was only just him. I could take him. Right?

"You're an abomination," he hissed in mashed-up English, but I could understand him perfectly.

I looked down at myself and shrugged. "Jeez. Okay. I'll admit it. The midnight snacks and wine are starting to take their toll, but I didn't think I looked *that* bad."

"I cannot permit you to live," he said.

My eyes widened in shock. "Wow. That's nice. And who decided this? You and the others? I like my life, thank you very much. And I'm not about to let you or any others change that. Got it?"

The demon's expression was unreadable. "You upset the balance."

"You mean like The Force?" I laughed. He didn't.

He watched me silently for a long moment. "We can't have mortals overthrow the natural order of our race. You're an insult to us and our kind. Your very existence is a series of contradictions. The blood must be pure. All bastards must be crushed."

Did he just call me a bastard? "Listen, Scarface. Can I call you Scarface? Great. I'd love to stay and chat, but I need to do something right now." Like, find my aunts before they did something insurmountably stupid.

I made to move but froze at the black energy spilling from his fingers. "Nice trick. Can you do it in pink?"

He tilted his head slightly; his face stretched into a smile that had the hairs on the back of my neck rising. "Nothing personal. I'm here to collect my quarry."

I felt my eyebrows go up. "Your *quarry*?" I didn't like the sound of that. "You mean like a bounty?" I blinked. "Is there a bounty on me?" Holy shit. "Are you some sort of hit man... hit demon?" Okay, now it was time to panic.

I could stay and fight, but let's face it, I really didn't want to.

The demon's red eye gleamed, and he muttered something in a language I didn't understand. Though I couldn't understand it, the tone and meaning of his words were as clear as day. They were words of hate, darkness, and death.

I drew in my will and reached out to tap the nearest ley line. A surge of energy hit me as it answered. Readying myself, I reached out and pulled the ley line toward me, feeling its power vibrating in my bones and bending it until it was nearly there.

With a sudden jerk, the ley line's power quivered and then disappeared, like the line had been cut.

What the hell?

Trembling with a mix of fear and rage, I drew up my will again, reaching out to the ley line's power. It felt shaky and uncertain, coming to me in drips, like a faulty faucet.

This had never happened to me before. Somehow, the demon was preventing me from using the ley line's power.

I narrowed my eyes at the demon. "What did you do? How are you doing this?" If he was blocking me from using the ley lines, this demon was no joke.

"You can't escape me." A dark dagger appeared in the demon's hand. It was black and matte and wasn't casting back any light. I'd never seen a blade like that. And I didn't like it.

Fear galvanized me. I had practically zero one-on-one combat skills. I was a witch. My one-on-one combat skills consisted of my ability to ugly cry, which always managed to get my rivals to run away from me.

The demon had somehow stopped me from using the ley lines. Did that mean I couldn't use the power from the elements?

One way to find out.

The demon lunged at me.

I stiffened, reaching out to the elements as I readied a power word. My pulse quickened, and I felt a sudden relief at the surge of magic, sending my skin riddling with goose bumps.

I focused my will, called forth the magic of the elements, and shouted, "Accendo!"

Twin fireballs hurled from my outstretched hands, flying straight and true right at the demon's head.

Scarface spun, bringing up his black cloak like a shield.

The fireballs hit the demon in a sudden blast of hot air, and they were extinguished into sizzling smoke. The demon pulled back his cloak, and a small, sly smile drew from his face.

"I'm going to enjoy gutting you, witch."

"Okay," I said, pissed. "So, you've got some skill with that cloak. But you're not coming near me with that thing." Okay, that sounded a little weird.

I was a Merlin, damn it. One demon didn't scare me. Right?

A push of air, and Scarface shot forward in a blur of limbs and black cloak. He moved like a shadow with that vampire speed Ronin had, which was utterly annoying.

I'd barely had time to register how quickly my plan had gone down the crapper as the demon came at me again. Forget calling up my magic.

So, what does a witch do when she's neck-deep in the crapper? The only thing she can.

She hides.

I flung myself to the side and rolled under the Volvo, twisting while ducking, barely missing a swipe of that black demon dagger.

Something grabbed hold of my left ankle. I kicked out, my foot making contact with something hard. His face hopefully. Better yet, his balls. I heard a yelp as Scarface let go. Scrambling, I managed to pull myself out from under the car on the other side.

I saw a blurred fist, and then agony exploded in my head as I stumbled. Damn. No one can prepare you for how much it hurt to get punched in the head. It hurt like a sonofabitch.

Scarface was suddenly next to me, his blade in his hand. Crap. I hadn't seen him coming.

"Inspiratione!" I howled, pulling on the elements as fractures of red energy blasted out of my hand.

It hit.

Scarface howled in pain as the red energy coiled around him like a rope. But one flick of his cloak, kind of like the swipe of a Spanish matador's cape, and they sizzled and popped and dwindled and then… died.

"I think I hate you," I told him.

And then I was running.

I wasn't a fool. If I couldn't ley line my butt away, and my magic was useless on him, my best course of action was to get inside the house.

Demons couldn't enter Davenport House, except for my father, of course. The multitude of wards and spells made it impossible. They couldn't penetrate it without suffering their true death.

I hit the flagstone walkway and ran toward the house. I wasn't known for my great sprinting speed, but with a nice bout of adrenaline, I surprised myself.

The porch bounded into view. Nearly there—

I cried out as searing pain exploded from the back of my head when I took another blow. I stumbled to my knees, my vision blurring.

This had gone from bad to worse in a matter of seconds.

Darkness shimmered at the edges of my mind, and I felt my strength weaken. I was in no shape to fight, but I had to.

Scarface came at me, swinging that damn blade of his. "Where do you think you're going, *witch*?" he mocked.

"Home," I shot back; no point in lying. I pushed myself up, which made my head pound even more. Where's the Tylenol when I needed it.

The demon grimaced and then he sprang. But I'd anticipated that. He wasn't exactly unpredictable.

Pulling on the elements, I sidestepped and spun around.

"Inflitus!" I shouted and landed a burst of kinetic force squarely in his gut.

I fell back on my butt from the impact, but who cared. It worked.

The demon pitched back with a grunt, landing hard and hitting his head on the flagstone walkway. His dagger slipped from his grip.

Panting, I scrambled to my feet. "Huh. Not so invincible, are you? Jackass."

I had no idea if I could kill a demon. Never had the pleasure. But after seeing Carrie, the Soul Collector's wife, and the pain she suffered at the hands of the angel Malak, I knew they could feel pain. And I was planning on giving him lots and lots of it.

In the blink of an eye, the demon did some fancy cloak work again and he was on his feet. A dark gray haze glowed around his hands, solidifying as his fingers manipulated his demonic magic, and his lips moved, giving it strength. The scent of sulfur was heavy, nearly making me choke. An ugly smile of anticipation came over him, widening as he held the beginnings of demonic energy of who knew what.

Oh… shit.

Scarface hurled his demon magic at me. His aim was spot on, no surprise there. But I was ready. I might not be able to beat it, but I could sure as hell contour it.

Gathering my will again, I cried, "Protego!"

A sphere-shaped shield of protection rolled up over my head.

The demon energy hit my sphere and I ducked. I found myself on my knees, the top of my hair sizzling as the energy pushed through the layers of my protection shield. Steam coiled from where an evil-looking, foaming mass slipped down the edge of my sphere. It hit the snow, burning a hole in the ground.

Damn. That could have been me.

And then the obvious happened.

My protection bubble warped and popped.

Fantastic.

Frantic, I was up on my feet again, a power word on my lips. Something flicked in my peripheral vision. I spun. A string of black energy was coming straight for me—again. I was a lucky girl tonight.

No way I could outrun this guy or outplay his demon magic. And the use of my power words was taking its toll on me. There was a limit to my magic, not to mention the two giant blows to the head I'd received weren't exactly helping my situation.

Eyes wide, I stared for a moment, dumb-struck, as the thread of black energy came closer and closer to my head—

"Ventum!"

A burst of wind rushed out and thrust upon the demon's magic, sending it away. It hit an electric pole with an explosion of green and white electricity.

But it had all been a trick. A diversion.

In that same fraction of a second, a blur of black knocked me down. Agony soared as scorching pain flared up from the right side of my waist. I heard a scream, my scream, as I fell, and pain from my hip bone sent my teeth clattering.

Something hot and wet dripped from my side. And when I looked up, I saw a red stain on the demon's blade as he sheathed it somewhere around his waist.

Panicked, I rolled around and pushed myself on my knees as a cry escaped me. I fell back on the snow, my breath shallow and harsh, like I was having an asthma attack. There wasn't enough air. Every muscle in my body was flaming. I was faltering. What was going on?

I felt my heart pounding where the demon's blade had perforated my skin and felt the searing pain of the deep gash.

And then the strangest thing happened.

Scarface upped and left.

I stared, my jaw somewhere around my middle, as the demon hit man from the Netherworld walked down Stardust Drive and disappeared into the cold night.

He was a hit man, hit demon, so why hadn't he finished the job?

My stomach twisted in a spasm of nausea. I rolled to my side as I vomited. Then came the fever of the century.

My skin blazed with fire as sweat broke from every single pore on my skin. I convulsed. My body was not my own as it lashed out in a writhing mess. Thank the cauldron Marcus wasn't here to see this because *that* would be embarrassing.

Marcus...

For a while, there was only nausea and a steady mounting of pain. Darkness was close. I could barely keep my eyes open. I knew what this was. And I knew why he'd done it.

He'd stabbed me and left because his blade was coated in poison. Nothing else could be done. Death was coming for me. It was near. I was going to die.

The last thing I heard was the sound of heavy footsteps, and my world turned to black.

CHAPTER
9

My dreams were dark and everlasting.

Death filled my head, and screams filled my ears. I wasn't sure if I was doing the screaming or not. It was just there and infinite. I lay in a coffin, I think. Something flat and hard pressed against my back. And I was cold. Really cold. Like I'd stripped down naked and fallen through the thin ice of a pond.

Fear comes in a variety of shapes and sizes, even in dreams. I was experiencing two at the moment. The fear that had me immobilized and the fear that had me screaming. Dreams were funny that way.

"Not too much or you'll kill her," said a stern voice in my dream.

"I can't work while you're screaming at me," came another voice, a little louder this time, and thick with fear. "Move. I need some space."

"Let me do it," said a third voice.

"Get out of my way." I heard the sound of a hard slap on skin. "Or so help me, you'll be bald for a year!"

I felt my head drift forward and something warm against my lips. Something hot, a liquid, poured down my throat.

Something wasn't right. Something was constricting my airway. I was going to choke to death in my sleep.

Panicked, I gripped my will and forced myself to wake up. The fog of sleep lifted. And I knew at that moment whatever I was experiencing wasn't a dream.

I peeled my eyes open. Three faces stared down at me.

"She opened her eyes!" Ruth clapped her hands together, tears welling up her eyes.

Dolores leaned over closer until her nose nearly brushed against mine. "Tessa? Can you hear me?"

I nodded, just as my body started convulsing. Gasping, a wave of cold hit me again, and I clenched in pain. Part of me wished I was in that dream again. Anything was better than this. I was dying from the inside out. Whatever poison the demon's blade was coated with was killing me.

Beverly pressed her hand on my head as my body jerked around like I was riding a bronc at a rodeo. "She's still really hot. Oh, girls. I'm really worried. She doesn't look good."

"I don't understand," whined Ruth, fear thick in her voice. "I stitched her up. The cut wasn't even that deep, and it didn't hit any major organs. She shouldn't be feverish like this. She should be getting better or, at least, not worse."

"Give her some more of the healing tonic," ordered Dolores.

Doing as she was told, Ruth carefully raised my head and placed a mug to my lips. "Drink this. It's full of good stuff. Oregano oil and rosemary. It'll help fight the infection, and it'll make you feel loads better." She smiled, though her eyes were sad and worried.

I swallowed, well, tried to swallow, but as my body shook, I sent more of Ruth's oregano oil down my front and neck. However, I still managed to get some in my mouth.

The tonic was warm and welcomed. I felt it working the second it went down my throat, filling my body with soothing warmth. The scent of earth magic filled my nose as it filled my body. I felt it in my mind, felt it flowing through me, vibrating with the current of raw earth magic. The well of energy was spinning and healing. Slowly, my pulse eased and soothed. My breath filled my lungs in a smooth, calm motion. My body still hurt as though Dolores had accidentally run me over with the Volvo, and the fever was still there along with the cold, but I wasn't a corpse. Not yet.

Once the convulsions lessened, I blinked and looked around. I was in Davenport House, in the kitchen. I felt the smoothness of wood against my back, and I realized I was lying flat on the kitchen table.

Something soft brushed the side of my cheek, and I turned my head to stare at a black cat.

"How you feeling, kid?" asked Hildo. The worry in his voice had my eyes burning. "Do you remember who did this to you?"

"Was it Allison or that witch you said was working for her?" asked Beverly.

Ruth bumped her hip on my other side. "Was it a curse? Do you remember what she said? The words she used?"

I shook my head and forced what little energy I had to form one single word. "Demon." Damn, my voice was harsh and sounded just like it did when I was eighty.

"Demon?" my three aunts said together.

I nodded, feeling another wave of fever lash through me. Taking a shaky breath I said, "Stabbed."

"Yes." Dolores exhaled. "We saw the blood. Why did the demon attack you?"

Because I'm an abomination, I wanted to say but only managed to utter, "Kill. Me." Every word took an enormous amount of energy, and I felt myself slipping into the darkness again. I was tired. So tired. My eyelids fluttered, the weight of them too much to keep open like they were coated with lead.

"Don't close your eyes, Tessa," urged Ruth. "You can't fall asleep. Sleep would be really, really bad. Do you understand? If you do, you might never wake up."

My eyes snapped open as I stared at her. I gave her a nod of my head. I was going to try not to sleep, for now. But if they didn't do something quickly, I didn't think I could keep them open much longer.

I felt a tug on my left hand as Beverly took it in hers. "You're all clammy and hot."

Hot? I felt like I was sitting in a freezer.

I blinked up at Beverly, leaning against the table next to me and looking spectacular in the dim light. The shadows accentuated the perfect angles on her flawless face. Ruth was propped up on my other side, biting her fingernails while Dolores had her head down in thought, worrying me.

"Why isn't Ruth's tonic working?" commented Beverly, her voice high and very unlike herself. "She should be up on her feet by now. Or at least the fever should be gone."

Ruth shrugged, looking defeated. "I don't know. I can try doubling the dose. I'll add more garlic extract and more honey this time. Oh. I've got some of my basil brew left over from when Karen Root had pneumonia. I can give that a try too."

"Wait." Dolores bumped her hip on the kitchen table as she moved closer to me. "Show me her wound again," she commanded. "Let's roll her on her left side."

Together, the three witches gently rolled me over. I felt warm fingers graze my skin and the tug of my sweater being hauled over my back.

"Cauldron save us," shrieked Beverly.

I heard the distinctive slap of someone covering their mouth to keep from screaming. Probably Ruth. And then I heard Dolores's sharp intake of breath. That was never good.

"What?" I managed to wheeze, though trying to stay awake was proving to be taxing. I gave myself another five minutes before I passed out. The fact that I was staring at a chair and not at whatever had them freaking out was bad. I should be panicking, but there wasn't much room in my mind for anything except sleep. Sleep to end the fever and the pain.

"Let me see." Hildo leaped over me, and I felt his light tread as he padded over to my back.

"Now we know why Ruth's healing potions aren't working," said Dolores. "This is why."

"What is that?" I heard Beverly ask, followed by the sound of her heels scratching the wood floors like she'd scurried back a step from whatever they were staring at. Oh yeah, me.

"Ruth, have you ever seen something like this?" asked Dolores, her voice edged with worry.

I hated that they were talking about me like I wasn't really there. But it's not like I could keep up a conversation. I struggled and fought against the pull of the poison. But each time it made me more susceptible to it, more vulnerable.

I felt warm fingers press around my wound, sending it ablaze again, and I cried out in pain.

Ruth was at my side in a second. "So, so sorry, Tessa." Her face was flushed as she rubbed my shoulder. "But I had to look and see if there was any pus."

"It's black. I've never seen black pus," came Beverly's voice from behind me, far away, like maybe she was in the living room.

Black pus? Dear God, I was dying for sure.

"Okay, it's black," pressed Dolores. "Have you seen this before?"

Ruth moved away from my side. "Well, see all those dark veins around the cut? That looks like septicemia. Blood poisoning. It happens when a bacterial infection enters the bloodstream." There was a pause. "But this is different."

97

"Because of the black pus?" asked Dolores.

"Yes. And my tonics would have cured it in no time."

"So, that demon's blade was poisoned," concluded Dolores. Good, they were catching on. But not fast enough. "If we know what poison was used, we can cure her. Right? Find the antidote?"

"Yes," answered Ruth. "But *which* poison? I'll have to take a sample of her pus. And then I'll have to test it against all the known poisons. It might take a while."

"How long?" asked Beverly.

"A few hours."

"A few hours and Tessa will be dead!" yelled Dolores. "She'll never make it. Look at her. She's *dying*. If we don't find something in the next few minutes, she's going to die."

Oh great. Even better.

"You've got a better idea?" howled Ruth. Man, I'd never heard her voice like that before. I didn't want them to start fighting because of me.

I heard the sound of nails scraping the wood top. "Uh-oh," came Hildo's voice. "I know what that is." I strained myself alert to hear more. "I've seen it before. That's poison from a demon's death blade."

Death blade? I'd never heard of it. I closed my eyes as another wave of dizziness shook me.

"A death blade?" came Beverly's voice, a little closer this time. "I don't like the sound of that."

Dolores let out a long breath. "Perhaps the word *death* gave it away."

"Do you know how to cure her? What poison this is?" asked Ruth, her voice high with hope and with obvious strain.

"No," answered the cat. "But her father will."

"Obiryn?" I heard Dolores say.

"Yes," replied the cat. "She told me her father was a demon. This is beyond your skill—no offense. Only a demon can help her now. You need to find him and bring him here. And you better do it quick," said Hildo, his voice growing fainter. "If he doesn't get here in the next five minutes, Tessa won't make it."

I wasn't going to make it.

I felt a faint need to giggle, and a smile curled over me. For some strange reason, the idea of dying seemed hilarious. I gave in to my desire to giggle. Yeah, I was losing it.

"Look at her! She's delirious," cried Beverly. "We have to hurry."

"It's the infection," said Ruth. "She's losing her mind over to it."

I took a labored breath and I let out another low chuckle. And another.

"Okay. How do we do this? Like in a summoning circle?" asked Dolores. "We know his name. That can work. Who can draw up a circle in a few minutes?"

"I've got a better idea." I heard Beverly's heels click on the hardwood floor and then the squeal of hinges as a door opened.

"Obiryn, darling," Beverly shouted. Was she in the basement? "We need you. Tessa needs you. She's in trouble. She's sick. No… she's dying. She's been stabbed by a demon's death blade. Please come."

There was a long pause and then, "I don't think that worked. Ruth, get on your knees and start drawing a circle—oh!"

"Hello, Beverly," came my father's voice. "Where is she?" I could hear the worry in his tone.

"Here," said Dolores.

The sound of shoes moving over the floor hit me, and then I was staring at a pair of luminous silver eyes, set inside a handsome face with dark graying hair and a meticulously trimmed beard.

"Dad," I managed.

"Don't speak. Keep your strength," he soothed.

"Can you help her?" Ruth appeared next to my father.

"Yes," he answered with absolute conviction. "You called me just in time. But I must warn you. It's going to be… *difficult*. Tessa will suffer greatly before she gets better. You need to prepare yourselves."

"We can handle it." Dolores's tone was both determined and anxious. "What are you going to do?"

He straightened and said, "I need to bleed her. Bleed out the poison from her body."

Oh goodie.

CHAPTER
10

Okay, not what I was expecting to hear, but… carry on.

"And then?" I heard Hildo ask.

"Then…" My father exhaled, his voice steady and not at all that of a man who was about to bleed his only daughter. "I need to give her some of my blood."

"Like a transfusion?" asked Ruth.

"Yes. Exactly. My blood will act as a cure for the infection. It'll bind the poison, stop it from being further absorbed into her blood. I'm going to need your help."

"Yes, of course," said Dolores. "We'll do anything for our Tessa."

Ruth pressed her hands on her hips, her face set in determination. "What do you need us to do?"

"I'll need a large pot for the infected blood," answered my father. "An IV line, a pump, tubes, catheters. Do you have those here?"

"I do," answered Ruth, which surprised me. "Be right back." I heard the slap of her bare feet as she rushed out of the kitchen.

"I'll get you the pot." I caught a glimpse of Dolores moving into the kitchen. She came back with a large stainless-steel mixing bowl.

"Tessa." My father's face was next to mine again. "I'm going to cut the stitches around your wound. You're going to feel some pressure. I need to push the poison out. I'm afraid it's going to hurt. But it has to be done. Okay?"

I nodded. "Okay," I panted.

"Okay." My father left my side and moved around the table to get to where my back was exposed. "Here I go."

Hildo popped into my line of sight. His whiskers brushed my face as he moved closer and sat next to me. Edgy, his tail flicked behind him. "It's going to feel like your blood is boiling, that your insides are on fire and want to squeeze out of your pores. You're going to feel like your bowels are going to come up and spew through your throat, choking you."

Nice. At least I could count on him for being truthful.

I could feel myself spinning, drifting into the darkness once more, the kitchen around me slowly shutting off. My trembling was worsening as Ruth's healing tonic was consumed by the blade's poison.

"Hurry! She's not going to make it," I heard Beverly cry out, but I was too tired to care anymore.

I felt a sudden tug on my skin where I'd been stabbed—and then buckets and buckets of pain.

I reared back as scorching pain slammed through my body. The blade's poison, a senseless fury, soaked into my body. I cried out in agony as the full effect of the poison hit me over and over again. I curled my mind around what was left and tried to see past the pain, to form another thought and prove I wasn't dead yet. Mindless from the pain, I felt my insides start to burn. I felt the blade's poison wrap around me, my soul, and yet I still burned. The sensation of my insides melting grew stronger. I felt the blade's poison from my side, hot and hateful. A putrid smell of rotten flesh and sulfur reached me. Where did that come from? Oh yeah. Me.

It burned, vicious and everlasting. I couldn't think fast enough.

"Arat h'uktak reyaudri," muttered my father, in a voice guttural and alien to me. Some demonic language.

The air shifted and sizzled with energy. My heart thrashed madly in my chest, the hairs at the nape of my neck prickling and standing on end. I felt a wave of energy cascade over me, cold and familiar. Demon magic.

My body trembled, and the same cold energy was sifting *through* me now, almost like a surge of adrenaline through my veins. It moved through me, alien and cold like a faint ache.

And then I felt a prick in my right arm like a needle. Something warm and pleasant entered my body, and I felt warm for the first time since the attack with the demon. Kind of like soaking in a hot tub, without the drink in my hand.

A sudden wind brushed my face, carrying the scent of sulfur, not repugnant like before but softer and more tolerable. My skin pricked as energy flowed with unusual sharpness.

After a moment, the pain in my body subsided, and with a final tug, it stopped completely as though it had never been there. After what felt like an eternity, the pressure around my wound disappeared.

"Did it work?" Came Dolores's anxious voice from somewhere behind me, just as I felt another prick from my arm and then nothing.

"Yes, I believe so," answered my father. "There's no more trace of the poison in her. But Tessa will tell us."

I blinked as Ruth, Beverly, Dolores, Hildo, and my father all appeared in my line of sight, their faces anxious and their bodies tightening with tension.

"Tessa? How do you feel?" Ruth pressed her hand on my forehead, and I saw the immediate relief on her face. "Thank the cauldron. Her fever broke."

I smiled despite the nauseated feeling I still had in me, though it now seemed manageable. Ruth's smiling face would do that to a person. Her happy spirit was contagious.

I took in a deep breath. "Like I swallowed some acid. But better. Much better. Thank you. If you hadn't found me when you did, I'd be dead by now." I tried not to think about it, but there it was. Without my aunts, I would have been a goner. For real this time.

The thought of never seeing Marcus again had my insides tightening around me, like I was wearing that Spanx bodywear again—and that was a scary thought.

"Let's get you in a chair," commanded Ruth. "You need to eat to replenish your strength." Both Ruth and Dolores helped me up off the table and eased me down into one of the chairs.

Off to the side were some long tubes connected to an IV stand. Next to it on the floor was a large stainless-steel bowl, almost entirely covered with black liquid that looked a lot like oil. The poison from the demon's blade.

"Damn. All that was in me?" Yikes. Utterly disgusting. The kitchen smelled sickly sweet, and my eyes watered at the stench of rot. It took immense self-control not to hurl.

Ruth caught me staring at the black liquid. "I'll get rid of that." She snatched up the bowl containing that vile substance along with the IV and tubing and disappeared down the hall. What she would do with the poison was beyond me, and I didn't care if she flushed it down the toilet. Though I was pretty sure she'd have to dispose of it properly, whatever that meant.

Beverly let herself fall in a chair next to me, her face flushed and a large glass of red wine in her hand. "All this stress is not good for my complexion," she said and took a large sip of wine. She tugged the skin on her forehead with her free hand. "I'm too young to have wrinkles." She looked at me and said, "It's amazing. Isn't it?"

I shrugged. "What is?"

Beverly flashed me a vibrant smile, her eyes bright. "That even under such duress, I still look *damn* good," she added with a laugh.

I pressed my lips together, not sure how to respond to that. I chose not to.

Hildo leaped onto my lap. "I'm glad you didn't die."

"Me too."

"You're one tough witch," said the cat. "You remind me of old witch Agatha Harper. I was her familiar for eighty years. Tough old broad, you know. And meaner than a badger on steroids. Loved that old witch." He settled himself and began purring. I raked my fingers through his silky fur, which was extremely therapeutic, and I was thankful to have him with me.

Ruth reappeared in the kitchen, her hands behind her as she tied an apron around her front with the words written in bold black letters, WITCH BY NATURE. BITCH BY CHOICE. "I'll heat up my vegetable minestrone soup I made yesterday," she said as she pulled out a large iron pot from the refrigerator and set it on the stove. "You need to hydrate your body, and it'll give your immune system a nice boost. Get your energy back too." Just the thought of her fabulous soup had me salivating. Damn, I hadn't realized how hungry I was.

"Sounds great. Thanks, Ruth," I told her, and she spun around and beamed at me, a pink wooden spoon in her hand, which she flicked as though it were a magic wand. Maybe it was.

Granted, I already felt better, but I still felt weak, like I was just coming out of a cold. Soup was just what I needed.

I met my father's silver gaze. "Thanks for saving my butt a second time. You should be awarded Father of the Year."

My father smiled, but I could see the worry lines etched around his eyes and mouth. He looked paler than usual as he ran his fingers through his short beard, a gesture I had come to understand was something he did when he was anxious or troubled.

"Can you tell us what happened?" My father pulled down the sleeve from his crisp white shirt where I assumed a catheter had been in his arm. He yanked a navy jacket from one of the chairs and put it on.

It occurred to me then that I had just received a dose of my father's blood. Being his biological daughter, I already had some, but now I had more. It was different. I couldn't help but wonder if it would *make* me different somehow... or perhaps stronger?

"Yes, I'd like to know this too." Dolores pulled out the chair across from the table from me and sat. "What was a demon doing in the middle of Hollow Cove? And on *our* street? And why, for cauldron's sake, did you decide to take him on yourself?"

"It's not like I had a choice." I took a breath and said, "Well, I went out looking for you." I glanced at my aunts, trying to see some guilt there but finding none. Just worried expressions aimed at me.

Beverly raised a brow and settled her wineglass. "Looking for us? Why?"

I contemplated whether or not to mention our issue with Silas having my father here and decided that was not my secret to tell.

"Never mind," I said, shaking my head. "The demon was here because he was looking for me."

"And he found you." Beverly took another mouthful of her wine.

Dolores frowned at her sister. She looked at me. "But why *you* specifically? Did he say why he wanted to kill you? Poison you with that blade?"

"Here comes the fun part," I told them. I waited a moment to get their full attention, even waited for Ruth to turn around, pink spoon at the ready. "Apparently, there's a hit on me."

My father hissed something in another language. He paced around the kitchen, running his fingers through his hair.

Worry pulled Dolores's long face. "I do believe I'll be needing a drink too." She jerked up from her seat, grabbed a wineglass from the cabinet, snatched the wine bottle Beverly had opened, and sat back down.

Ruth screwed up her face and made circles in the air with her spoon. "That sounds really bad."

"No! Ya think?" snapped Dolores, making Ruth narrow her eyes at her. "I'd never realized there're such things as demon hit men," she continued and finished pouring her wine.

"Me neither." I stroked the top of Hildo's head, smiling as he closed his eyes.

The scent of Ruth's minestrone soup was heavy in the air. Within moments, she placed a bowl of steaming, delicious soup in front of me, the spoon propped against the side of the bowl inviting me to grab it.

"Some fresh homemade bread with that?" she asked, her smiling face looking down at me.

I nodded. "Load on the butter, please," I answered, making Hildo snort. I realized that the extra butter would most definitely clog up some arteries, but I'd nearly died tonight. I deserved extra butter. Besides, weren't bread, butter, and wine life's essentials? Well, they were to me.

A moment later, I was the owner of two slices of homemade bread topped with a heavy layer of butter. Yum. This gal was in heaven.

Hildo had crept up closer to the table's edge, eyeing my bread like a sad, starving feral street cat. That kind of talent would land him the starring role in Disney's remake of *The Aristocats*. I tore off a piece and gave it to him.

Next, it was my turn as I tore into the bread like some famished animal. The butter and bread combination made my taste buds dance a disco before swallowing.

"Ruth," I mumbled. "Have I ever told you that you're the best cook ever?"

Ruth's cheeks turned bright red. "Oh." She shrugged, looking down, though her smile was spread from ear to ear. "Don't be silly. This is nothing."

It wasn't nothing. Quite the opposite. It was heaven in my mouth.

Beverly leaned back in her chair with a frown. "Hit men are usually paid for their services. So, who hired him?"

I shrugged, grabbing the spoon, taking my first spoonful of soup, and feeling the warmth sink into me. "My guess would be these *others* my mother had mentioned to me before. They want me dead." I looked over to my father to see if he'd come to the same conclusion as I did, but he was staring at his feet, marching through the kitchen with his face twisted up in fury.

"Obiryn, will you sit down," ordered Dolores, having caught my gaze as she rubbed her temples. "Your pacing is giving me a headache."

It worked.

My father drew up a chair on my other side, his legs fidgeting. His face was definitely paler, a result of all the blood he gave me that saved my life.

"Obi-Wan, relax," I told him, trying to lighten the mood a little. "I'm all right. It's fine."

His silver eyes met mine, his expression serious. "It's not." His lips twitched like he was about to say more but didn't.

Dolores stared at my father. "Do you know why there's a demon trying to kill my niece? If you do, please explain this to us."

"Oh. I can answer that," I said between chews. "Apparently, I'm an abomination."

Ruth dropped some plates in the kitchen sink. She looked up, her face screwed up in anger. "That's a horrible thing to say."

"Maybe," I answered. "But there you have it. These *others* hate me because of what I am. Because my mother is a mortal witch and my father a demon. I mean… why do they even care? Why is that such a big deal? I'm nobody."

"Good question." Dolores was eyeing my father, waiting for him to answer. He didn't. In fact, he avoided her gaze altogether.

I stared at the last of my soup. Forget using a spoon. I grabbed the bowl with both hands and tipped the edge to my lips, downing the entire contents like it was my last meal.

"What did he look like? The hit man that stabbed you?" asked my father, a worried edge to his tone. He'd gone completely still, waiting on my every word as though he feared what I was about to say.

I set the bowl down and wiped my mouth with my napkin. "Average height. Build. Ugly bastard. With one red eye and a nasty scar that ripped into the other eye down to his jaw. Oh yeah. He wore this special cloak that acted as a shield against my magic." I exhaled, remembering how he'd done something to the ley lines. "I don't know how, but he prevented me from using the ley lines, like he was jamming the signals with some sort of demonic ward, blocking them."

My father was silent for a long while, absorbing what I'd just told him. "I know who he is," he answered, his expression dark and strained. "He calls himself Vorkan, though no one knows his true name. He's one of the most infamous demon hit men in the Netherworld. The most expensive. He's legendary because he's never failed a target. *Ever*."

The hair on the back of my neck rose at the tone in my father's voice. "Well, he failed tonight. I'm still alive. He needs to brush up on his skills."

My father was shaking his head. "He'll be back, Tessa. Once he gets word that you're still alive, you'll see him again. And this time if his blade doesn't kill you, he'll use something else. Something worse."

"Great. I love being popular."

"You'll have to stay inside Davenport House," he said, and I didn't like the finality in his tone.

"Okay. Until when?"

He shrugged and said, "Forever."

My lips parted and I laughed. "Listen, Dad, I'm grateful for your help. Grateful for saving my life—twice—but you can't expect me to stay in this house forever. I can't live like that. I have things to do. People to see." Like a sexy wereape naked on his bed waiting for a naked me to join him.

"Your father's right." Dolores gave me her signature authoritative frown that would have had grown men scampering away. "You need to stay *inside*. It's the safest place for you. He can't reach you here. Like I told you before, this place is like a bunker against all those soul-sucker devils." She looked at my father and added, "No offense."

He gave her a tight smile. "None taken."

I couldn't help but notice how Beverly and Ruth weren't saying anything to come to my defense (or just to contradict Dolores because, let's face it, they loved to argue). Their silence said it all. They agreed with Dolores and my father.

Now I was a little ticked. "I'm sorry, but… I'm not going to be a prisoner in this house. And I'm not going to live in fear of this demon either. That's giving him way too much power over me. Not going to happen."

My father's jaw clenched. "If you leave this house, he will find you and he *will* kill you."

I took a deep breath and let it out, trying to reel in my anger. This was not my father's fault. I just didn't appreciate how he thought trapping me in this house for the rest of my existence would help. "I'll be more prepared next time. Now that I know he'll be out there, lurking. I *can* defend myself. I'm not weak."

The wrinkles around my father's eyes deepened. "I'm not saying that you are. But you don't understand. Vorkan won't *ever* stop. Not until you're dead. It might not be tomorrow or even next month or next year. For him, twenty or fifty years is nothing to wait out a mark. And then one day, when you're least expecting it, and when you think he's finally given up—he'll strike hard and kill you." His silver eyes pinned me. "He nearly succeeded tonight."

Okay, he had a point. But I wasn't going to make it any easier. "I'm not agreeing to this. I can't be locked in here for the rest of my life. Especially when things finally started to feel normal again. I won't do it."

"It won't be for forever." My father got to his feet and started to button his jacket. "Just give me a few days, and I'll figure something out."

I leaned back in my chair and crossed my arms over my chest. "Like what?"

"Vorkan's a hit man. But he's also a businessman. I just need to give him something more substantial than what they've offered him."

I blinked. "Do the others have a name, or do we continue to call them just that?"

"The leaders of my world," he answered, looking more tired. "The heads of state, if you will. Think of them as a council. Similar to your witch courts. Only this one is governed by demons."

It wasn't that I was surprised the Netherworld had bodies of government. I was surprised they knew of my existence and cared

116

enough to want me dead. That was the real surprise.

My father walked over to the basement door and pulled it open. He stood there a moment and then turned to face me, his hand still on the handle. "Just… stay here, okay? Just until I get back."

I raised a brow. "And when will that be?"

"A few days."

I shifted in my chair. "I can try, but I'm not making any promises."

"We'll look after her," said Beverly, having noticed my father's resistance to leave. "She's safe with us."

My father seemed to have accepted Beverly's offer and stepped through the threshold, closing the basement door behind him.

I didn't have to look to know that he was already gone, somewhere in the Netherworld, to his house or whatever living arrangements were in that world.

I felt eyes on me, and I turned my gaze to my three aunts. Part of me wanted to ask my aunts about their plan on using the kiss-of-death curse on Silas. But I could tell after what happened tonight, it sort of put a damper on their murderous scheme. Well, at least I knew they weren't going anywhere tonight. Not after what happened. But tomorrow was a different story.

Right now, I was exhausted. "I'm going to bed." I pushed my chair back, and Hildo leaped off my lap as I stood.

"Good idea," said Dolores. "A good night's sleep will do you some good. Would do all of us some good."

Beverly gave a snort. "A good night's sleep with Dennis Taylor would do *me* some good too."

Dolores laughed, surprising me. But what surprised me more was when they clinked their wineglasses together in a toast. Guess these ladies were all worn out too.

Ruth came over and picked up my empty bowl. "I'll be up in a minute with some chamomile tea to help you sleep."

"Thanks, Ruth." I smiled and squeezed her arm. "You spoil me, but I like it."

Ruth laughed. "You deserve to be spoiled a little from time to time. There's no crime in that."

"Me too. I deserve to be spoiled," said Hildo at my feet, a hopeful gleam in his eyes.

"I'll bring you up some of my chocolate chips," Ruth told the cat.

Hildo showed his teeth in a smile. "Ruth... I love you."

I laughed. Hildo laughed. Ruth laughed.

Okay, time for bed.

"Good night," I told my aunts as I shuffled my way out the kitchen, my legs seemingly heavier than I remembered, or I'd just gained thirty pounds from eating all that butter. Totally worth it.

"I'm coming with you," meowed Hildo, and I smiled down at him. With his tail high in the air and that glossy black fur with those gleaming yellow eyes, he was truly a handsome cat. And a very good friend to want to accompany me. Yeah, I was really happy to have him around. Besides, I was going to need a pal on my side if I was going to be on house arrest for a while, though they really couldn't keep me locked up forever.

Despite my father's overprotective tendencies, I did agree with him on one account. I knew this Vorkan would be back.

But this time, I'd be ready for him.

CHAPTER
11

I woke the next morning, afternoon rather, according to Hildo who'd walked over my face, in way of an alarm clock, feeling like I'd slept for a week.

The first thing that surprised me was how rejuvenated I felt, as though I'd downed a few of Ruth's healing tonics for breakfast. But I hadn't.

No doubt this had something to do with my father—his blood, specifically. The transfusion had not only saved my life, but it had also revived me, healing all my aches and pains from the night before. Weeks before, really, if the disappearing of those bruises I'd gotten last week were any indication. I hadn't felt this good in years.

It made me wonder what else this transfusion had done to me. Guess I'd find out later.

Despite my demon upgrade (what else was I supposed to call it), I wasn't perfectly happy. This whole contract on my life left a damper on my spirit. More like it kicked it around even when it was down. Having a demon on my tail made things complicated. More than complicated, it made everything worse, dangerous. Especially now with what my aunts and I had to deal with, not to mention Silas. Because we all knew he wasn't going to go away anytime soon.

I'm not going to lie. The demon's timing sucked. Okay, so he might have nearly killed me. But he didn't. I wasn't afraid either. I was pissed because I'd only just gotten my life back, and I wasn't about to let Scarface take it away.

And this newly returned life had plans that included a sexy-as-hell and uber-virile chief who thought *I* was *beautiful*. Yeah, no one was going to mess with that.

Vorkan might be a skilled demon hit man with a magical, protective cloak and a poisonous dagger, but I had brains and wit. I was strong, and I knew I'd only just hit the tip of the iceberg on what I could do with my magic.

Maybe my father might be able to sway Vorkan. Though I wasn't getting my hopes up.

But first, I needed to deal with my aunts.

Swinging my legs off my bed, I grabbed my phone and checked my messages. I stared at the screen. No new messages. I glanced at the text I'd gotten from Marcus last night.

Marcus: *If you don't have dinner with me tomorrow, I'm coming over there and ripping all your clothes off. Miss you. Night.*

A stupid grin spread over my face as I'd texted him back.

Me: *Do you promise? Miss you too.*

I tossed my phone on my bed and practically skipped my way to the bathroom. I turned the shower on while I brushed my teeth to get the water nice and hot. Then I stripped and slipped under the water—

And howled like the queen of all banshees.

Cold, icy water splashed over my naked body like I'd jumped into an arctic pond in the middle of January.

"Cold! Cold! Cold!" I pushed the showerhead to the side so the water hit the tile and not me and turned the knob again, checking the water with my now-trembling hand. Nope. Still cold. There wasn't a drop of hot water.

"Great. Just freaking great."

Mood souring, I took the fastest shower in history. All thirty-two seconds of it.

After I washed every part of my body as well as I could under the circumstances—forget washing my hair… I'd do that later once the hot water was back on—I got dressed with a pair of jeans and a cozy gray sweater. Still feeling the cold of the shower on my icy and very red skin, I grabbed my phone and walked over to the open bedroom door. I remembered closing it last night when I went to bed.

"Hildo, you clever little furball."

I knew he'd done it. Probably magicked it to open for him. Or maybe House opened it for him. I made a mental note to ask him about that later.

Just when I reached the threshold—the door slammed in my face.

I jerked back, the panel nearly taking my nose off.

"This is really *not* my morning."

I let out a frustrated breath, reached for the door handle, and turned.

Only the door handle wouldn't turn. The door was locked.

"House," I voiced. "Open the door. This isn't funny." I needed to get downstairs. I could hear the sounds of my aunts' voices coming through the door from somewhere downstairs, so I knew they were still here. But that didn't mean they hadn't snuck out last night after I went to bed or early this morning to carry out their kissing scheme with Silas.

I yanked on the door handle again, twisting it as I pulled. "House. Open the door!" I growled, my anger rising. "What the hell is wrong with you? Open this door right now!"

Blood pumping, I let it go and stepped back, my hands balled into fists. "I swear. If you don't open this door now at once, I'm going to burn it down." As soon as the words left my lips, I was reminded of Gran the first time I'd seen her on the porch that night when she rose from the dead and Davenport House wouldn't let her in.

It hadn't worked though.

With a swoosh of energy and a click, my bedroom door swung open.

"Thanks," I said, irritated as I made my way out and down the stairs. I had no idea why House had done that. But right now I had more important matters to attend to.

"Thanks for using up all the hot water," I grumbled as I entered the kitchen.

Beverly and Dolores sat at their usual spots around the kitchen table while Ruth worked at the stove, standing over a sizzling pan of vegetables and something that smelled of Mexican spices. Hildo was on the counter next to the stove, his yellow eyes pinned to Ruth's pan.

Ruth let out a laugh and looked over her shoulder at me. "That's impossible, silly. We've never run out of hot water. House would never let that happen. House is magical, you see," she added as though I had no idea I'd been living in a magical house for months.

Frowning, I moved to the coffee machine and poured myself a cup. "Tell that to the icy shower I just had. I'll have to drink some antifreeze to thaw out my intestines." I gave her a tight-lipped smile to soften the shortness of my answer.

Ruth continued to smile like I was joking. "Sit. I'm making Mexican vegetarian burritos. After what happened to you last night, well, you need to feed your body with nutrition."

"Yeah. You need to feed the beast," said Hildo, although I think he was referring to himself. He swiped a finger in the steaming pan and then dabbed it on his tongue. "Needs more salt."

"What you need is a nutritional arsenal," Ruth continued. "Superfood."

I frowned at her. "Superfood?"

She nodded. "Food with capes."

Dolores set her mug down as she and Beverly exchanged a look. Then Dolores put her elbows on the table and leaned forward. "Anything else that's happened that is a little strange?"

Strange was our normal in this house. Still...

"Yes, actually." I pulled out the chair next to Beverly and sat. "House slammed the door in my face just now. And when I tried to open my bedroom door, it was locked. I had to threaten House to let me out. Maybe House needs a vacation."

Again, the aunts shared a look, and this time Ruth was involved too as she whirled around, her eyebrows high.

"What?" I asked, running my gaze over the witches and seeing the tension rise between them.

Dolores sighed. "I was afraid of this."

I frowned. "Afraid of what?"

"That House might have an issue with you."

I glanced back and forth between them for a moment before I said, "Excuse me?"

Ruth shrugged like it was no big deal. "It's because of your father's blood." With a pan in her hand, she poured the contents over the platter of tortillas.

"But I've always had my father's blood in me, and House never had a problem with me before," I said, watching Ruth roll the first burrito. "He's my dad. I've got his DNA. This isn't new."

"Yes, but last night you got an *extra* dose," said Beverly and took a sip of her coffee. "Your father gave you a lot of his blood."

"And now House thinks you're a threat," commented Dolores, a forced smile on her lips.

"You mean, House thinks I'm a demon." I stared at my coffee, my stomach churning. I was certain this was why House was acting up. It made sense. House was only protecting its members from evil. Only this time, the evil was me.

"It could have been worse," said Dolores. "House could have thrown you out the minute you woke up."

"Out naked in the snow," added Beverly, with a seductive smile.

"Or obliterated you into nothingness," offered Ruth, nodding her head.

Dolores glared at Ruth. "So, that's good," she added, her eyes back to me. "It knows you're you... only..."

"Different," I finished.

Beverly leaned over and patted my arm. "But don't worry, darling. House knows you're a Davenport witch. It's just a temporary glitch. I'm sure it'll pass."

"How sure?"

My pretty aunt shrugged. "Pretty sure. I mean, it's never happened before. But you're a Davenport witch. It'll be fine." Again, she and Dolores shared a look that I didn't like. Translation—they had no idea if things would get better or worse for me.

"Great. So now I have no idea what to expect from House." My eyes moved to the basement where on many occasions Beverly pushed a few cheating husbands and wife beaters to get lobotomized. I was going to stay clear of the basement for a while.

"While you're all here, I have something to ask." I waited to get their full attention. "What are you planning on doing to Silas?"

Beverly spat some of her coffee. "What are you talking about?"

I wrapped my fingers around my hot mug. "You can stop the act. I know all about it."

"Know about what?" Dolores's eyes narrowed. "What are you getting at, Tessa?" She brought her coffee mug to her lips and took a sip.

I looked at each aunt in turn and said, "Did you kill him?"

It was Dolores's time to spit out her coffee in a shower over the table. "What? Are you insane? Why on earth would you think that?"

Maybe Dolores and Beverly were more skilled at controlling their emotions. Their faces were expertly pulled into very convincing shocked expressions with a dab of indignance. But Ruth, well, Ruth was an open spellbook. She looked guilty as hell.

My heart stopped. "Oh, my, God. You did! You killed him!"

"Stop this nonsense." Dolores slapped an open hand on the table, making me jerk. "We didn't *kill* anyone."

Except for Nathaniel. "I saw the book in the potions room. I saw the page with the kiss-of-death curse. It's why I came looking for you last night and got my ass kicked by that demon. You can't deny it?"

Beverly brushed a strand of blonde hair from her face. "I won't deny that you saw one of the many spellbooks we own. But you're mistaken, darling. We were interested in what was on the *other* page."

Huh. I never thought of looking at the other page. "What was on the other page?"

"The kiss of the forgetful curse," answered Dolores.

Beverly flashed one of her famous smiles. "It spells a person to forget."

"Like amnesia," volunteered Ruth. "Only it lasts forever."

"It makes them forget why they're here and drives them to move on," continued Dolores. "To leave. To leave town and forget everything about Beverly. About Nathaniel."

I leaned forward, curious. "And did you?"

Dolores pressed her lips together. "We had you to fix. So, no, we didn't."

The idea of Dolores kissing Silas made me smile. "So, who was going to pucker up and kiss the sonofabitch?"

"Me." Beverly straightened in her seat. "And I was really looking forward to pressing my plump, sensuous, expert lips on that handsome devil." She let out a low breath tinged with a throaty growl. "I love a man who uses his body as a canvas. Just like me. Only my art lasts for a few hours," she added with a giggle.

I nearly threw up in my mouth. "That's nice." I was relieved that they didn't find him. I had this feeling Silas was somewhat immune to curses and hexes. If they'd tried and failed to curse him, things would have taken a turn for the worse.

"Listen. You have to *promise* not to do anything like that again," I said, and before Dolores could protest, I continued, "I think he might be resistant to some curses. Just forget about curses. Let's just concentrate on getting him out of here another way."

"How?" asked Ruth.

My train of thought was interrupted by the sound of a phone ringing.

"I'll get it." Dolores walked down the hallway to the small side table where the landline was.

Ruth came over and set a plate with a juicy Mexican veggie burrito in front of me. "Hope you like it."

"I know I will. Thanks."

My aunt beamed. "There's lots more. So, don't be shy."

I tore into my burrito, and yummy spicy sauce dripped from the corners of my mouth as I chewed and moaned. Yup. This was really good. Before I knew it, my plate was empty. The only evidence of my burrito was my sticky fingers and my face. Thank God Marcus wasn't here to see me like this. He might rethink his text from last night.

"You eat like a five-year-old," commented Hildo.

I laughed and shot him a look. "And I pet cats like a five-year-old too."

The cat's eyes widened, but he didn't say anything after that.

From the hallway, Dolores's voice rose in irritation.

Ruth stopped in mid-tortilla roll and stared in that direction. "I wonder what that's about?"

Beverly's expression was cautious. "Well. You won't have to wait long. Here she comes."

Wiping my mouth and then my fingers on my napkin, I watched as the tall witch marched back into the kitchen. Her frown and worried expression had my pulse rising.

"That was Martha on the phone," said Dolores as she stood, her hands on her hips.

"Oh," said Ruth, rolling a mini burrito and giving it to Hildo on a plate. "What does Martha have to say?"

"Apparently Silas was just at her beauty salon," answered Dolores, her dark eyes moving to Beverly, who'd stiffened. "And he wasn't there for a bikini wax."

"Oh? What was he there for?" asked Ruth, as though bikini waxing was something she thought Silas had done regularly.

Dolores scowled at her. "He was drilling her for questions about us. About you mostly, Beverly."

Beverly threw up her hands. "Great. That gossip queen was probably thrilled to have an audience. Now everyone in town will know about Nathaniel being missing and me in the middle of it."

My aunt was right. Martha was probably ecstatic to have someone new listen to her gossip. Though I wasn't surprised Silas was going around town getting dirt on Beverly. It was his purpose here.

"What kinds of questions did he ask her?" I pressed, a nervous feeling bubbling up inside me. I didn't trust Silas. He was up to something. I could feel it in my bones. The longer he stayed in town, the worse it would be.

"He asked her if she knew who Nathaniel was," answered Dolores, making Beverly whine. "If she ever met him. Stuff like that. She was too busy telling me how handsome and exotic he was—her words, not mine—for me to get more information out of her."

Beverly scrunched up her face. "What? Why do you look like there's more?"

Dolores pulled out her chair and sat back down in her seat. "He's on his way to see Gilbert next."

"What!"

At the sound of panic in her voice, we all stopped what we were doing and looked at Beverly.

Dolores cocked her head to the side. "Beverly? What is it?"

Beverly's perfect rosy complexion had gone ghostly white. Stress and fear made her features sharp and her green eyes pop. She looked stunning even when she looked like she might bolt out of her chair. Me? I looked like a crazed hag when I got scared. Can't have it all.

Despite all that, I'd never seen her look so... defeated. And I didn't like that look on her. She didn't look like herself.

"Does Gilbert know something?" I asked Beverly, my tension rising. "If that little shifter owl thinks he's going to spew garbage about my family, I'm going to pluck every single feather off his body." That shifter knew how to push my buttons. Because of him, I was now working for the town for free while my salary went to pay for the new gazebo. Yes, I'd burned the old one down, but it had been an accident. I had been trying to fry the Soul Collector demon's ass, who was now my friend. Yeah, my world was a strange one.

My aunt shook her head very slowly. "No." She took a deep breath. "Gilbert was at the same hotel where Nathaniel and I were staying last year. On that night. On the night he..."

Shit.

My curse overpowered Ruth's and Dolores's intake of breaths. "Did he see you?"

Beverly wiped the corner of her brow with a trembling finger. "I don't know. He could have. I mean..." She smiled forcefully. "I'm hard to miss." But her smile faded just as fast as it had appeared.

"If Gilbert tells Silas about the hotel..." started Dolores.

"Then all he has to do is check with the hotel's bookings. He'll see your names. The hotel probably has cameras too."

"Oh no. They'll see us!" shouted Ruth.

"They'll see us coming into the hotel," agreed Dolores. "But I put an invisibility spell on us when we left. Even if Silas looks at the footage, he won't see us leaving with Nathaniel's body."

I'd always wondered how they'd sneaked Nathaniel's body into the Volvo. Guess that story would be for another time.

Tears fell from Beverly's face. She didn't even bother wiping them away. Those beautiful green eyes that were always filled with playful laughter were now consumed with fear.

"It's over," she stammered, and my heart gave a tug. "I'm finished. I should have never been on that date with him. I should have listened to my instincts. I knew something was off about him. This is all because of me."

I felt a surge of overprotectiveness for my Aunt Beverly. I'd never let anyone harm her, let alone Silas. Regrettably, Nathaniel died. True, if he wasn't dead, none of this would be happening. But then Beverly would be dead, and the bastard would probably be doing the same thing he tried on Beverly to someone else.

I jumped to my feet. "It's not over. And none of what happened is your fault. *If* Gilbert did see you, all we have to do is stop him from telling Silas."

Silent, desperate tears marked Beverly's face. "How do you propose to do that?"

I smiled. "Leave Gilbert to me."

Dolores stood up and pointed a finger at me. "Where do you think you're going, missy?"

I flashed my teeth. "This missy is going with you to stop Gilbert."

Ruth rushed over. "But you can't. That demon's still out there. You heard your father. You have to stay inside the house for your own protection."

"I know what he said," I told them. "But it's daylight. Vorkan can't walk around in broad daylight unless he wants to commit demon suicide." I grinned.

Dolores raised a brow. "She has a point."

I beamed as excitement spread through my middle. "Let's go, ladies. Let's fetch ourselves a little owl."

CHAPTER
12

After a quick ride in the Volvo, Dolores parked it at the curb right in front of Gilbert's Grocer & Gifts. Beverly was in no shape to walk, and the faster we got there, and the sooner we could stop Gilbert from blabbing, the better.

There was nothing I wanted more than to strangle that little shifter. Okay, maybe an owl stew in one of Ruth's cauldrons was up there as a first choice, but for now, I'd settle for strangulation. He made it so easy for me to hate him, really easy. But I wasn't here for me. I was here for Beverly. And I was going to make things right for her. It was the least I could do. My aunts had been so good to me since I'd arrived

in Hollow Cove six months ago. It was my turn
to give something back.

I clambered out of the car behind Ruth. Hildo
was perched on Ruth's shoulder, his tail curled
around her neck like a scarf. He hadn't asked
me if he could come. He'd just leaped on Ruth's
shoulder like that was his designated spot, like
it had *always* been where he was meant to be.
And it didn't bother me one bit. In fact, it made
me happy.

The two of them were obviously better
suited. Since his arrival, Hildo had been hanging out with Ruth more often than me or my
other two aunts. He seemed genuinely interested in her cooking and potion making. And it
wasn't like I had chosen my familiar, or him
choosing me, I sort of rescued Hildo from the in-
between with the rest of the familiars and
brought him back to the world of the living.

Looking at him now, I thought he'd made his
choice of witch, and I was glad for him and
Ruth. I would never come between that.

A buzz of voices rose as some townspeople
circled the streets, doing their shopping while
popping in and out of coffee shops and pubs.
Several of them nodded as they passed my
aunts, a gesture of acknowledgment and respect
for the witches who have been keeping their
town safe over the years from all those who'd
want to harm it.

"I'm so sorry to get you involved in all this, Tessa," said Beverly, appearing next to me. "This is our mess. You shouldn't have been involved in the first place."

My expression softened into a smile. "I'm family. That makes me involved by blood. Your mess is my mess. Your murders are now my murders."

Beverly nodded silently. She blinked rapidly and turned away, seemingly trying to hold it together.

"Let's go, girls." With a swing of her hip, Dolores shut her car door and headed for the front door. Beverly was right behind her, followed by Ruth and Hildo. I brought up the rear and shadowed my aunts through the glass door and into the store.

The small grocery shop was packed with customers. I recognized a few faces, but I wasn't here on a social call. I looked past the aisles to the back of the store and spotted a single closed door. And it so happened to be the very same door Dolores was making a beeline for.

When we reached it, raised voices from Gilbert's office pricked my ears.

Dolores turned to look at us. "Should we knock?"

"We're way past knocking." I brushed past Dolores, pushed the door open, and strode into a small office-like room that acted as both an office and storage.

My eyes found Silas first. He sat in one of the only two chairs that could fit in the tiny space. When his eyes found mine, his expression turned hard, his brows inched up knowingly, and a quick understanding laced his gaze. Either he was expecting us to show up or he knew why we were here.

Behind a desk littered with papers and stacked with boxes sat Gilbert. A frown screwed up his face at our intrusion, which had me all giddy inside.

"Hey, Gilly." I gave him a smile and a finger wave. "Sorry to barge in like that." Not really.

Gilbert leaped to his feet, fists clenched, which wasn't much of a threat seeing as he was the size of a hobbit. The buttons of his brown suit that looked and smelled like it belonged to the seventies threatened to pop under the pressure of his large middle. The frown on his face vanished at the sight of me, pulling his features in a broad smile.

That was unexpected. I was anticipating his usual frown at the sight of us, of me. Instead, the shifter looked… happy. No, he looked *thrilled*.

"I had no idea your face could do that," I told him truthfully. I really didn't. And I didn't like it. Because if he was smiling, then that meant he had something on us.

His expression twitched, and he placed his hands on his hips. "Do what?"

"Smile," I replied, making Dolores snort.

Gilbert's joy brought his thick eyebrows high. "You're too late," proclaimed the owl shifter, his face showing a twisted pleasure while deepening in color along with his wrinkles. "I told him *everything*."

Oh... shit.

Panic hit hard. I looked at Silas, but his expression was blank and passive, impossible to know what he was thinking, impossible to know what incriminating evidence Gilbert had told him. Had he seen Beverly? Is that why that stupid smile was plastered all over his face?

Whatever war of words Dolores had prepared seemed to have vanished and she paled. So did Ruth. So did Beverly.

Gilbert's smile showed some teeth. He was getting too much joy from seeing the open despair on my aunts' faces. A dark flame burned inside my chest.

Even if he told Silas that he'd seen Beverly at the hotel, it didn't prove anything. And I wasn't about to give up.

I took a deep breath and narrowed the inflow of my magic before it overflowed and I couldn't get a grip on it. I didn't want to accidentally have a roasted owl instead of a mayor. I would have gladly strangled the little shifter owl, given the chance. But now wasn't the time. I needed to know *exactly* what he'd told Silas.

My aunts had shut down. It was up to me now. And I gladly stepped up to the challenge.

Mimicking his posture, I put my hands on my hips. "What's that, Gilly? What did you tell Uncle Silas? Did you have to sit on his lap?" My heart was thrashing. I couldn't help it. I just hoped Gilbert and Silas couldn't hear it.

Gilbert looked at Silas and then back at me. "I told him about your lack of professionalism and your inept skills at protecting our town from threats," he accused, his gaze moving from each of my aunts and then finally me. "I've told him since *you* arrived, the town's been in complete disarray."

"Nice. I can always count on you to roll out the compliments."

"We've been attacked by demons," continued the town mayor, his voice rising to match the redness on his neck and face. "We've been overrun by the dead—*the dead*—and our souls were stolen by a Soul Collector because of you!"

Okay, now I was pissed. "How the hell is that *my* fault? I protected the town. I saved lives. I never made this happen."

Gilbert pointed a grubby finger in my direction. "And do you know what these things all have in common?"

I shrugged and said, "Penises?"

Gilbert's face took on another shade of red. "You," he accused.

"Tessa's right." Dolores seemed to have finally found her voice. "None of those things are her fault. She has no control over what the universe throws at us. Come on, Gilbert. You know this. As someone who's lived here his entire life, you've seen your share of evil threats. Tessa is not responsible."

Gilbert clenched his jaw; his eyes narrowed at her harsh tone. "*She* burned down the town's gazebo."

I cursed, rolling my eyes. "Not *this* again. How many times do I have to tell you that it was an *accident*."

"It was *no* accident," he shrieked. "I was a witness. I *saw* what you did." Spit flew from his mouth from those last words. Man, this little guy held a giant grudge.

My eyes moved to Silas. The fact that he looked bored had my anger surging. "Tell me, Gilly, why is it that ever since I stepped into this town you've been a giant pain in my ass?"

This time the snort came from Hildo. Gilbert's eyes zipped to the cat on Ruth's shoulder. His eyes tightened, and I could see plans formulating behind them. If he kept staring at Hildo for more than a few more seconds, I was going to lose it.

My pulse hammered as I tried to get control of my emotions. I shouldn't let this guy get me all riled up. I had to focus on what was important—my aunts, my Aunt Beverly, and her future. My fight with Gilly could wait.

All the while, Silas hadn't even uttered a single word. The fact that he was just sitting there, seemingly enjoying this personal attack, was ticking me off. I don't know why, but part of me wanted to pull on that goatee of his. Just saying.

Gilbert's frown curled into that smile again. "Mr. Cardinal asked about you. And I told him about what you've done." When his eyes flicked to Beverly and I heard the meaning behind his words, my heart nearly split out of my chest to land at my feet.

My eyes found Beverly. She was visibly shaking. Damn.

I cringed. "Oh yeah?" I said, turning my attention back on Gilbert as I shrugged, trying to look innocent and not on the defensive. "What's that?"

The tiny shifter straightened his shoulders and said, "It so happens that Beverly has been sending secret payments to the town treasurer to pay for the new gazebo, which is a breach of contract. That should not be allowed."

I looked at Beverly, who gave me a warm smile. "You did that?"

"We all did," replied Dolores, winning a nod from Ruth. "Put aside half of our pays from the town each month to help pay for it. You shouldn't be paying for it alone. That's just ridiculous. The Soul Collector and the damage he caused was a Merlin affair, and we Merlins pay our debts. Together."

"Should be paid in full by the end of this month," said Ruth, her blue eyes twinkling.

"Thank you." A warmth of gratitude spread through my gut. These ladies were a class act, and they were my aunts.

And this, my friends, was the best news ever.

"That's it?" I asked, and Silas's gaze flicked to mine. The slight narrowing of his eyes spoke of his suspicion that I was hiding something. Too bad I wasn't about to share.

But good for us that it appeared Gilbert hadn't seen Beverly at the hotel. If he had, he would have blabbed by now. He would have loved to see the look on Beverly's face.

Yeah. He had nothing on her.

I gave Gilbert a thumbs-up. "Good talk." I spun around, seeing the color returning to my aunts' faces, and their relaxed postures told me they'd come to the same conclusion. "Well, this was *exciting*." I shook my shoulders. "But we should go." No need for Silas to stare at us some more in his silence. I wish I knew what he was thinking. The guy was giving me the creeps.

The sound of a chair scratching the floor derailed my train of thought.

"Thank you, Gilbert. I'll be in touch," said Silas, speaking for the first time since we'd arrived and removing himself from the meeting.

"Glad to be of service to the MIAD," answered Gilbert proudly. He then gave my aunts and me a smile, the kind that said he was happy to have ditched the dirt on us.

I stepped in Silas's way. "Who's on your list of people to harass next? Care to share?" I doubted he was going to answer, but the guy was a pompous ass, so he just might.

Silas smiled, his dark eyes filled with threat. "Wouldn't you like to know?" And with that, he slipped around me and walked out.

"Come on," I urged my aunts and followed the tattooed witch out the office.

Dolores hurried to catch up to me. "What are you doing?" she asked, her voice low.

"He's up to something. The only way to know what, is to follow him."

"Good plan," exclaimed Ruth, Hildo bouncing on her shoulder as she rushed alongside us. "The best plans are the good ones."

Dolores scoffed. "Guess that leaves you out of the planning, genius."

I sneaked a glance at Beverly. She was really quiet, and the frown that pulled on her pretty features worried me.

Silas reached the front entrance to the grocery store and stepped out. We weren't far behind. A moment later I arrived first at the front door. Keeping my eyes on the witch, I raised my hands to grab the handle—

The glass door swung open.

I fell forward and caught myself before I fell flat on my face on the hard concrete, just as a tall blonde let go of the door, nearly causing me to smash into her.

"You," seethed Allison, looking gorgeous and annoyingly perfect in her casual jeans and short, pink puffer jacket.

I straightened and grinned. "Me."

"Watch where you're going," she snapped as my aunts all filed out behind me.

"Well, it's hard to see anything with your giant head in the way." I slipped past her. I didn't have time to argue with gorilla Barbie right now. I needed to find Silas.

Allison stepped in my way, an amused, dangerous smile on her pretty face. "This isn't over."

I arched a brow. "This conversation is over."

"You think you can curse me and that I won't retaliate? Then you know nothing of our kind."

"I never cursed you," I told her, which was the honest truth. But I wasn't about to betray Iris, not when the Dark witch had done this for me. "Listen, there's nothing I'd love more than to throw insults at each other, but right now, I have more important things to do."

Allison's face got dangerously close to mine. "You think you're so smart. Don't you? Well, let me tell you. You're not," she said, a trace of a winning smile on her face.

"Um… Tessa…" came Beverly's voice from behind me. There was a tinge of warning in her tone, but I kept my eyes on the wereape. I don't know why my aunt was so worried. It's not like I was going to beat her. Not yet.

I didn't know what it was about Allison that had me ready to drop the leash on my inner beast. It was like I couldn't help but want this war with her. She made me want to go all primal witch on her ass. Her having a past relationship with Marcus had nothing to do with it. More like her relentless, manipulative schemes to take Marcus from me. That wasn't going to happen.

Allison smiled at something she saw behind me. "The game is still in play, and I never lose."

I knew which *game* she was referring to. I'd had just about enough of her. I felt my composure disappear before I could get a handle on it.

I got right into her face and looked up. Yeah, she was that tall. "How about you go back to the zoo. Everybody *loves* the monkey exhibit."

"Tessa."

I turned my head at the sound of my name. Marcus was standing behind me, and a woman stood with him.

She was a few inches shorter than him, wearing a tasteful white wool winter coat that hit just above her knee, tailored to the curves of her well-proportioned body. In her hand was a white leather clutch purse. She looked to be in her early fifties. Her dark hair was pulled back into an elegant low bun, accentuating her high cheekbones, perfect straight nose, and oval face. Thick dark lashes framed a pair of gray eyes. Strangely familiar eyes…

"Tessa." A tight smile appeared on the chief's face. "I'd like you to meet my mother."

Oh… fu-u-u-u-ck!

CHAPTER
13

Okay, not exactly the *best* first impression. Who was I kidding? That was a total and epic failure. Marcus's mother was a wereape, and I'd just made a complete ass of myself.

Nice going, Tessa.

In-laws weren't my forte. They never seemed to warm up to me. My ex's parents always referred to me as "the weird one" and laughed in my face as though my very existence was a joke. More like me being with their son was the joke.

Nervous, I said nothing. We all know what happens to me when I'm nervous. I open my mouth and the word vomit comes spewing out. That was not an option.

I could feel my aunts bristling uneasily behind me, having heard and seen the exchange with Allison.

Marcus's mother's gray eyes were filled with contempt at my expense. I didn't blame her. I'd be staring at me too in that exact way after what I'd said.

I didn't have to look at Allison to feel the smile on her face. Yeah. She'd played me this time. She got me good.

Again, I stayed silent.

Marcus's mother held herself with a similar predatory grace that commanded attention—one I'd grown accustomed to with Marcus. From what I'd gathered with my limited knowledge of wereapes, the males were rougher around the edges. The females, well, they were more deadly looking.

His mother raised a perfectly manicured dark brow. "Is she mute, or does she just like to be insulting and rude to strangers."

Shoot. Me. Now.

Marcus was shaking his head and glaring at me like I'd gone completely mad. That gave me a little push and shook me out of my mortifying stupor.

"Hello, Mrs. Durand," I finally said, my face warming and probably matching the same red as Beverly's coat. "It's nice to finally meet you."

Marcus let out a breath. "Mom, this is, Tessa. My girlfriend."

I should have been thrilled he called me his girlfriend in front of his mother, in front of Allison. Hell, I should have been doing cartwheels naked down the main road. But I just stood there, like an idiot, feeling my one time to make a good impression had gone down the crapper.

Feeling like the fool of the century, I stuck out my hand, thinking it was the proper thing to do.

Mrs. Durand didn't even acknowledge my hand just dangling there. She looked me over, her delicate nose wrinkling like she'd just taken in my scent, and it didn't agree with her.

I dropped my arm, feeling a nervous sweat accumulate under my armpits. Nice. Now I would be a real stinker.

Seeing my embarrassment, Allison smiled at me, all mocking and confident. I narrowed my eyes, giving her the "we're not done" look.

"Now, look who's being rude, *Katherine*." Beverly moved to stand next to me, and I felt a small sense of gratitude at her pulling Mrs. Durand's attention away from me for a few seconds.

Mrs. Durand raised a brow. "Beverly? How nice to see you again. Still dressing up as a twenty-year-old in heat."

Beverly threw back her head and laughed. "Yes, well. When you've got it, flaunt it." My aunt's face pulled into one of her infamous, sensuous smiles and said, "Tell me. How is Martin? I do miss his laugh… among *other* things."

Beverly did tell me more than once that she'd slept with Marcus's father. Now, that was an interesting thing.

Katherine, Marcus's mom, didn't miss that either. In fact, her eyes narrowed at the suggestion of past carnal knowledge and activities. And then, you guessed it, she turned her icy gray gaze on me again. Swell.

I don't know why though. *I* didn't sleep with him.

Mrs. Durand's painted lips were pressed together tightly. "You didn't tell me she was a *Davenport* witch," she told her son, as though I wasn't just standing there in front of her. She'd said it as a slight, as though being one of the Davenport witches was something dreadful, lesser.

This was going really, really well.

Marcus shrugged. "I didn't think it was important."

Clearly, it was. And clearly, there was a history with Beverly.

I felt like a complete moron, yes, but I wasn't about to let Mrs. Durand's scowl frighten me. If she despised one of us Davenport witches, she despised us all. We came as a unit.

"Being a witch is one thing, but being a *Davenport* witch... well... that's an entirely different matter," answered Mrs. Durand, like that was supposed to mean something.

I had no idea where she was going with this, but it had my aunts all stiffening around me.

"She's the worst kind of witch there is," declared Allison, leaning close to Marcus's mother. "The ones that curse you when your back is turned. I've always said… you can't trust a witch."

"Wow," I mocked, eyebrows high. "Did you make that up yourself? I'm impressed."

"Tessa," said Marcus, getting between us. "I came looking for you. My mother's having a dinner party tonight, and I'd like you to be there."

Dread shot through me, pulling my insides tight. "A dinner party? Tonight?" I repeated like a simpleton as I tried to pull off the perfect lie. I couldn't leave Davenport House at night, not unless I wanted to dance with Vorkan again.

"That's right. Will you come?" His smile had me weak in the knees. Damn. Why did he have to be so beautiful?

I shifted my gaze to my aunts, and my face went cold. Beverly had lost that winning, seductive smile she had reserved for Katherine. Dolores's eyes were stern with the warning to keep my mouth shut. And Ruth, well, she just stood there, eyes wide as saucers while Hildo kept giving quick shakes of his head.

Well, I was in a tight spot, and all without the help from my faithful Spanx.

I'd already insulted Marcus's mother once. Now, I was going to have to do it again by refusing this dining party, probably making Marcus hate me in the process.

I couldn't just tell Marcus's mother and Allison that I was a demon half-breed, and by being so, a demon hit man was trying to kill me. I would tell Marcus about the demon hit man eventually, but now wasn't the time.

I stilled myself, preparing for the shit show that was about to blow up in my face for what I was about to say. "That sounds really lovely." I thought it best to start with a compliment. "But unfortunately, I can't."

Emotions crossed Marcus's features, and I didn't miss the hardness in his eyes. "What do you mean you can't?" His voice was a mix of confusion, forced laughter, and maybe even embarrassment. "It won't just be us," he said, mistaking my hesitancy for not wanting to have all the attention. "My mother's invited some of her friends. I'd like you to meet them too. You told me you wanted to see the house I grew up in."

"I did. I'm sorry. But I really can't." God, that sounded lame, but I couldn't come up with a better excuse than that.

"That's a shame," said Mrs. Durand, not caring to hide her irritation. "Can't you make an exception tonight? Surely, you can get out of whatever plans you have, for my son."

Oh yeah. She hates me. "It's not possible. I can't. I'm sorry."

"Tessa." Marcus leaned closer and added in a low voice, "The dinner is sort of for you. To get to know you. You have to come. It's important to me."

I felt like my heart was being trampled on. "I'm sorry. I wish I could, but I really can't."

Marcus's expression went cold. "You *can't*." He said it more like a statement. "Why's that?" He tightened his jaw, clearly angry that I had just refused his mother's invitation and, in the process, humiliated him.

My lips parted, but nothing came out. What the hell was I supposed to tell him?

"Tessa's working on a job with us tonight," Dolores blurted, and I felt a little relief sift through me. "It's a hard case, I'm afraid. One that requires the four of us."

The chief's attention moved to Dolores. "What kind of job? Is there something I need to know?"

Dolores waved him off. "No, no. Nothing that needs to involve the chief."

"White-witch business," added Beverly, with a genuine expression.

"Magic stuff," offered Ruth, eyes wide as though that would make it more believable.

Call it wereape or being the chief's instincts, but I could tell Marcus wasn't buying it. He had that look about him, the one where I was sure his wereape senses acted like a lie detector.

I swallowed. "Maybe some other time? Maybe we could do dinner at Davenport House—"

"There won't be another time. I'm leaving for France in a few days. I was told you'd come to-night." Mrs. Durand's hands gripped her white leather clutch almost as though she were imagining it being my neck she was twisting, her expression a mix of mistrust and anger.

I looked over at Marcus, but he wouldn't look at me.

"I can help you with the dinner preparations, Katherine. You know you can count on me." Allison hooked her arm around Marcus's mother's—a gesture she'd done loads of times before, no doubt. I hated to admit it, but they looked… they looked completely natural like that.

When she caught me staring, she smiled at me, the smile of a winner, of someone who'd just witnessed the failure of another.

"Thank you, Allison. I don't know what I'd do without you." Mrs. Durand beamed, squeezing Allison's arm with affection.

I was going to be sick. I felt ill with dread and shame and hurt. I felt like I was back on my way to the in-between, being pulled in every direction at once and not able to do anything about it.

"Okay," Marcus said after a long moment, finally meeting my eyes, though I wasn't sure what I saw in them. "Have it your way." Saying nothing else, he turned on his heel and walked away, tearing a tiny piece of my heart with him.

His mother followed her son without another word, though not before giving me her icy gray stare. And Allison, her triumphant sneer, waltzed away with her like they couldn't wait to put as much distance between us as possible.

"That went well." I laughed bitterly. "I couldn't have done it better if I was standing here naked." I exhaled, letting go of some of that pent-up emotion. "What a mess. If they're giving out awards for best new girlfriend of the year"—I hooked thumbs at myself—"I'm the clear winner."

Beverly wrapped her arm around me. "Oh, darling. You're exaggerating. It wasn't *that* bad. Katherine's a bitch. It's in her nature. She can't help herself."

"Oh, it was *that* bad. She'll always remember me as the girlfriend who *refused* the dinner she was preparing *for* me. You can't beat that. It was a disaster." Remembering Allison's cunning smile had my blood boiling on high. I couldn't be certain she hadn't planned it all. She wasn't that smart, but women were conniving tricksters and masters of manipulation when it came to the men they loved.

157

I needed a drink. Preferably a whole damn bottle.

"She'll come around when she knows you," offered Dolores, giving me a weak smile. "She'll see what a wonderful and kind person you are. She'll grow to love you. You just wait."

I shook my head. "I doubt it. The woman hates me. *I* hate me right now."

Ruth laughed. "Don't be silly. It's not as bad as all that. Katherine loves to be overly dramatic. It'll pass. Trust me, she'll have forgotten all of this later." Though the shaking of Hildo's head said otherwise.

"Ruth's right," said Beverly. "Katherine always gave herself airs that she has no proper claim to. She's just trying to downplay the size of her ass."

"What?" Dolores sputtered out.

Beverly ignored her. "But the truth is, she's always hated the Davenport witches because of me. You see, Martin picked me over her, and she always harbored harsh feelings because of it. I dumped him a few years ago—"

"More like centuries ago," remarked Dolores.

"I mean, yes, they got married. But I know he still secretly desires me." Beverly laughed and winked at me. "And that has her all wound up tight."

At another time I would have laughed with her, but all I felt was numb.

Marcus's mother hated me. That was pretty clear. And it was obvious she preferred Allison over me. Worse, though, I'd hurt and humiliated Marcus. And that stung like a bitch.

Worse than that? In all the commotion with Marcus's mother, I'd forgotten why we were out here in the first place.

Silas, that oily, tattooed witch, was gone.

CHAPTER
14

"**I** need your help to break out of my house."

Iris stared at me as though some fungus was starting to grow on my forehead. "Have you been in Ruth's jar of magic mushrooms?"

"No." I exhaled. I stood with my hands on my hips, staring at the tiny Dark witch sitting at the edge of my bed.

"Tess, you do understand the concept of breaking and entering, right?" Ronin stretched out on my chair, his hands behind his head. "Usually you break *in*. Not out. Not unless you're in jail or something."

I cocked my head. "I'm kinda in jail at the moment."

Iris frowned. "What's happened? Does this have to do with Silas?"

"No." I quickly recounted the events of my encounter with the demon hit man and how my father's blood saved me.

Ronin leaned forward, his elbows on his thighs. "Damn, girl. You've been busy."

"Tell me about it."

"And your father says to stay inside." A frown pulled Iris's pretty features tight. "For your own protection."

My pulse was pounding and I wasn't even moving. "He did. But I can't stay here tonight. Not after what happened with Marcus and his mother. You should have seen him." I swallowed the hurt in my throat and shook my head. "He was so angry… disappointed. I need to make this right. I need to be there." For him, but also for me.

Iris leaned back and crossed her legs. "So you need us to help break you out so your aunts don't see you? Because I'm pretty sure they're adamant on you staying inside until your father figures something out with this demon hit man."

"Yes." I nodded. "There's more." I cast my gaze around my room. "House's been acting weird since my father gave me some of his blood. It's almost as though House's not sure about me. Doesn't trust me."

Ronin shook his head. "This is such a strange conversation. Can't we talk about something else? Like lingerie and skinny-dipping?"

Iris picked at her fingernails, her face pinched as she thought about what I'd just said. "Tessa, you almost died yesterday." Her dark eyes met mine. "It must have been pretty serious if you needed a blood transfusion. Are you sure you want to risk it again, just for a dinner? I'm sure Marcus will understand. Why don't you just call him or invite him over?"

I shook my head again. "If you were me and had seen the look on Marcus's face, you'd go too. This needs to be done face-to-face. I'm not a coward." And there was also the question of Allison. I knew she would be cozying up to his mother, and at the same time, cozying up to him as well. Guess I had some insecurities to work on.

Brows knitting, Iris crossed her arms over her chest. "What about the demon?"

"I'm more prepared now to face this demon." Not really. "Now that I know he's out there after me, I can handle it." Again, not really. "Besides, I mean, what are the odds that the demon will show up again tonight?"

"I'd say, *very* good odds," stated Ronin. "The dude probably only gets full payment once the job is done. He's going to keeping showing up until you're dead."

"Thanks, Ronin." I glared at him, recalling those exact words from my father. "I can always count on you to give it to me straight."

"You can stop with your *angry eyes*," said the half-vampire. "I'm only pointing out the obvious. Someone has to. You're acting like having a demon hit man after you is no big deal. It's a big deal. A *very* big deal."

He had a point. "Fine. It's a big deal. But Marcus is also a big deal to me. He deserves to know the truth why I refused this dinner thing."

The thought of the chief had my insides binding into a tight ball. Marcus had come out of nowhere to be tossed into the madness of my life, dangerous and soothing.

The wereape was strong, independent, surprisingly sensitive to the pain of others, and sexy as hell. He could have any female he wanted. He could have gone back to Allison, but he'd picked me.

He'd managed to sneak around my heart and broke down my protective walls without me noticing. I knew I was falling for him. The chief was the best thing that had happened to me in years. Perhaps even my entire life. And I wasn't going to risk something coming between us. Especially if that something was me.

"Do you know the demon's name?" asked Iris.

KIM RICHARDSON

"My father says he thinks it's the demon that goes by the name Vorkan. Not his real name, obviously. Have you ever heard of him?"

Iris shook her head, sending her black, chin-length bob to brush against her face. "No. Never. He could be a lower demon or even a mid-demon. But if he's able to manipulate magic with that cloak, the way you described it... he's probably a mid-demon. Or higher."

"Great." I let out a breath and stared out my window. The evening sun had disappeared prematurely under the growing thick clouds, casting odd lights and spectral shadows through the roiling overcast so it appeared to be around midnight when the clock on my phone said it was only about half past five. Those were some heavy snow clouds. Or my favorite. Freezing rain.

"Tessa," said Iris, and the tension in her voice pulled my eyes back to her. "Maybe you should stay..."

"No." I rubbed my eyes. "I made a giant ass of myself to his mother," I said, recalling the use of the words gorilla, monkey, and zoo. Yeah, not good. "I'm going. There's no telling when Vorkan'll show his ugly face again. Tonight? Tomorrow? In a week? I'm not going to live my life in fear. I'm not going to be a prisoner in my own home after dark. I won't."

164

"I kind of agree with Tess on that point," Ronin stated and clamped his mouth shut at the look he got from Iris.

I glanced at my friends. "And, if you drive me there… because I have no idea where Marcus's mother lives… you'll have my back. It'll be a lot safer than traveling alone." I stared at Ronin. "You do know where she lives. Don't you?"

Ronin inclined his head, looking devilish and seductive. "Am I not the hottest male alive?"

"No. But close." I laughed. "If I use a ley line, my father will know. He'll show up here. My aunts will freak out. I just want to clear the air with Marcus." I searched their faces, my pulse increasing in tempo. "So. Are you in or out?"

Iris smiled. "You're totally insane. Of course, I'm in."

"Me too." Ronin jumped to his feet. "How do we do this? Your aunts are downstairs."

"Right." I stared at my bedroom door. "Well, I can't use the front door unless I want my aunts to see me." I let out a breath. "I'll have to use the window."

Ronin stared at me for a beat, incredulously. He pointed to the only window in my room. "Not *that* window? Not the one on the *top* floor? The one in the freaking *attic*?"

I shrugged and smiled. "The very same."

Ronin blinked and then moved forward, grabbed me by the shoulders, and turned me around so he was behind me.

"What are you doing?"

"I'm looking for your wings," he said.

I turned and pushed him away playfully. "Very funny."

Ronin crossed his arms over his chest. "Okay. So, how are you going to get down three stories from that itty-bitty window in the middle of winter? Jump? And hope to land in a pile of snow without breaking your neck?"

I pursed my lips. "Hey. That's not a bad idea?" I laughed. "Just kidding. I might be crazy, but I'm not psychotic. I'm going to *climb* down." I moved over to the window. "I've been working on this new levitation power word for a few hours in case I slip. I can do this. Plus, every floor has a roof hip so I can take a break and then climb down to the next one. How hard can it be?"

The half-vampire grinned. "Depends. Are you afraid of heights?"

"Not sure." I looked up at him. "Guess I'm about to find out."

"What about your aunts?" asked Iris. "Won't they suspect anything? Won't they notice you're gone? What if they come up to see if you're hungry or something?"

I shook my head at her. "They won't. I've already eaten, and I told them that I have work to do and not to disturb me. Once the two of you leave, they'll think I'll be working. I know my aunts. They won't bother me."

"You've thought this through. Haven't you?" asked the half-vampire.

"I have." I moved to my bed and grabbed my winter coat. "You guys should leave now. While you're distracting my aunts, I'll climb out the window."

"Wait." Iris leaped to her feet. "Is that what you're wearing?"

I looked down at my casual jeans and black shirt. "Yeah. Why? You think I should change?"

"If you want to smooth things over with Mrs. Durand, then yeah. You need to look like you're trying."

"You mean you want me to look like Allison? I don't think so."

Iris rolled her eyes. "Of course not. But you have to look a little more… put together." She disappeared into my walk-in closet and came out with a pair of straight-legged black pants that I hadn't even worn yet and a nice silk burgundy blouse. "This will look great with your complexion." She stared at me. "Can you do a smoky eye?"

"I think so…"

"Good. Do that and a dab of lip gloss. Not too much. But enough to make a statement. And do your hair up."

"Yes, Mom." I took the clothes from the Dark witch. "Okay. Thanks. Meet me in the car," I told them and ushered them out so I could get dressed.

After I finished my makeup and hair, I threw on my coat, pulled on my new flat ankle boots that looked fabulous with those pants, and moved to the window. I took a breath. Then another. House hadn't pulled anything on me since I came back with my aunts. No slamming doors in my face or anything like it. But now, staring at the window, my guts rolled. If House had been waiting for the perfect moment to sabotage me, this would be it.

"House?" I called, my heart slamming against my chest. "You know it's me. Right? Tessa?" I waited for an answer, like the squeaking of expanding pipes, but got only silence. Using those few seconds, I pulled on my gloves. "Just… please don't do anything to me. I'm just sneaking out the window. Yes, I know how this looks, but if you've been listening, you know I have to do this."

Still nothing.

"Here goes."

I placed my gloved fingers on the window's lower sill and lifted it. Cold January air seeped through, in and around me. I stuck my head out the window and saw Ronin's car parked out front. No sign of him or Iris yet. They were probably still chatting with the aunts to give me enough time to reach the bottom.

The bottom.

I stared at the snow-covered front lawn, thirty feet below. Yeah. I was crazy. But I was still going to do it. I stared into the darkness, looking for a sign of Vorkan, but the street was deserted.

Steeling myself, I let out a long breath. Adrenaline sparked through me as I clambered out the window, my boots hitting the roof hip below the attic window. With my boots firmly placed on the roof shingles, I yanked the window back down and turned.

Next came the hard part. I had to lower myself to the next roof hip, which was connected to the front porch's roof, without slipping and killing myself. No problem.

I lowered to my butt and slowly dragged myself over the ice-covered shingles to the eave of the roof and turned on my belly. My heart thrashed in my chest. I was having a bit of a panic attack, but it was too late to turn back around. I didn't think I could climb back up on the ice-covered roof.

"I can do this."

Gripping the edge of the eaves and the gutter, I lowered myself down, my boots wiggling below as I searched for the next roofline. Only I couldn't feel it.

Okay, *now* it was time to panic.

Shit. Shit. Shit.

The sound of metal grinding hit me, and the next thing I knew, the gutter came away.

Me with it.

My fingers slipped just as I felt my body move away from the house. I fell. I screamed. But my witch instincts came into play.

I gathered in my will as I reached out to the elements around me and shouted, "Volito!"

Power rushed around me. A gust of kinetic force wrapped around me, holding me up for a moment. I wasn't falling anymore.

"It worked," I said, proud of myself for working a new power word so quickly. "Look at me. Badass witch—"

Then there was a sudden feeling of release, and I was falling again.

Crap.

My boots hit the porch's roof with a bang, making my right ankle cry out in pain. Thrashing my arms wildly, I tried to grab on to something, but I slid down fast like I was tobogganing down a hill.

The next thing I knew, I was airborne again. The porch roof slipped from my line of sight and then I fell.

Right into something soft that smelled of pine.

I blinked at the juniper bushes that had probably just saved my life. I needed to work on that new power word if I ever wanted to use it again.

"If this is your way of sneaking out without the entire town hearing you," said Ronin standing above me, "you need to up your game, witch."

I stuck out my hand. "Oh, shut up and help me up."

Laughing, Ronin hauled me out of the juniper bushes. As Iris picked juniper twigs from my hair, I took a moment to watch the front door in case my aunts had heard me and came bustling out. But after a few seconds, the front door remained closed.

I pulled away from the house. "Come on. Let's go."

And together the three of us made for Ronin's car.

CHAPTER
15

"You sure this is the one?" I asked, my voice high with emotion as I stared out the car window at the large, three-story, mountain-style mansion.

It was a perfect collaboration of wood and stone, nestled in the middle of a sprawling estate framed by woods. It didn't have the charm of Davenport House, but it was just as lovely. My awe might have calmed my anxiety, had I any room left for that emotion. I didn't.

"That's the one." The sound of leather pulling was loud as Ronin turned in his seat. "If I ever had to build a house, I'd build one just like that. Look at this baby. It screams Ronin."

"I love it. If you build one like this, I'm moving in," said Iris, her arms dangling out her window as she started snapping pictures with her phone.

A dozen cars filled the long and curved driveway. It was obvious a party was here. My eyes settled on a burgundy Jeep and my stomach clenched. I'd gone over and over again in my head what I was going to say to Marcus when I saw him. But now, all those preparations just vanished. It didn't matter what came out of my mouth as long as it was honest. As long as I came clean with everything that's happened to me, things would be right again between us.

There I went with the wishful thinking. The truth was, after seeing that look of disappointment on Marcus's face earlier today, I wasn't so sure anymore.

My nerves hit hard, and I knew the longer I sat in Ronin's car, the harder it was going to be for me to get out. I just had to rip off the Band-Aid. Quick.

Iris turned around in her seat to look at me. "You nervous? You look nervous."

"No." I lied. "Yes. I should have brought something. Who goes to a dinner party without bringing the host something? I'm such an idiot. I should have brought wine. Why didn't I bring wine?"

"Because you're a basket case." Worry creased Iris's pretty face. "I don't think Marcus will care that you didn't bring anything. He's going to be so happy that you came. That's all he's going to think about. And your ass in those pants. Trust me."

I forced a smile. "We'll see." That's *if* he wants to see me. He hadn't texted or called since I'd seen him this afternoon. He was angry. I got that. And I was just about to get a front-row-seat perspective of that anger.

"You want me to come with you?" said Iris gently. "I don't mind."

"I'll come too," said Ronin. "Besides, I've always wanted to see the inside of this beauty. You don't see houses built like that anymore. It's a rare gift."

My heart leaped at their offer, at their concern for me. "Thanks. But I need to go in there on my own. I don't want Mrs. Durand to think I'm too afraid to come alone. That I needed backup. That would make Allison's day. I'm a grown-ass woman. I can deal with Mrs. Durand." Though her hating me was a little awkward. But I was here to fix my situation with Marcus. Once that was done, it would be a lot easier to fix things with his mother, with him now on my side.

"Well, I'll be at Ronin's place," said Iris. "If you need us to pick you up, just text me. Okay?"

"Thanks."

Iris narrowed her eyes at me and pointed a finger. "I don't want you to ley line your way home. Got it? Not with that demon after you."

"I won't."

"And be careful," she continued. "Davenport House might be warded against demons, but not this house. It's pretty. But it's open to all things Netherworld. So stay alert. He could come for you, you know." She paused. "You're better off telling Marcus. You shouldn't be on your own tonight. I'd feel a lot better if you told him."

I tried a smile. "That's the plan. I'm telling him tonight." Part of me was also hoping Marcus would take me back to his place. The thought of that beautiful man naked next to me was enough to endure whatever insults his mother would throw my way.

But it wasn't just the sex, though still amazing. Marcus deserved to know the truth. I had to tell him about the demon. Even if I knew he'd go all protective on me, at least then he'd understand why I had to refuse his mother's offer in the first place.

With that plan in mind, I said, "See you guys later," and climbed out of the car.

The sound of Ronin's car driving away rang out as I made my way across the driveway toward the elegant mountain home. My pulse quickened, my boots crunching on the gravel path that separated what looked like a large flower garden under heaps of snow.

Orange light spilled from the many windows as I stepped up to the impressive double doors with my heart in my throat. Why was I so nervous? Maybe it was because part of me didn't want Marcus's mother to hate me. Too late for that.

I pressed my finger on the doorbell, which was in the form of a gorilla's head. Nice touch. At another time, I would have taken a few minutes to admire the home's architectural beauty because it was spectacular, but the tension had manifested into a throbbing headache.

The sound of music and voices drifted through.

The door swung open.

A woman stepped from the threshold. I was expecting to see Marcus's mother, having mentally prepared for her surprised frown. What I got was an older woman in a dark skirt suit with a pair of black flats. Her plum-colored hair was cut short in modern style, giving her a bit of an edge. She was older than Mrs. Durand but just as fit, though in a much smaller frame. She didn't look an inch past five feet.

I was shocked when her wrinkled face creased into a genuine smile. "Don't worry. You're not late at all. Everyone's in the drawing room. Come in. Come in." She ushered me inside.

Huh. Not what I was expecting.

If I thought the exterior was incredible, the inside was just as stunning. A grand, double-sided staircase split the house in half, surrounded by miles of crafted wood paneling, all polished and glowing. The walls were decorated with paintings and warm wainscoting. All the furniture was in a cabin style with lots of wood detail, yet with clean lines and not too bulky.

"It's so nice to finally meet you," said the nice lady, speaking fast. A familiar wave of energy rolled in the air, mixed with the scent of pine needles, wet earth, and leaves mixed in a wildflower meadow—the scent of White witches.

Now, *that* was a surprise. I was under the impression that Marcus's mother hated witches.

"I'm Audrey, Mrs. Durand's assistant," said the witch, with that rapid voice again, and I had a feeling she was one of those fast talkers. "Here. I'll take your coat."

Before I could protest, the older witch yanked off my coat and hung it over her arm.

"I'm—"

"Tessa Davenport," answered Audrey. "I know." She beamed, making her light-brown eyes sparkle. "I knew you'd come. I told them you would."

"You did?" Maybe Audrey was a psychic. Some witches were.

"I'm not a psychic," the witch said suddenly, as though she'd just read my mind. "I just had a feeling, you know? Marcus is going to be so glad you've come."

I had no idea if that was true so I just nodded. My eyes found the gleaming wood floors, and my heart sank at the idea of me leaving a trail of wet snow and dirt. "Oh no. I forgot to bring my shoes."

Audrey snapped her fingers at my feet, and I felt a sprinkling of energy wash over my skin. "There. All clean. No more worries. Come with me."

I took a second to check my boots, and yup, they were dry and shiny as though I'd just polished them. I needed to learn that trick.

I followed Audrey down a long hallway decorated with paintings of landscapes and horses, lots and lots of horses. A few had wolves, but most of them were paintings of landscapes with horses. It was quite beautiful and tastefully done.

"Thank God. No creepy family portraits," I blurted before I could stop myself.

Audrey laughed, the kind of laugh that immediately made you feel at ease. I liked her already. "I know what you mean," she said. "I worked for a couple in Burnsall, Yorkshire, where all of the family portrait paintings, dating back hundreds of years, all kept staring at me. It didn't matter where I was in a room or a hall-way. Their eyes always followed."

"Yikes."

"I think it was spelled that way to keep the human burglars out."

"That would do it." My eyes found one paint-ing of a beautiful black horse in a meadow sur-rounded by mountains. The orange and yellow leaves were a clear indicator that it was painted in the fall. It was incredible, the kind of painting I would love to have but couldn't afford. "This one's amazing. Who's the artist?"

"Mrs. Durand. Good, aren't they? Marcus didn't inherit that gift. His hands are too big." Audrey laughed.

Just big enough. I leaned closer and saw the small signature on the bottom right of the paint-ing. I could make out the initials K.D. Again, this woman was not what I was expecting, espe-cially not her artistic talent or her love of horses.

Looks like we had two things in common—art and Marcus. I could work with that.

"Here we are," said the witch.

I followed Audrey into a room left of the hall-way. It had a very masculine feel with lots of brown leather sofas and chairs and dark pol-ished wood, stark against the white walls. A massive Persian carpet in deep shades of red, blue, and gold spread out against the wood floors. It drew my eye to the grand stone fireplace across the room, lit with yellow and orange flames.

"Do you prefer red or white wine?" asked Audrey.

"Red," I told her.

"I'll be right back with your drink." She skipped out of the room and disappeared around the corner.

I looked around, feeling awkward, now that I was alone in a strange house filled with strangers. The room was full of about twenty people I'd never seen before. Some were my age, but most of them were older, hovering between my aunts' ages and older. They talked and laughed and drank, all to some soft classical music. When I quickly threw my gaze over the crowd, seeing their stylish and expensive-looking clothes, I was grateful Iris had made me change out of my jeans and casual top. I'm all about being comfortable in my clothes, but that doesn't mean I needed to look like I just got back from the gym.

While I watched, I nearly laughed at the shock and ugly frown on Allison's face when she saw me. I didn't even mind the low-cut, black minidress she was wearing that barely contained all of her voluptuous, womanly parts. Though I did offer her a flash of teeth and finger wave.

My heart leaped when I found a pair of gray eyes watching me from across the room. Marcus looked amazing in a dark gray shirt that was snug over his wide shoulders tucked into a pair of black dress pants that hugged his toned thighs. My eyes rolled over his ridiculously muscular biceps, and I imagined my fingers curling over them.

A smile marred his clean-shaven face as he started for me, a glass of red wine in his big manly hand. Loved those hands. Butterflies did a line dance in my belly. Damn, this virile man was hot.

I was still amazed that just the sight of this sexy man did that to me. But this was also because of what had happened earlier. It was time to clear the air and make things right if I ever wanted to be with him again.

His eyes locked on mine again, which sent waves of heat unfurling through me. I didn't even care about the demon hit man on my ass that could take me out at any moment. This was *loads* better.

But when Marcus came my way, he cleared the path behind him.

And when my eyes settled on a pair of dark eyes next to the fireplace, all my thoughts of Marcus vanished.

The man's gaze swept along the others, evaluating, searching, the kind of gaze you'd expect from a cop. Only he wasn't. He was much worse.

Silas had been invited to the party.

CHAPTER
16

"You came?"

I pulled my attention back to Marcus as he stepped into me. With his free hand at my waist, his touch heating my skin through the fabric of my blouse, he placed the softest of kisses on my cheek, sending tiny pricks of electricity to my belly. Damn. I might have moaned.

I swallowed and blinked, trying to focus. "Umm. Yeah. I did."

Though Marcus pulled back from that kiss, he stayed close, leaving me to enjoy his scent of male and some musky cologne that was intoxicating. I think I might have drooled. "I'm glad you did," he said, his voice rumbling over my skin as though he were touching me.

"Me too." He looked damned fine in that shirt. And I smiled as I imagined ripping it off him. What? You would have too if you knew what was under there.

"Your aunts didn't mind you coming?" he asked, his eyes dropping to my lips and sending those butterflies from before doing the cha-cha inside the walls of my stomach.

"Hmmm. Why would they mind?" I laughed.

A tiny frown crossed his forehead. "That family emergency you had to help them with? You're all done with that?"

Right. Ooopsy. "Not completely," I told him, which was the honest truth. "But my aunts can handle a few hours without me." But if they noticed I was gone, they were about to crash this party.

I felt eyes on me and looked past Marcus's shoulder to find Silas watching. What a creep. He was probably one of those creeps who liked to watch.

"What's the matter?" Marcus followed my gaze. "Oh. Him. This guy's something else."

"What's he doing here?" I asked, my voice low.

Marcus turned to look at me. The slight tightening of his brow told me he wasn't thrilled to see him either. "My mother invited him."

"Why?"

"No idea. She likes to invite eccentric types to her parties. I think she likes the energy they give off."

"He's not giving off the right kind of energy." When I looked at Silas again, he was still watching us. "He's a creep. He's foul. He threatened to have my Merlin license revoked. Says I cheated because I used a ley line in the trials."

"You're kidding? Can he do that?"

I shrugged. "Not sure. My aunts don't think so. But I don't trust him. He's had it in for me since the first day of the trials. No idea why."

Marcus's eyes were bright. "Maybe he likes you," he said, his voice as smooth as water. "I don't blame him. You are… extremely beautiful."

I punched him playfully on the chest. "I think I just threw up in my mouth."

Marcus laughed. "Are you going to tell me why he's here?"

"You say it like I'm supposed to know. Your mother invited him."

The chief sighed through his nose. "I know he's here because he's trying to get some information about Beverly." His gray eyes searched my face. "I don't like the way he's watching you."

"Me neither. You think he's trying to undress me with his eyes or thinking up ways to dispose of my body?" I asked, trying to smooth the mood.

Marcus frowned. "You know what I mean. I know there's something you're not telling me. What's going on, Tessa? Why are you all acting weird and secretive?"

My pulse jumped. "Right. About that." Here it comes. "Listen. There's something I need to tell you about—"

"Here you go, Tessa." Audrey appeared in a space next to us, a large glass of wine in her hand. "It's a Merlot. Not too strong, and slightly fruitier, but still lovely."

I took the wineglass from the witch. "Thank you, Audrey."

She grinned. "My pleasure." She looked at Marcus and said, "Your mother owes me fifty dollars." Eyes alight with mischief, she winked at me and strolled out of the room again.

My mouth fell open. "Did I miss something? Or did your mother and Audrey have a bet going on me?"

Marcus took a sip of his wine, clearly trying to avoid the question.

Come to think of it, I hadn't seen Mrs. Durand yet. No doubt she was busy preparing for this dinner or rather ordering her cooks in some massive kitchen.

A laugh pulled my attention back to the crowd. Allison was tossing her long blonde hair and batting her eyelashes as some handsome guy in a suit, her hand pressed against his chest in a flirty—let's be honest, slutty—manner. She kept throwing glances our way. Yeah, she was trying to make Marcus jealous. It wasn't working.

Marcus leaned forward. "What did you want to tell me?"

I met his gaze. "The thing is," I tried again, "something happened last night—"

"Dinner is served," announced a loud voice.

Mrs. Durand appeared in the room wearing a rich burgundy and black, flowing dress that had a bohemian flair to it and a radiant smile. Her long dark hair flowed in loose waves down her back. Her glowing smile reminded me of Marcus's. Eyes bright, she glanced around the room, and when they settled on me, she didn't look surprised to see me standing there. Guess Audrey had told her. She'd bet that I wouldn't show.

Mrs. Durand whirled around and ushered her guests to follow her. They did.

Marcus took my hand and pulled me with him. His rough, callused hand sent tiny thrills through me and I gladly followed.

We entered a large dining room with dark wood paneling and a table that could fit, you guessed it, twenty people. A large iron chandelier hung from a twelve-foot ceiling above the table laden with expensive-looking plates and silverware. Three centerpieces of a mix of orchids set in a wooden log carved with the images of gorillas were placed on the table over a crisp white tablecloth. It was a gorgeous arrangement. My aunts would have been envious.

Voices bustled as the guests all moved around the table finding seats, Marcus tugging me along and moving toward two empty seats. This was nice. I could get used to this.

"This is really lovely," I told him as he pulled one out for me.

"My mother likes to show off," he said, leaning on the chair's backrest. "She loves to entertain."

I moved around the chair Marcus was offering me and sat.

"Tessa," called Mrs. Durand from the head of the table. "I have a spot for you right here"—she pointed to her right—"next to Mr. Cardinal."

The dining room went silent. When I looked around, everyone's attention was on me, silently waiting to see what I was about to do.

Okay. Not awkward at all. Silas was my least favorite, creepy-staring witch in the universe. I did not want to sit next to him and share the air he breathed.

Mrs. Durand's face was expectant. Clearly, the woman wasn't used to being told no. Not wanting to make a scene, and since I'd always had one strike against me, I wasn't planning on making it two.

Stomach twisting, I pushed my chair back and stood, aware that everyone was still watching me.

"You don't have to, you know," said Marcus, his hand on my lower back.

I gave him a tight smile. "But I do."

The chief grinned at me. "Thanks for doing this." The guy had no clue.

Feeling like the elephant in the room, I made my way to my designated chair next to Silas, who had this weird smile on his face, clearly enjoying this situation.

"What are you smiling about?" I sat down, scooting over in my chair so that I wouldn't accidentally brush my thigh against his.

"Who says I'm smiling," answered the witch.

"It's a stupid look on you," I shot back, knowing he was smiling at my expense. I really hated sitting next to the guy who was trying to find dirt on my Aunt Beverly. I had to be careful what I said to him.

A familiar laugh that sent my blood boiling sounded, and I leaned over to look down at the table. Allison was sitting next to Marcus. When she caught me looking, she put a hand on his arm. I tensed. I was going to murder that bitch. So far my plan of being open with Marcus wasn't going down like I had hoped it would. I had to find a way to talk to him somehow.

"Careful now," said Silas as I leaned back. "Someone might think you want to harm that pretty blonde over there."

"How about you mind your own damn business," I told him, scrambling to realign my emotions.

"Jealousy runs deep in the Davenport family. Doesn't it? It's an ugly emotion. Gets lots of people in trouble."

I whirled on him, seeing that smile still showing on his face. It was all I could do not to spit in it. "What the hell are you getting at? You're making things up as you go because you've got nothing. You're pathetic. You know that?"

Silas snickered. "Families like yours ruin it for the rest of us."

"The rest of us?" I rolled my eyes and took a sip of my wine. "You've lost me. But then again, I don't care what you have to say. How about you do us both a favor and shut the hell up."

"The older, more privileged families," Silas continued. "You think because of a name, it makes you untouchable. Like cheating to get your Merlin license."

"Great. This again. You really don't know when to give up. Do you? You need some new material, buddy."

I looked around the table. Audrey sat across from me. She was in a conversation with Mrs. Durand, who was laughing, clearly enjoying herself. Better than her shooting daggers at me with her eyes.

I took another gulp of wine as six waiters and waitresses in white shirts came in with plates topped with steaming vegetables and something else I couldn't see, though the scent of spices had me practically salivating.

The polite chatter stopped as the meals were served. Guess everyone was just as hungry as I was. One of the waitresses lowered a plate on the table in front of me and moved away.

My smile vanished. I stared down at my plate, at the large, steaming round disk of fleshy meat. Filet mignon. Mrs. Durand didn't know I didn't eat meat.

The snort that came from Silas told me he'd done his research.

"What's the matter, Tessa?"

I looked up to find Mrs. Durand's gray eyes pinned on me. "Allison told me this was your favorite. Did I get it wrong?"

Right. Of course she did. I turned my head just in time to meet the blonde's gaze and see her cunning smile. Yup. There it was, all wide and dazzling, showing off her teeth. Damn. I had to up my game. That's twice she'd gotten me today. I was losing my touch.

Marcus was watching me, and then he shifted in his chair, his hand up, trying to get the attention of one of the waiters.

I quickly shook my head and mouthed, "It's fine." He watched me for a beat longer and then dropped his arm, his lips twisted in a worried smile.

I took a breath. I had two choices. One, I eat the meat and then quickly excuse myself as I made friends with the toilet. Or two, I eat only the vegetables and hope Mrs. Durand wouldn't notice. Who was I kidding? The woman's eyes were practically glued to my every move.

The last thing I wanted was to insult the hostess. But I drew the line with meat, especially cow. Just like my aunts, I didn't eat things with souls.

Guess I was just about to be rude.

Speaking of rude, a phone started ringing, loudly, over the sound of the happy chatter and of people eating.

Silas pulled out his cell phone and brought it to his ear. I found myself leaning over to the right, trying to eavesdrop on his conversation. But I couldn't hear anything.

"Are you not hungry?" Mrs. Durand's expression was unreadable. Either she was pissed and hiding it well, or she was truly concerned that I didn't want to touch that chunk of flesh on my plate.

I forced a smile and jabbed my fork into some asparagus. "Starving. Looks delicious."

A smile formed on Mrs. Durand before she turned back her attention to Audrey again.

"… music to my ears, Shane," Silas was saying. "Yes. I'll inform them." He paused, listening, just as I was listening. Anything that made him this happy could only be bad. And the wider his smile, the more teeth he showed, and the more my tension rose.

"Call me if you find out anything else." Silas hung up his phone and stuffed it in his pocket. He looked at me, his lips parting in a smile that was one part amusement to two parts wicked. "My night's full of surprises."

"What? Did your hooker bail on you again? Next time use more lube. Working girls need a little help from time to time."

He leaned forward and addressed Mrs. Durand. "I'm afraid I must be going. Something's come up."

Mrs. Durand's mouth clamped shut. "But you barely touched your food," she said, a crease forming on her manicured brow. I could see the shadow of muscles twitching along her face as she tried to control her emotions.

"MIAD business." Silas stood up and tossed his white napkin over his untouched plate, which was all kinds of rude. "I have an arrest to make," he said loudly so everyone in the room could hear.

Fear slid through me at his words. My heart jumped into my throat as I stared at the tattooed witch. Did he mean me?

Suddenly Marcus was on his feet, a shocking amount of anger flicking through him as he made his way over, his gray eyes pinned on Silas. Guess the wereape had come to the same conclusion as me. But arrest me for what?

192

Silas finally turned his attention back to me, his expression showing a winning delight, kind of like what Allison had been doing to me for the past few minutes.

I felt a chill crawl over my skin as I found my voice. "What are you talking about?"

Silas grabbed his wineglass off the table, threw back his head, and downed it. Smacking his lips in a vulgar way, he placed the glass on the table and said with a sneer, "I'm arresting your Aunt Beverly for the murder of Nathaniel Vandenberg."

Ah, hell.

CHAPTER
17

Needless to say, the first thing I did was rush out of that house and call my aunts. And by rushing out, I mean I *forgot* to thank the hostess for the lovely dinner party.

Yeah, I didn't think I'd get another invite to any of her dinner parties in the foreseeable future.

But I had bigger problems to worry about than Mrs. Durand's outrage toward me. Said problem was Silas arresting my Aunt Beverly.

I had to find her before he did.

I stood in the driveway, a mix of panic and anger making me breathe hard like I'd just run around the block for fun. I watched as Silas strolled down the driveway, taking his sweet, lanky-ass time, as though he didn't need to hurry, like it was already too late for Beverly.

My anger shifted to worry, and I barely registered the energy that was emitting from me, making some of my loose strands of hair float up around my head. Eyes narrowing, I watched as Silas got behind the wheel of his black Escalate SUV and drove off.

I texted Iris a 911 in the hopes that she'd seen my aunts, giving her a quick breakdown of what Silas was about to do. But she'd quickly texted back that she hadn't seen them but she and Ronin were on their way.

Next, I tried my aunts again, but my second call went straight to voice mail again. Damn it. Where the hell were they?

I shook with adrenaline. My heart pounded with nervous fear, making it hard to focus. And then it hit me. Maybe they were out looking for me? No. They would have shown up by now.

Gripping my phone with trembling fingers, I pressed the redial button again.

"What's going on, Tessa?"

I looked up to find Marcus marching my way, his face darkening under that beautiful golden tan. His movements were intense, though still moving with the grace of a predator.

I hung up just before it went to voice mail again. "I know. I'm sorry I had to leave like that.

I'm sure your mother despises me now. If she didn't already hate me before."

He shook his head, and the exterior lights made deep shadows on his face. "My mother doesn't hate you. Family means everything to her. She understands why you had to leave. Trust me."

I wasn't so sure about that, but I wasn't about to contradict him either. "Well, I'm sure it'll give the guests something to talk about." Especially Allison, who was incognito for the moment, but I was pretty sure she'd show her face soon.

"Here," he said, clouds of white mist shooting from his mouth as he handed me my coat. "Witches aren't immune to the cold. Not like us."

I grabbed my coat and hauled it on. "Thanks," I answered, only then realizing how cold it was and how my coat added some much-needed warmth.

"What's going on with Beverly?" he asked again. "Who's Nathaniel Vandenberg? And why is that MIAD guy going to arrest her for his murder?" His eyes were hard. "Does this have to do with why you wouldn't come to my mother's dinner party originally?"

"Kinda," I answered. I tried my aunts again, and again it went to voice mail.

Marcus moved closer. "If you know something, you need to tell me now." I felt a jolt at the concern in his tone. He was worried. So was I.

I wasn't sure what to tell him. My aunts had made it very clear they didn't want the chief involved. But seeing as we were going up shit creek without a paddle, having the chief on our side was better than dealing with Silas on our own. The fact was, we needed help.

"They killed him," I said, watching as his eyes widened in shock beneath his dark brows. "Nathaniel Vandenberg. He's dead."

"What?"

"It was self-defense," I blurted and told him exactly what happened according to what my aunts had told me. "Beverly would have died if Dolores and Ruth hadn't killed him. He would have killed them too. They didn't have a choice."

Marcus stood facing me, his expression assessing. "Why didn't you tell me all this before?" His voice rose as he ran his fingers through his thick locks of dark hair leaving it attractively tousled. "I could have helped. I'm the goddamn chief."

My brow narrowed at his tone. "It wasn't my secret to tell. If they wanted you to know, they would have told you. This happened before I moved here. Your beef is with my aunts, not me."

"But you knew about this. And you still didn't tell me. When I could have helped? When

I could have done something about it?" Marcus, being Marcus, was a natural protector, predator, yes, but he had an innate urge to protect the people of this town. Especially those he cared for, like my aunts. It was an extremely attractive quality. What woman didn't desire a strong, protective type? I would have been totally turned on if he wasn't so angry with me.

His anger was nearly palpable. He felt the threat to a member of his community, and he looked like he was about to beast out into his King Kong alter ego.

Okay, this was not going as I had hoped it would. "Look..." I sighed. "You can bite my head off later. Right now, I need to find them before Silas does."

Marcus was silent for a while. "What are you going to do if you find her?"

"Hide," I answered, a smile tugging on my lips. He didn't smile back. "Let me find her first, and then I'll figure something out."

The chief rubbed his jaw with his fingers. "What did you do with the body?"

I didn't miss the fact that he'd just said *you* like I had been involved with the killing in the first place. "Why?"

"Because without any evidence on the body or a murder weapon, he can't charge her. He must have something."

I took a breath, anticipating his reaction. "He's in... he's in the town's cemetery." I didn't think mentioning that he'd been buried in our backyard for the past year was a good idea, seeing how angry he was.

"What?" Marcus growled, and he began to pace around the driveway, the muscles around his neck and back popping under his shirt.

I shrugged. "It was the best place to hide him, with all things considered," I said, realizing how guilty I sounded. "There isn't a murder weapon." I tried to keep my voice as low as I could and strained to keep from staring at all those muscles shifting under his shirt. "They used magic. That's the weapon."

"So what does he have on your aunt?"

"Maybe Silas is lying." The realization dawned on me. "He's just clever enough to make something up like this. Maybe to trap us somehow? Waiting for us to make a mistake?" I wouldn't put it past the tattooed witch. The guy was as ugly as he was smart; maybe this was part of his plan to trap Beverly.

The sound of tires scratching the pavement had me look over my shoulder. A black BMW 7 Series drove up the street and pulled into the driveway.

Iris's head and most of her upper body hung out the front passenger window. "Did you get in touch with them?" she asked, her face flushed. "I tried calling too. Nothing."

I shook my head. "Nothing yet." My heart started to race. Where the hell were my aunts?

Iris's eyes moved from Marcus to me, her face worried. "Um. You okay?" She made a weird thing with her mouth. She did that when she was trying to communicate mutely with me, covert like. But all it did was make her look like she was trying not to pass gas.

"I'm great." I couldn't stand here any longer. I needed to move. If my aunts weren't at the house, there was only one other place I could think of they could be. "Iris. Can you guys do me a favor?" I asked, seeing Ronin behind the wheel, bending his head to get a better look.

"Depends on the favor," said Ronin, raising his brows suggestively.

Iris tsked and smacked him on the arm. She turned back around and said, "Anything. Shoot."

I gave her a tight smile, though my nerves were shot. "Can you go and stay at the house in case they come back? I need to go check on something first."

"You're going to the cemetery." Marcus had worded that as a statement.

No point in lying now. "I am."

"Tessa, no," warned Iris, her pretty face tight with worry. She pulled herself farther out of the car window, nearly at the waist. "You can't go alone. Let us give you a lift."

"Yeah," called Ronin. "Hop in."

"It'll take too long. It's faster if I use a ley line." I needed to move. I needed to move fast.

Iris's lips parted in a silent *oh*. "But what about the demon? If he finds you again… you barely survived the last time."

"What demon?" Moving with the speed and precision of a predator, Marcus was next to me in a blur. "What does she mean by you *barely* survived. What the hell is going on, Tessa?"

Well, crapola.

Iris clamped her mouth shut, but it was too late. Her eyes moved from me to Marcus and back to me as she mouthed, *"Sorry."*

"Ah…" I answered, trying to find an excuse that would explain why a demon had nearly killed me last night. I was all out of excuses to pull out of my butt. "Well, apparently, there's a demon hit man on me."

"Apparently?" he growled.

"We met yesterday," I said. "It didn't go so well." I cocked my head. "For me, that is. But, as you can see, I'm all good now."

"Thanks to a blood transfusion from your ol' daddio," said Ronin, making a large vein on Marcus's forehead throb.

"Thanks, Ronin."

"No problem," answered the half-vampire. "Glad I could help. See? I'm not just a pretty face."

Marcus's shoulders twitched, and so did a muscle along his jaw. Damn. If I didn't know any better, it was as though he was trying to control his inner beast. And he didn't look like he had it under control either.

"How are we supposed to have a relationship if you can't trust me?" asked the chief, his gray eyes darkening with a hard tension to the point where they appeared black. "If you can't even trust me with something this important? Trust me when your life's at stake? How do you see this working if there's no trust?"

My heart squeezed, like a boa constrictor tightened around it, ready to swallow it. "But I do trust you."

"No, you don't." His eyes were wild with anger. "You would have come to me if you did."

O-o-o-o-h, crap.

"We should go," I heard Iris say, and I turned to look at her. "I'll text you if they're there."

I watched Iris slip back into the car as it moved away. Part of me wanted to just pull a ley line and jump. To get away. A few seconds might make a difference in Beverly's life, but I had to deal with Marcus. This was the worst time to have our first real fight.

"It's not like that," I told him, trying to ease my tension before I said something I might regret. "Of course I trust you." I could feel myself losing it, losing my cool. I cared about Marcus. Hell, I was falling for him. But I needed to get my ass moving and find my aunts before it was too late.

Muscles played along his jaw. "Well, not enough to tell me about that demon that's trying to kill you," he replied, his voice like venom.

Man, that wereape was insufferable. I was kind of ticked off. "You don't get it. This has nothing to do with you."

The chief's eyes narrowed further. I guessed that was the *wrong* thing to say.

I sighed through my nose and tried again. "Can we *not* do this now? I need to find Beverly." And the more I stood here arguing with him, the slimmer my chances became.

He glared at me. "I'm the chief. Chief of this town. How could you not tell me?"

"Do you have to know everything?" I shot back, irritated. What was his problem? I needed to leave. Like, right now.

A growl tore out of his throat, making my skin erupt in goose bumps. "A demon in my town *is* my business. As chief, every single soul in this town is my responsibility. Don't confuse being a Merlin and chief as the same. They're not. This is *my* town. Merlins answer to me."

I gritted my teeth. It seemed as though the more I opened my mouth, the worse it got. But I couldn't help myself. "No one died, okay. I've got everything under control." Yeah, who was I kidding?

A faint grimace skewed his face. "How can you screw around with your life like that? How can you gamble with it? It's selfish."

Okay. Now I'd had enough. "You don't own me. I can do whatever I want with *my* life. It's mine. If I want to *screw* it up, that's up to me." Yup, that sounded lame, but I was beyond being reasonable at this point. I couldn't think straight.

Marcus just watched me, and I saw something across his face snap. I knew it was bad. And I knew, somehow, there was no coming back from it.

"Marcus? What's going on here?"

Mrs. Durand stood outside the front entrance, her perfect brows pinched in a frown. Allison stood next to her. The smile on her face was an indicator that she'd heard at least part of our conversion. God, that wereape was getting on my nerves.

Marcus glanced over at his mother. "Nothing. Go back inside."

Mrs. Durand placed her hands on her hips. "Doesn't seem like nothing. You're arguing in the middle of my driveway while I have guests. Marcus?"

The chief was staring straight ahead at nothing, but I could see his mind working. "It's over. Go back to your guests."

Marcus turned his back on me and walked to his Jeep. He climbed in behind the wheel and swerved out of the driveway, his brake lights shining on the pavement. He turned the corner at the end of the street, sped off into the darkness, and disappeared.

I stood there, shaking, half in anger, half in despair, and my eyes burned, not fully comprehending what the hell had just happened.

But, of course, Allison was there to fill me in.

"I told you," she said, appearing right in front of me, that smug smile firmly on her face.

Blinking fast, I glared at the tall wereape. "Told me what?" My voice cracked, and I hated it. Hated this place. I had to leave.

"You're not his match. You never were." Her words hit like a physical blow. The glee all over her face made me want to spit in it. "You've barely been dating a few weeks, and you can't even hold on to him. You witches are too independent. Take your aunts, for example. Their husbands have been dead awhile. Right? And still, none of them are with a mate. Sure, your Aunt Beverly likes to bed a few different men a week, but they always leave in the morning."

I felt the last of my cool evaporate. Hell, I'd lost my cool a while ago, and it was already halfway to Greenland. "Shut up. Shut the hell up. You don't know anything about my family."

Allison shifted her weight, her stance domineering, territorial. "Being a wereape's mate means you must surrender to him. Let him protect you. Take care of you. It's in his nature. That's how he's programmed. You share everything. You become a single unit. And you, well, you can't even be honest with him."

"Go to hell," I hissed. "You don't know what we have." It took all of my efforts not to shed a tear. I would not shed a single one in front of that bitch. Not. One. Tear.

Allison snickered. "What you *have?* Witch, the way it looks, you have *nothing*."

Anger flared deep inside my gut. "Stop talking, or I won't be responsible for what I'm about to do to you."

"Face it, witch, it's never going to work. Might as well get used to the idea. And the way it looked to me, it's already over. You've lost him." With a last gleaming smile, Allison waltzed away, right back up the steps where Mrs. Durand was still waiting. She was watching me strangely. I had no idea what I saw on her face.

I shook it off. I didn't care. I was done.

I sensed my determination being battered as I stood there in the driveway. Clenching my jaw, trying to keep it together, I turned away.

With a deep breath, I gathered my will and reached out to the nearest ley line. A blast of energy hit me, and I vibrated with its power.

I felt the last of my resolve breaking down. The tears fell. They just fell, buckets of them, until my cheeks were soaked with them and they fell off my jaw to land somewhere around my boots.

And just as I felt my knees buckle, I jumped.

CHAPTER
18

*I*t's over...

Was it really over? Had I screwed things up so royally they were irreversible? Things had spiraled down the crapper so fast, I barely had time to register what exactly happened. I was still confused. In shock mostly. There was a bit of denial too.

How could an evening that had started out so well go so wrong so quickly?

It's over.

Marcus had said those words to his mother, but he could have been saying them to me. That's how it felt. There was a finality to them. A stinging finish. And when he turned his back and walked away, well, that was also a dead giveaway.

It's over.

If I had told Marcus about the demon, none of this would have happened. We'd probably be up in his apartment, having some hot, really hot, makeup sex.

I was getting a whole lot of nothing tonight.

With Silas being in town, I'd been more focused on helping Beverly than on the demon that wanted me dead. Maybe I'd been overestimating my abilities. Maybe I was the biggest fool who ever lived. But seeing the despair on my aunt's face, the fear of being sent to the witch prison for only defending herself, it was all I could think of. I'd wanted to come clean to Marcus. I'd planned to. Despite my intentions, things happened, and I never got my chance to explain properly.

But it was too late for second-guessing my decisions. I had to own up to it. Accept it and the consequences of my actions. If Marcus was pissed because I didn't share every single detail of my life with him, then so be it. I was my own person.

I'm not going to lie, this spat with Marcus hurt. Hurt like a sonofabitch. But I had enough life experience, with some serious lady balls, to know when to shut it off. This wasn't the time to cry. I needed to be strong. Beverly needed me to be strong.

Perhaps Allison was right. Marcus and I were never meant to be. Maybe I'd been lying to myself this whole time.

Using a ley line to travel to the cemetery wasn't very smart. I was undoubtedly alerting my daddy dearest that I wasn't shackled to Davenport House like he wanted me to be. He was going to have a fit. But worse, I was now free game for my lovely, scarred demon friend, Vorkan.

But I wasn't a total fool. Just a tad foolish. Now that I knew I had a demon on my tail, I was pulling on the elements around me, keeping them close. If he came at me, I'd be ready this time.

When I reached the cemetery, I slowed the ley line near a line of trees. There was just enough light from the moon reflecting off the snow to let me see the spot where we'd buried Nathaniel's body. I jumped off, landing somewhat easily, thanks to the snowbank that cushioned my fall.

The cemetery looked exactly the same as it did the night before.

All except for one thing.

One *major* thing.

Nathaniel Vandenberg's grave was empty.

Where there'd been snow covering an earthy grave that my aunts and I had taken great care to cover up, I was now staring down an empty and very rough, dug-up hole in the ground.

210

And Nathaniel was a no-show.

My pulse went into overdrive. Now I was panicking.

"He's gone," said a voice behind me.

"Ah!" I spun around and landed in a crouch, fists out like I was in a boxing match.

Dolores waved her hand dismissively at me. "Put those away before you hurt yourself."

I lowered my hands. "Right," I said, my face warming with my humiliation, though if that had been the demon, I'd be dead by now. "What are *you* doing here, sneaking up on me like that? And where the hell have you been? I've been trying to reach you?"

"We came here when we saw that you weren't in your room." Beverly stepped out from behind a tall gravestone, her face pale and drawn, with Ruth following closely behind her.

Okay, I was found out. "You thought I'd come here? To the cemetery? Why?"

The aunts shared a sidelong glance, and then Dolores said, "The way you and Marcus had that argument. We thought for sure you'd want to make up. To make things right with him. And that meant…"

"You thought I'd tell him about Nathaniel." They were right, though, but I didn't say anything. Not yet.

Dolores nodded. "We did."

Beverly winked at me. "Not me. I thought you'd be having lots and lots of makeup sex."

211

She giggled. "If it were me, that's what I'd be doing."

Dolores threw up her hands in the air, frustrated. "So we panicked. And came here."

"*You* panicked," accused Beverly, pulling a piece of lint from her red coat and flicking it, which she must have had super night vision to see. She pressed a hand on her cocked hip. "It's not a good look on you, Dolores. Makes all those *thousands* of lines on your face pull and stretch."

Dolores exhaled heavily. "We came here to move the body elsewhere. So Marcus wouldn't find it."

"But someone beat us to it," commented Beverly, her beautiful face agonized.

I stared at the grave again. Piles of earth were everywhere, thrown all over the place. Whoever had done it had been in a hurry.

Ruth moved to stand at the edge of the grave and looked down. "You think he came back?"

"Came back?" questioned Dolores. "What do you mean *came back*?"

"Like the others?" said Ruth, her eyebrows high in question. "Like Mum and the others? Maybe he woke up and crawled out." Her eyes, suddenly haunted, snapped to Beverly. "Maybe he's looking for *you*. To finish the job."

Beverly lost her smile. "You know, Ruth, I really hate you sometimes."

I shook my head. "The grave's too clean for someone to have crawled out. This looks like someone *dug* him out."

Fear had drawn Beverly's face into lines. "But... who would have dug him out? And why?"

That's what I wanted to know too.

"I'll give you a guess," said Dolores, hands on her hips, her face darkened into a scowl. "He's rude and has a tattoo fetish."

"No, it's not him," I told them. "Silas was at Mrs. Durand's dinner party. There's no way he could have done this. Unless he can be in two places at once, though I highly doubt it."

"He was at the dinner party?" questioned Dolores. "You went?"

"I did."

Dolores gave me a sour look. "I can't believe Katherine would invite him."

"I believe it," said Beverly, pressing her hands on her hips. "She heard that he was looking for dirt on me. I'm sure she had *plenty* to tell. And I'm sure she was happy to *give* it to him too."

O-o-o-kay. "Well, he was there. No idea why. Don't care. He even sat next to me. Long story," I told Dolores at the question on her face. "But he didn't do this. Someone else did."

"But who?" Ruth stared at the hole in the ground as though she expected to see someone crawl back out of it.

"We're the only ones who knew who was in that grave." Dolores's dark eyes searched us each in turn. "Did you tell anyone?" she asked us.

"No," said Ruth and Beverly at the same time, shaking their heads.

I opened my mouth, about to tell them that I'd told Marcus, but Ruth beat me to it.

"Maybe someone *saw* us." Ruth's voice was high, the whites of her eyes showing and reflecting in the moonlight.

"No. We were careful," answered Dolores, though by the tone of her voice, she didn't sound so convinced. "My invisibility bubble was perfect. I tripled-checked the spell before we left. I don't make that kind of mistake."

"No, that's true. Only with your wardrobe," noted Beverly.

I looked over my shoulder at the sea of headstones, gravestones, leafless trees, and a few mausoleums and crypts. If we'd been hidden by Dolores's spell, it was something else. If someone did see us, they saw us another way.

Or after we were done.

It hit me. "He has people working for him. He didn't come here alone," I said, remembering the feeling of being watched at the cemetery and thinking it was a squirrel.

Dolores stared at me for a long second. "What are you talking about?"

214

"If he had people following us," I said. "All they had to do was wait. They waited. Probably followed our footprints in the snow to this area right here. Saw us with our shovels too."

Dolores cursed. "Put three and three together," she said, her pale face growing paler by the second with a hand pressed on her forehead.

Everything started to fall into place. "They probably waited for it to be dark to dig him out. They either did it last night or we just missed them."

Beverly tensed, panic sliding behind her green eyes. "So, if they have Nathaniel's body… What does that mean for me?"

Fear was heavy in my gut, but my anger was heavier. "I'm not sure."

"Tessa?" Dolores dipped her head, her brows knitted in the middle as they always did when she was on to something. "Why did you come here? You never said?"

"Right." I took a deep breath. "I came to check Nathaniel's grave. Silas got a phone call when we were just starting to eat," I continued. "He was thrilled. My guess is they called him after they dug up Nathaniel and said they found something." I looked at Beverly. "Whatever they found, it's enough to make an arrest."

"What?" Beverly's face was pinched in fear and horror. "No. No. They can't. He can't. It… it was self-defense. Nathaniel's a monster. He tried to kill me."

"I know." I swallowed and said, "But Silas doesn't know that." I took a deep breath and added, "He's going to arrest you for Nathaniel's murder. He said so himself. In front of everyone."

"Did Katherine hear him?" asked Beverly, her voice pained, and I felt a pang in my heart at the distress I saw on her face. It was obvious she cared what that other woman thought of her. Or maybe she didn't want that bit of information to get back to her husband.

I nodded. "She did. Everyone did."

"Cauldron save us," said Ruth, and she let herself fall on top of a heap of snow. "We're doomed. We're all doomed."

"Wait. Wait. Just wait a second." Dolores paced around us, her fingers pinching the bridge of her nose. "There are rules to follow. Even this Silas must follow rules, a code, or something. Let's all just relax and think. We need a plan."

"Maybe Marcus can help us," offered Ruth.

"He won't." I didn't think Marcus would want anything to do with me or my aunts for a very long time. Not after tonight.

Beverly stared at me for a moment. "Something happened between you two. Didn't it? I can tell. I can always tell."

Dolores huffed. "Not this again." She looked at me. "Well? Did it?"

I didn't have the energy to tell them about the horrible fight. So I decided to stick to the facts, of what I knew. "It's over between us."

They all stared at me like I'd lost my mind.

"Did you hear me?" I tried again. "I'm almost positive it's finished. We're done. It's over."

Ruth laughed and dismissed me with a wave of her hand. "Don't be silly. I'm sure it's nothing to worry about. These things have a way of working themselves out. They always do."

"Oh, I seriously doubt that. He'll never want to see me again."

"Nonsense," said Ruth.

"I have a feeling." A gut-wrenching, tearing-at-my-soul feeling.

"You'll see him again soon. I promise."

I stared at my aunt. "How would you know?"

Ruth looked past me. "Because here he comes."

I froze. Then I swore as I turned around, my eyes immediately drawn to the wereape, to the way he was walking over, the way his large shoulders swung as he walked. As much as I hated to admit it, his tousled dark hair, his thickly muscled body under his short winter jacket, pegged my attraction meter.

He decided to follow me to the cemetery, and I didn't think it was because he wanted to apologize. "U-umm…" I stammered. "By the way. Marcus knows."

"What?" my three aunts said in unison.

"I was going to tell you."

Dolores glared at me. "What stopped you?"

I pointed. "That hole in the ground. That's what."

Marcus's face was pulled tightly, his motions sharp and aggressive. He stopped before us, a good distance from me. His eyes dropped to the large six-foot hole in the ground. He looked up, his gaze traveling over my aunts. Marcus never looked in my direction, not once. It stung. I won't lie. He was acting as though I didn't even exist.

After a moment, his eyes settled on Beverly. "Beverly. You're coming with me."

My aunt cocked a hip and smiled seductively. "I am? Why ever for?"

Marcus's face was stone cold as he moved and grabbed Beverly by the arm. "Because you're under arrest."

CHAPTER

19

I snapped.

"Have you lost your mind!" I howled, running after Marcus who was hauling my Aunt Beverly by the arm down the snow-plowed path to the entrance of the cemetery. Ruth and Dolores were both shouting, but I couldn't make anything out over the angry, white noise in my ears.

Marcus had just arrested my Aunt Beverly. The world was turning to shit before my eyes.

I ran and placed myself in front of him, walking backward, which was harder than I thought when you were trekking through snow at a fast pace.

"Are you crazy! What the hell are you doing?" I shouted. Beverly's face was pale, and she looked as shaky as I felt.

"What I must," said the chief, still not making eye contact.

"You *have* to arrest her?" I trudged backward as fast as I could without falling. "I thought you were on our side. I thought you cared about my aunts. But you're just as bad as Silas."

At that Marcus halted, his beautiful gray eyes filled with fury. "I'm *protecting* her. It's what I do," he growled, his posture holding repressed anger.

I held my ground. "Really? By *arresting* her? Explain that, *chief*."

The chief moved past me, steering Beverly by the arm, her face confused and helpless—the fear real and full. I didn't like that look on her.

Had the chief lost it? Was he so enraged with me that he was taking out his frustration on Beverly? No. That wasn't him. Something else was up.

"How is arresting her helping her?" I tried again, not giving up and following him to the burgundy Jeep parked at the curb.

"Marcus." Dolores ran past me to the Jeep. "I demand you explain yourself this minute! You can't just arrest my sister without an explanation."

And then Ruth was there, planting herself in front of the Jeep, arms out, a determined look in her eye. "You'll have to get past me. I'm stronger than I look."

Ruth had read my mind. I wasn't about to let Marcus haul my Aunt Beverly to jail, not when she was the victim here. We might have been a thing only a few hours ago, but nothing was stopping me from spelling his ass, though a really hot ass.

Despite his said hot ass, arresting my aunt was not in character for him. This was not the Marcus I knew. The Marcus I knew would do everything in his power to protect my aunt.

The chief sighed, visibly stressed by this whole situation. "I'm doing this *for* her. By my arresting her first, Silas can't touch her."

Oh. Okay. Had not thought of that. "Really?" I felt some of my tension leave my body. He was helping her?

Ruth lowered her arms. "I'm confused."

"I am too," said Beverly, some of that fear gone from her eyes as well.

Dolores let out a frustrated breath. "He's saying that Silas can't make an arrest if Beverly's already being detained by Marcus. He's saying that he's going to keep her safe."

Wish I had thought of that before.

The chief opened the passenger door and helped Beverly inside. She went in without a fuss. Guess she realized this was her best option.

"Yes. Exactly." He shut the door of his Jeep and glared at each of us in turn. "But if you had told me, I could have helped her. I could have had the charges dropped. And you wouldn't be in this mess. It's too late for that now."

I looked over at my aunts, guilt rising thick in me and on their faces. The decision to keep Marcus out of it had been theirs. I'd felt it had been the best option at the time. But now, seeing this, I wasn't so sure anymore.

I swallowed hard. "What happens now?"

Marcus's face was heavy with concern as he looked at me. "I'll do what I can. She'll be safe tonight."

"And tomorrow?"

Marcus held his gaze to mine for a moment. "Better start praying to your goddess."

The three of us watched in silence as the chief got behind the wheel of his Jeep, started the engine, and pulled away. The last thing I saw was Beverly's frightened face staring back at us from the front passenger's side window.

Despite the obvious desperate situation we'd found ourselves in, I refused to accept that this was the end of it. Where there was despair, there was hope. And where there was darkness, there was light. I was going to find that light.

I was grateful for Marcus. Just the thought of him had my gut tightening. I was still in shock at how quickly and messy things had gone between us. I'd never realized how easy it was to lose someone, especially once you had them. A dull ache throbbed in my chest at his loss, but I stifled those feelings. There would be time to wallow about that later.

The chief had saved Beverly for now and might have given us some time. But sooner or later, Silas would eventually get his arrest. He'd made it clear that he had something on my aunt, enough to arrest her for murder, he'd said. The said something was Nathaniel's body.

"I can't believe this is happening." Ruth wiped her eyes with her blue wool mittens. The light from the streetlamp cast heavy shadows over her face, making her look gaunt and tired. "Our Beverly. Arrested. What will the town think when they hear the news?"

"They've already heard the news," growled Dolores. "Haven't you been paying attention? Silas told everyone at Katherine's party. Everyone will know by now."

"You don't have to yell," snapped Ruth. "I'm standing right here."

"We should have never buried the body in the cemetery," Dolores was saying. "We should have left him where he was." Her dark eyes pinned me.

Okay, I know there were a lot of emotions going around, but I didn't appreciate the accusation in her eyes.

"Don't start," I warned. "I'm not to blame for this. I didn't *murder* anyone."

Dolores's face twisted in a way that scared me. "No. But *you* told us to put him there!"

"You kind of did," agreed Ruth.

"Yeah, I did." I pressed my hands on my hips. "And if we hadn't moved Nathaniel from the backyard when we did, Silas would have found him. Beverly would be on her way to the witch prison by now, and we'd all be helpless to do anything about it. At least Marcus has given us some time to think." I tried to keep my voice down, but all that pent-up anger from what happened with Marcus was spewing out before I could get control.

Ruth nodded. "She's right about that."

Dolores was shaking her head like she was about to lose it. Either that or her head was about to pull a three-hundred-and-sixty-degree turn, like the little possessed girl in *The Exorcist* movie.

"Look..." I let out a sigh. "How about we use all that anger and put it toward helping Beverly? Fighting now isn't going to help."

When Dolores pulled her eyes on me, they were filled with tears. "How? How can we help her?"

Where there's a will, there's a way, right? "I have a plan." I'd just thought about it now, but who cared?

"What?"

Ruth and Dolores edged closer to me, and I said, "Without a body, Silas's got nothing on

Beverly. Right? It's probably his entire case against her."

Dolores crossed her arms over her chest. "Yes. That makes sense. So, what's this plan of yours?"

There was only one place in Hollow Cove to stash a dead body until it was ready for transport—a place I knew well, where I'd been before with Iris.

I searched my aunts' faces, my heart thumping with excitement. "Simple. We're going to steal the body."

Both stared at me, their expressions bland. It was impossible to tell what they were thinking. Both were speechless, which I wasn't sure was a good sign or a bad one. But when Dolores pinched her face in thought, nodding her head in agreement, a tiny smile spread across Ruth's face. I knew they were with me on this.

It was a crazy, stupid plan. But it was the only thing that made sense if that made any sense.

I grinned, adrenaline soaring. "So, ladies. What do you say about breaking into a morgue?"

"I'd say," commented Dolores, a wicked gleam in her eye. "That's the smartest thing you've said all night, m'dear."

Ruth threw her fist in the air. "This is going to be so much fun!"

All righty then.

CHAPTER
20

The thing with breaking and entering is that you have to make sure no one's home. Otherwise, it's just an awkward visit to a midnight soirée you weren't invited to.

In our case, we had to be sure no one was at the town morgue, which so happened to be in the chief's Hollow Cove Security Agency building. More specifically, in the basement level.

By the time Dolores drove us there, it was half past 11:00 p.m. From where I sat in the Volvo, I couldn't see a single illegally parked car or even a single soul walking the dark street. I blamed it on the weather. It was fifteen below on a Monday night. Smart people stayed indoors when it was cold enough to steal the breath from your lungs.

No lights shone from the apartment above the agency's building, Marcus's apartment. Either he was sleeping, or he wasn't there. A sudden pang hit my chest, and I pushed it away quickly and focused on my task. I was not going to go there now.

After Beverly's arrest, we'd all gone home to get something to eat and to formulate our body-snatching plan, though none of us could swallow anything. It was an impossible task to steal a body from a morgue and hope nobody saw us. We were also just crazy enough and desperate enough to attempt it. And we needed all hands on deck. More specifically, I needed Iris and Ronin.

That being said, I needed Iris and Ronin to follow Silas. I wanted eyes and ears on him the entire night we were planning our body snatching.

"We found him. He's at the Hairy Dragon Pub," came Iris's voice in my phone's speaker.

"Are you sure? How do you know?" I asked. Both Dolores and Ruth turned around in their seats to look at me.

"Because I'm staring right at him," answered Iris.

"Okay." I laughed. "Stay on him. And call me if he moves."

I could hear the sound of voices and the hum of music in the background. "Don't worry, Tess," Ronin's voice blared from the speaker. "We're on him like flies on shit."

Nice. "You do that." I hung up and looked up at my aunts. "You guys ready? We need to do this now."

"I'm ready." Ruth's white hair was hidden under a black wool hat that hit just above her brows, and a black wool coat hung over her small frame, three sizes too big. If I were to guess, I'd say it used to belong to her dead husband.

A black fedora hat sat on Dolores's head. She matched it with a black raincoat that was way too thin for this kind of cold weather and way too small for her wide shoulders. She reminded me of Jack, the Soul Collector demon, in that outfit, but I wasn't about to tell her.

Me, well, I just opted for whatever was comfortable and not restricting in case I needed to run or drag a dead body around, which was a dark hoodie, jeans, and a short winter jacket.

I was the first one out of the car, and I gave my car door a soft push until it closed properly. My aunts did the same. Next, I turned my phone to vibrate and slipped it into my coat pocket.

Dolores gave us the once-over. "We look like the Three Stooges on our way to Oz to see the Wizard."

I choked on my air, though Ruth looked pleased. "Let's go."

Together, the three of us hurried across the street and made it to the front doors without a problem.

Dolores moved past us and pulled open the front door like she knew it wouldn't be locked. This wasn't the first time this happened—the door not being locked. When I came to snoop around Marcus's office with Ronin a few months back, the doors weren't locked either. Who doesn't lock up their offices at night? Apparently Marcus.

I was hit with a serious case of déjà vu as I slipped inside behind Dolores with Ruth at my back. Adrenaline pumped through my veins as I crept along the dark hallway of the HOLLOW COVE SECURITY AGENCY, and our boots tapped softly against the hard-tiled floors. All the main lights were off except for a few night-lights along the walls, which gave us enough illumination to see where we were going. Still, I was pretty sure Dolores had packed one of her witch lights with her, just in case.

"The morgue's through that door behind Grace's desk," I whispered, remembering coming this way with Iris when we'd transported Bernard's body, the town's baker, on a gurney.

Dolores whipped her head at me, and I could see her deep frown even in the semidarkness. "I know that. This isn't my first time visiting the

morgue." She turned around and rushed toward said, door like she was in charge.

Right. Guess killing Nathaniel gave her that
right. I wasn't about to argue with that.

Yes, what we were doing was stupid, insane,
and unethical, but the idea of Beverly locked up
in a cell somewhere made me ill. Come to think
of it, I had no idea where Marcus held his de-
tainees. Where the hell was his lockup? Did he
even have one? And where was Beverly?

"Do you know where Beverly is?" I asked,
not to anyone in particular. "Where does Marcus hold his prisoners?" Maybe we could break
her out while we were here? Yeah, I didn't think
that would go well for her. Not to mention it
would make her look guilty.

Dolores halted. Slowly, she turned her gaze
around across the lobby to the left of the entrance. I followed her gaze. Directly across from
Marcus's office was a gray metal door with a
small slit window at eye level.

"I've never noticed it before," I said, my voice
a little loud and I immediately lowered it. I
didn't want Beverly to hear us. I didn't want her
to get her hopes up. At least I knew now where
she was. If things got worse, or if we could get
rid of the evidence, I was breaking her out.

Pain flashed across Dolores's face as she spun
back around and hurried out the door, as
though she had to physically make herself
leave. Ruth just stood there, her bottom lip

trembling as she stared at that gray door, un-willing to move.

I slipped my fingers through hers. "Come. She'll be okay. She's safe for now." I had no idea if that was true, and I said it for me as well, but Ruth let me pull her along with me, looking small and fragile in that oversized coat. I also knew that one look at Beverly sitting in a cell, and my thoughts about stealing Nathaniel would evaporate. The only thing I'd want to do was get her out of there.

Together, we rushed through the door Dolores had just disappeared through, down the stairs to the basement level, and stepped into a dark hallway. Soft-red emergency lights gleamed on the polished floors and white walls, our only source of illumination.

Pulse racing, I let go of Ruth's hand once I figured she wasn't going to bolt back upstairs and headed down the dark hallway behind Dolores. We went through a pair of double doors with the word MORGUE painted in large, black letters on the right one.

Plain white walls, with matching boring white tiles surrounded us, all lit with fluorescent lights from above. I swept my gaze across the room to the metal refrigerator doors on the opposite wall and to the stainless-steel autopsy table next to a rolling medical cart, covered with gleaming, sharp medical tools and devices.

A single gurney occupied the space. And on it lay Nathaniel's dead body.

The air was cool and stank of disinfectant and the sweetish odor of dead flesh. And something else.

Magic.

More specifically, wards. Lots and lots of powerful wards.

The air hissed and popped with static electricity.

"I smell magic," I announced, looking around.

"I smell poop," said Ruth, and I had to agree with her.

My eyes settled on a ring of red, glowing wards on the floor below the gurney. Within the wards were hand-drawn squiggly sigils of fire along with some I didn't recognize. Though they looked familiar... like... the tatts on Silas's skin.

"Stop!" Dolores threw her hand in the air like an army hand signal, and both me and Ruth froze. Ruth held her pose like a store mannequin.

Dolores's gaze was fixed on the wards below the gurney. "What kind of wards are those?" I asked her.

"Barriers," she answered, taking a careful step closer while Ruth and I were still frozen in place, not daring to move. "Aligned energy that blocks physical or magical intrusion, turning the energy back upon itself."

I frowned. "And what does that mean exactly?" I really needed to study more.

Dolores let out a puff of frustrated air. "It means… a small push would result in a similar push back against whatever is trying to get it out. A harder push, then, a much bigger push back of energy."

"So if we were to try and take Nathaniel's body?"

Dolores looked over at me and said, "We'd be hit with a force of destructive energy about as powerful as your average homemade bomb."

Swell.

CHAPTER
21

The realization that Silas had placed some explosive-type wards made the whole *body-snatching* experience a whole lot worse.

It never occurred to me that we'd be faced with wards. My plan was suddenly feeling even more ridiculous now, seeing that it wasn't going to work.

I sighed and moved to stand next to Dolores. "Silas did this. I recognize his tatts in those runes and sigils."

Dolores nodded, standing over the gurney. "Yes. You can move now, Ruth," said her sister. "The wards are only for the body."

"Okey dokey." Ruth released out of her mannequin pose, rolling her shoulders and neck. "So?" She stood next to us, looking down at Nathaniel's body. "What do we do now?"

If we couldn't take Nathaniel's body out of here, we were royally screwed. "Can you do a counter ward or something?" I wanted to help, but this magic was beyond my training.

Heavy lines marred Dolores's face as she thought about it. "Possibly. Ruth and I can try. But it'll take hours."

Shit. We didn't have hours. "Well, if there's no other way to get him out, you better start now. What can I do to help?"

Dolores retrieved a small leather pouch from the folds of her raincoat. "Just keep an eye out in case someone comes. Ruth. I need you."

I stood back while my aunts began chanting as they walked around the gurney spreading herbs and powders on the floor, careful not to accidentally touch the dead man's body. My skin tingled with energy as I felt the magic of the elements soar into the room, driven by my aunts.

A half hour later, my aunts' chanting grew louder, just as my patience grew thin.

"Any luck?" My nerves were shot, and just standing around doing nothing wasn't doing me any favors.

"Patience, Tessa," growled Dolores. "These things take time. You can't just rush into a counter ward. It takes skill. Patience. And extreme concentration."

Ruth made a series of swift gestures with her hand, and the wards beneath the gurney burned a bright red, just like Silas's tatts when he tapped into their power.

And then one of the wards shimmered and went black.

It was working.

Relief swept over me and I sighed. We were going to do this. We were going to get rid of Nathaniel's body, and then everything would be fine.

Except for one small thing, I had no idea where we were going to put the dead bastard this time. We'd figure it out when the time came.

A buzzing sound came from my pocket and I pulled out my phone. Seeing Iris's name, I swiped the screen. "What's up?"

"Tessa? Oh my God. I'm sorry, I lost him," said Iris's panicked voice. "A loud group of young werewolves came in. I couldn't see him anymore. And then he was just gone. Just gone."

My breath caught. "What? Are you serious?" My voice rose as a thread of panic shot through me and wrapped around my chest. I spun around and stared at the morgue's doors, knowing he might be on his way here.

"I'm sorry," said Iris again, and I felt a slip of guilt at the worry in her voice. None of this was her fault, and I was grateful for her help.

"It's fine," I told her. "Don't worry about it. Thanks for calling."

I stuffed my phone in my pocket and looked at my aunts, who were both staring at me with their eyes as wide as I'd ever seen them. "Change of plans," I told my aunts. "You have to work faster. Silas is on his way here now." Call it my witchy instincts, but I knew the bastard was on his way.

"Now?" shouted Dolores. She pointed at the dead witch. "There's no way we can have all the wards removed in time. I'm sorry, Tessa. This isn't going to work."

Ruth was shifting from foot to foot. "If he finds us here…"

She didn't have to finish that sentence. I knew what would happen if he did.

"There's got to be another way." I rubbed my forehead with my fingers. *Think. Tessa. Think!*

"We need to leave. Now!" shouted Dolores, no more trying to keep things on the down-low. She and Ruth sprinted for the doors.

Instead of following them, I moved closer to the body. There was a reason Silas needed the body. Why? What could he possibly have on Beverly? The body had been dead for over a year. Sure, she had her DNA on his, and her witch imprint, which was more of a magical

237

mark, but that was it. It wasn't enough for a murder conviction. It only proved that they were together. Where was the proof she had killed him?

There wasn't any.

It begged the question, without a murder weapon and no apparent cause of death on the body that I could see, what had Silas found to link Beverly to this killing?

Something occurred to me. "Is there a way to see how Nathaniel died? Like a spell that would show us his last living moments?"

"Yes. It's called a 'see beyond' spell," answered Ruth, surprising me.

"And how does that work, exactly?"

"Well." Ruth cocked her head to the side. "The spell would allow us to see what Nathaniel saw before he died."

"Like in a vision?"

Ruth nodded. "Yes. Exactly like a vision."

A sudden wash of cold reasoning shocked through me. This was it. "That's what Silas has. It has to be. He saw something, and he's using it against Beverly." It was the only thing that made any sense.

"But she didn't kill him," expressed Dolores, looking grim. "We did. If that were true, he'd be arresting us, not her."

"That's true." That part was still foggy, but I knew I was onto something. "Still, if we could

238

see what Silas has on Beverly, we'd be that much closer to helping her."

"It doesn't matter." Dolores's eyes settled on Nathaniel's body and let out a breath. "Without the body, we can't do much of anything. We don't have time for this. And if we get caught, it'll be all for nothing. He'll see that we removed one ward. He can arrest us for that."

"We just need more time," I snapped back, knowing I'd need more time to think of plan B, which was usually done on a whim.

"We don't have time!" Dolores threw up her hands. "You said it yourself. Silas is coming! We can't move the body. We only managed to remove one ward. It's over. We failed."

My eyes moved to the blackened ward. And then I had a flash of insight.

"Wait a minute. To make the see-beyond spell," I asked, pulse thrashing with adrenaline. "Would it work with just a part of the body?"

Dolores made a face. "What are you saying?"

"Well, would it?"

The tall witch shrugged. "Theoretically, I'd have to say yes, since you only need a portion of the subject in question."

Holding my breath, I glanced one more time at the blackened ward. This had to work.

Hoping I was right, I reached out my hand over Nathaniel's body.

"Tessa! What do you think you're doing?" howled Dolores, seemingly having caught on to my plan.

And then I touched his right arm.

I stiffened. And nothing. I wasn't obliterated into smithereens. I exhaled. "So far so good."

"If you're thinking of using his hair," Dolores was saying as she appeared next to me. "It won't work. You need something more substantial."

"I wasn't thinking about hair."

My gaze fell to the tray of silver, shining, sharp medical tools and grabbed a small saw.

I whipped it in the air, feeling a little mad. "We need a finger."

"Are you crazy?" shouted Dolores, her eyes practically bugging out of her head.

"Little bit."

Ruth's mouth fell open, but she didn't say anything.

Yeah, I was crazy. I stifled the urge of manic laughter that threatened to bubble up.

I grabbed Nathaniel's right hand with my left and spread out his fingers so I had room to work and cut his index finger. I cringed. They were cold and stiff, and it took some effort just to spread them out.

Dolores was shaking her head. "Clearly, you've lost your mind. You're not actually going to go through with this?"

"I think she is," said Ruth, who looked a little impressed and intrigued at my mad attempt of cutting off a dead guy's finger.

I pointed my saw over Nathaniel's groin. "I can think of something else to cut off. I really don't mind. Your choice. Dick or finger?"

"Dick!" cried Ruth, a fierce gleam in her eye. Yeah. Not going there.

Dolores made a face. "Don't be ridiculous."

By the look on her face, she thought I was joking. I really wasn't.

"Fine. Take a finger." Dolores huffed out a breath. "But they're going to notice it's missing," said Dolores. "Silas isn't stupid."

"Not if I pull down his jacket. And not if they're not looking for it. They won't notice." At least, not until we were miles away and had already performed the see-beyond spell.

I swallowed hard and placed the saw on the dead witch's right index finger, right between the knuckles. Part of me couldn't believe I was mad enough to do this. But the other part, the one that kept visualizing Beverly in some remote, dark, and dingy cell was the winning one.

"Just like cutting carrots, right?" I laughed. Damn. I truly sounded insane.

"Oh, my cauldron, I can't look." Dolores covered her eyes with her hands, though Ruth bumped her shoulder against mine, totally immersed in my Dr. Frankenstein behavior. Yeah, don't let the little-old-lady shell fool you. Ruth was a badass, through and through.

Swallowing down the urge to vomit, I applied pressure—and began to cut. Moving the saw back and forth, I concentrated on making a clean cut as fast as I could without cutting my own finger.

Sawing the finger of a dead person was a lot easier than you might think. Especially post-mortem, and post-magical preservation. There was no blood. And I gagged as it came clean off.

"Holy shit," I breathed, slightly disgusted and slightly impressed at myself. "I did it."

"You did. You really did," agreed Ruth, leaning forward to get a better look. "And a very nice cut too."

Dolores moved her hands from her face. "Great. Now. Let's get out of here."

She didn't have to tell me twice.

Grabbing a cloth from a nearby table, I wrapped the finger in it and dropped it into my jacket pocket. Next, I placed Nathaniel's hand with the severed finger closer to his body and pulled on his sleeve to hide the missing finger.

"Good enough. Let's go." Heart pounding in my ear, I spun around and rushed toward the double doors, me first this time, too excited to be disgusted that I was carrying the finger of the witch who had tried to kill Beverly.

I would have gotten out of there faster.

Only someone was blocking our way.

CHAPTER
22

Marcus stepped into the morgue, the doors closing behind him with a sharp bang. "I thought I heard something."

I froze, slightly shocked at the deep frown that marred the chief's face but mostly surprised that we'd been caught.

Marcus reached behind him and flicked on the lights, flooding the morgue in sudden bright white light. "What are you doing here?"

Ruth threw up her hands in the air. "We didn't steal the body," she blurted.

"Thanks for clearing that up, genius," snapped Dolores.

Marcus's gray eyes moved to each of us in turn, searching. His nostrils flared like he was taking in a scent, and then his gaze snapped to me, or rather, to my pocket where I'd stuffed Nathaniel's finger. Damn. I tensed. Could he smell the finger in my pocket?

Without the finger, we had nothing to help Beverly.

If Marcus knew I had Nathaniel's finger in my pocket, he didn't mention it.

"Are you going to arrest us?" I hadn't intended for my voice to come out so harshly, but apparently seeing Marcus now, I still had some unresolved issues about how things had ended between us. I ran my eyes over him, hating how rattled he made me feel. I blamed it on his attractiveness.

He looked at me, his face unreadable. "Should I? Were you involved in any *illegal* activity?"

Breaking and entering was one, and I was almost positive cutting off the finger of a dead guy was another. But since he wasn't saying anything, I didn't either.

His eyes glanced at my pocket again, and he raised an eyebrow at me. Yeah, he knew about the finger. The question was, what was he going to do about it?

"Beverly's innocent," I said tightly. It was the only thing I could think of.

Marcus crossed his arms over his large chest, his pec muscles bulging and drawing my eyes to them. He did that on purpose.

The chief cocked his head to the side and said, "I know."

My mouth fell open. "You do?"

"I had a nice long chat with Beverly," said the chief, and I noticed that he was now looking at Dolores and Ruth. "I know she acted in self-defense. And I also know your involvement in all this."

Dolores moved in next to me. "Then why isn't she at home with us?"

Worry crossed Marcus's brow. "Because the MIAD case against her is still open. As long as she's in my custody, that agent can't touch her. I'll need some time to go through all the evidence. It's hard to prove self-defense when the alleged victim has no defense wounds. It's even harder when the suspect has been dead for over a year."

"You have witnesses," I pointed out. "Dolores and Ruth were there."

Marcus nodded. "I know. And I'll need both of your testimonies," he said to Dolores and Ruth. "I've got Beverly's on the night in question. For now, the best thing I can do for her is to build a strong case against Nathaniel. Prove that he was a violent witch."

"How are you going to do that?" I asked.

His eyes pinned mine, and I felt a flutter in my belly. "Usually, these types have done it before. They get off on it. If he hurt other women like what he did to Beverly, somebody knows something. It'll take some digging, considering who his family is, but I'm owed a few favors. If someone made a complaint about Nathaniel Vandenberg, I'll find it."

"That's good. I guess." The idea that this Nathaniel had hurt more women made me ill.

Ruth walked over and squeezed Marcus's arm. "I knew you'd help. I knew you'd find a way to bring our Beverly back to us."

Marcus smiled. He opened his mouth to say something, but he frowned instead and whipped his head back like he'd heard something.

Just when I was about to ask what he'd heard, the doors swung open.

"I knew you'd try something."

Silas waltzed into the morgue, the tatts on his neck glowing red and ugly under the fluorescent lights. A black coat draped over his shoulders, brushing against his tight leather black pants. A twisted smile materialized on his face when he caught sight of the body still on the gurney.

A man and a woman followed him in. Scratch that. A male and female *witch*, by the scent of wet leaves and by the powerful witchy vibes they were giving off. The female's black hair was cropped short. She was fit and nearly as tall as Silas. She caught me staring and flashed me her teeth, white against her dark skin.

The male was short, his head and face covered by a dark hoodie, and as ordinary as a potato. I couldn't see anything interesting about him, but perhaps that was his angle. Look weak. Strike hard.

The air sizzled with their magic. It was obvious they wanted us to know their strengths, but I saw that as a weakness. I wasn't afraid of them.

"Your gravediggers?" I pointed out and then gave them a finger wave as they positioned themselves across from us, their backs to the wall, to get a better view of the room. Their eyes took it all in, their expressions unreadable and alien.

My breath caught as Silas examined the body, his eyes moving along Nathaniel's right side. If he saw the missing finger, it was over.

Silas caught sight of the blackened ward on the ground. He let out a deep, amused chuckle. "Your spells are no match for my wards, *little* witches."

Dolores put a hand on her hip and straightened to her full height. She gave him a false smile. "I would have destroyed your *little* wards in about an hour," she countered.

"Yeah," offered Ruth, a confident swing to her hip. "Wasn't even that hard to break one."

Silas smiled, showing teeth, and positioned himself next to the gurney, his leather pants creaking. "So you fully admit to tampering with evidence?" He smiled at the thwarted expressions on Dolores and Ruth. "That's an arrestable offense."

"So are the clothes you're wearing," I shot at him. "Mötley Crüe called. They want their leather pants back."

Marcus snorted. Too bad he hated me right now because there was no bigger turn-on than when a guy thought *I* was funny.

But Ruth's panicked expression sobered me right up. She was terrified that we couldn't help Beverly and that perhaps we'd be joining her.

"Laugh all you want," said Silas, his expression condescending. "But I have the power to arrest *all* of you if I want. You tampered with my wards. Only the guilty would want to do that. Interfering with an ongoing investigation? Well, that's your one-way ticket to Grimway Citadel. To take down all of the Davenport witches?" His face twisted in a nefarious delight. "That's a real promotion."

Yup. I really, really hated this guy. Guess I cut off the wrong part on the wrong bastard.

Marcus uncrossed his arms and stepped to put himself right in front of Silas. "No one is arresting anyone."

The tatts on Silas's neck shone brighter until they looked like burning coals. "You can't stop me this time, Chief. Especially since you seem to be *involved*."

The chief clenched his jaw. "Involved?"

"Letting these witches do whatever they want," answered Silas, a slight tightening to his eyes. "Helping them cover up murders? Well, when this is over, I'll have your job too, I think. Better yet… I know I will."

Marcus inched closer until his nose was nearly touching Silas's forehead. Yeah. He was taller and nearly two times thicker. "Is that a threat?" growled the chief, his voice tinged with amusement.

Silas never stopped smiling. "It is."

Silas's gravediggers pushed off the wall and came to stand on either side of him. Marcus never even moved a muscle. Except that his smile twerked his lips like he was enjoying himself. I could also read that exciting tension rolling off his body and see the muscles of his neck and shoulders contract. He wanted to fight him. The wereape wanted to take on the witch.

Oh boy.

There was nothing I'd enjoy more than the sight of Marcus ripping off his clothes and then pounding Silas's head into the ground. But if he fought the MIAD agents, I was pretty sure he'd lose his job.

Damn. The last thing I wanted was for Marcus to lose his job. Our relationship might be over, but I knew the wereape was doing the best he could to help Beverly. Now us. I wasn't going to let him ruin his career over this.

Dolores and Ruth both shot me worried looks like it was up to me to do something as though I was supposed to be in control of the wereape. I really wasn't. But someone had to stop this before it got out of control.

"Marcus isn't involved," I said, adrenaline scouring through me and making my pulse jump. "This is all me. All of it. Just me." Yeah, I'd take all the blame. This was my idea after all. I wouldn't let my aunts take the fall or Marcus. I'd never be able to forgive myself if Marcus was fired because of me.

"That's right," said Ruth as she moved to stand on my right, surprising me. "We did this."

"We did," agreed Dolores, stepping to my left. "Marcus was on his way to show us out. His only crime was doing his job."

Silas laughed, his eyes alight. "You expect me to believe that?" A snarl of anger touched his voice.

"It's the truth," I shot back.

But Silas wasn't paying any attention to me. His dark eyes flashed with fury. "Where is she?" he growled at the chief, spit flying from his mouth. His fingers were splayed out on either side of him, readying some spell no doubt. If he spelled the chief, I was going to lose it.

"Who?" Marcus shifted his body a little, a predator's stance.

Silas's face twitched into an ugly grimace. "The Davenport witch. She's not in any of the holding cells. Where is she?"

My aunts and I exchanged a look. What the hell? Beverly wasn't even here?

"I assure you that Beverly Davenport is indeed in holding." Marcus's voice was calm despite the primal threat his body was giving off.

Damn, he was hot. *Focus, Tessa. Focus!*

Silas made an ugly noise deep in his throat. I could see sweat forming on his brow. "She's not here. Where is she!" he yelled, losing some of his cool composure.

Clever, clever Marcus. He'd hidden her away. He knew Silas would eventually come and try to take her. But if he didn't know where she was, he couldn't.

My chest swelled with emotion. God, why did he have to be so goddamn nice?

Silas made a nasty noise in his throat. "Doesn't matter. I'm going to find her. And when I do, her life is over." His dark eyes moved past Marcus and settled on me. "And then I'll be coming for you."

I hooked a thumb at myself. "Me? Bring it on, pants."

"Ladies, I think it's time you leave," warned the chief. He was looking at Silas with a smile, like a cat who ate the chipmunk. "I'll take care of this. You should go now."

The last thing I wanted was to leave Marcus alone with three witches. But I had a finger in my pocket—a finger that needed to tell a story.

I opened my mouth to tell him to call me later, only to realize there would be no call from him later. A feeling of loss rose to squeeze around my lungs.

"Come on. Let's go." Pushing down that little crack in my heart, I whirled around and ushered my aunts out of the morgue with me.

I'd deal with my heart later. Too many unanswered questions required my full attention.

But the one question that dominated them all was, if Beverly wasn't in Marcus's lockup, where the hell was she?

CHAPTER
23

I stared at the severed finger resting on a white plate with painted pictures of pink kittens. I wasn't sure what was more disturbing, the dead guy's finger or the fact that someone thought adding pink kittens to a plate was a good design choice.

"The pink kitties are freaking me out," grumbled Hildo, sitting on the kitchen table and eyeing the plate like it was about to sprout legs and run off.

"Really?" Ruth smiled down at the plate. "I think they're cute. It's why a bought a whole set. Makes me happy when I look at them." Ruth rubbed a finger over one of the kittens' faces.

"Here, kitty, kitty." She laughed while Hildo frowned at her, his tail whipping behind him in irritation.

"Who cares about the stupid plate." Dolores let out a frustrated sigh as she finished drawing a rune on the table with a piece of chalk. "There. It's done. Are you all ready?"

"Ready," I replied, and Ruth nodded.

My gaze traveled over the table. Runes and sigils of intricate designs were scrawled over the table's surface, circling the plate with Nathaniel's finger.

My chest twisted. I felt a little ill about what we were about to see. If it worked, we were going to witness Nathaniel's last moments. That's not what disturbed me. What disturbed me was seeing what he did to Beverly, seeing her pain and suffering, the fear on her face as the man she thought cared for her wanted her dead.

This spell was the only way to know what Silas had on Beverly. Before we could help her, before we could go forward with anything, we needed to know what that was. I just hoped it wasn't as bad as I feared it would be.

I cast my gaze around my aunts. Their faces were drawn with dark shadows under their eyes. Dolores's tall frame hunched in exhaustion, her eyes traveling over an old book bound in red leather set precisely next to the dish. The pages were yellowed with age and edged in gold foil.

With a match, Ruth lit the last of the candles on the table placed strategically next to each rune. When she was done, she rubbed her eyes and shook her head like she was trying to stay awake. And no wonder. The clock on my phone said it was one in the morning, and we hadn't even taken a break yet. We were all exhausted.

A wave of dizziness hit me, and I grabbed the edge of the table to steady myself before my aunts noticed anything. Guess the effects of being attacked by the demon yesterday were now taking their toll on me. My father's blood had helped a great deal, but I wasn't immortal. I needed to rest and let my body recuperate. But I couldn't.

"Here." Ruth held a fat chocolate chip cookie at me. She broke it in half and gave me one piece. "You've got low blood sugar. I can tell. Eat this. It'll give you a little boost and make you feel better."

"Thanks." I shoved half the cookie in my mouth while Ruth ate the other. After I swallowed, I immediately felt better, more alert, more energized. The constantly growing aches and pains were gone.

Loved my little Ruth.

Dolores removed her reading glasses and looked at me. "This is going to be *extremely* unpleasant," she said, her brows etched in worry.

"I know. I'll never be able to *unsee* what I see tonight," I answered.

"I just want you to be prepared. Ruth and I… well… we were there. We know what happened. Most of it is just a blur. It happened so fast. If that Silas says he has evidence that incriminates Beverly, maybe we missed something. Something we don't remember."

"I try to forget," said Ruth. "It was awful. I still get the nightmares," she said and wrapped her arms around her middle, her body shaking at the memory.

The three of us were silent for a little while.

"Will the finger be enough?" I asked.

"We're about to find out. Let's begin," instructed Dolores. She looked at us and added, "Do you both remember the see-beyond spell?" When we both nodded, she let out a breath and said, "Then, let us begin."

"In this darkest hour," we chanted together, "we call upon the goddess and her sacred power. Reveal to us what can't be seen and show us the unseen. Give us sight through the night you died, show us the faces that cannot hide."

I felt the magic gathering at once. The air hummed with a buzz of energy as the power of the elements soared through our kitchen. The candles flickered as a gust of wind whipped around and then settled. After a flash of light, a wave of golden illumination flooded over the table to the runes, lighting them as though they were on fire.

And then something disturbing happened.

Nathaniel's finger rose about twelve inches in the air from the kitty plate and began spinning. Like a top, the severed finger spun on its axis. The dull, dead gray color of the finger blazed into a fiery red color, and then multicolored rays of fractal light shot out of the finger, weaving a web throughout the kitchen.

And then the images came flooding in.

To say I wasn't prepared for that was an understatement.

Like a movie projector, the finger shot out beams of color that coalesced into images around the kitchen. Unlike a movie screen, the projected images weren't flat but more three-dimensional and see-through, like a hologram.

Images and silhouettes molded into recognizable shapes. A figure moved and turned. It was Beverly.

It hit me. We were seeing through Nathaniel's eyes, seeing what *he* saw.

Holy crap. I was seriously impressed… and a little freaked out.

Beverly stood in her black bra and underwear. She lifted her hands, tears running down her face with a look of pure terror in her eyes as she backed away from us, from Nathaniel. I could vaguely make out shapes and walls, a chair, a bed. I realized this must be that hotel room.

Did I forget to mention there was audio? Yeah. In surround sound.

"Get away from me, you bastard!" cried Beverly as she ran across the room.

A hand shot out. Must have been Nathaniel's, though we couldn't see his face. A blur of movement, and his other fist connected with the side of Beverly's face. She went limp and he caught her.

"Mother fu—"

"Shhh!" snapped Dolores.

I clamped my mouth shut and watched as Nathaniel carried Beverly in his arms and dropped her on the bed. Then he climbed over her and pinned her arms with his hands.

At that moment, Beverly's eyes snapped open. They widened in fear at whatever she saw on his face.

My skin riddled in goose bumps as Beverly's terrified scream filled the kitchen. She kicked and screamed, and then her cry shut off abruptly as Nathaniel's hands wrapped around her throat. Her face contorted, and her beautiful green eyes bulged as she desperately tried to breathe.

Instinctively, I shot forward toward the images, only to find Dolores's iron grip on my arm, pulling me back.

I watched horrified as my Aunt Beverly fought for her life. The bastard was choking her to death. Then he released his hold and the image moved. We saw a glimpse of the hotel door, as though Nathaniel had heard something. He turned back around. Beverly had a table lamp in her hand and with a powerful strike, she hit him.

Then the images flickered and faded until nothing was left. With a sudden whoosh of energy, we heard the soft tap of Nathaniel's finger hitting the kitty plate.

"What?" I looked around the kitchen. "That's it? That can't be it? There's got to be more. Do it again."

Dolores shook her head. "That's it, Tessa. There is no more. If there was, we would have seen it. That's it."

I couldn't stop shaking. "But… it makes her look…"

"Guilty," commented Ruth, her mouth pinched tight. "It makes her look like she killed Nathaniel with that lamp."

Cauldron save us. It's what Silas had. It was why he was looking to arrest Beverly and looking so smug about it.

"But what about you? You came in there to save her. Where's that feed, that part? The part where he tried to kill you both?"

Ruth shrugged. "Spells don't always work the way we want them to, and we don't always know why. It could be because Beverly hit him."

Dolores slammed her spellbook shut. "When we came in, he wasn't unconscious anymore. Beverly was."

I slumped into the nearest chair. "But we do see that he was trying to kill her. She was trying to fight him off. She was fighting for her life. And then she hit him. Anyone in her place would have done the same. If anything, it was self-defense."

"Maybe. But it could also be construed as involuntary manslaughter." Dolores turned around and rested her behind on the table. "Nathaniel did let go of Beverly's neck. Then she hit him. I don't know what angle the agent is going to use, but this is enough for a conviction. He has a strong case."

A strong case. I stared at the finger, recalling what Marcus had said about Nathaniel and types like him. I sat straighter. "Wait a minute," I said, my heart pounding. Before I knew what I was doing, I grabbed the severed finger. "How far back can we go?" I asked, pointing it at Dolores.

Dolores made a face and moved away. "Don't point that thing at me."

"It's a finger," said Ruth.

"No. Ya think," Dolores growled. "Here I thought it was a kitten."

"Can we stop with the kitty jokes," grumbled Hildo. "I don't feel so good."

"Seriously," I asked, wiggling the finger like it could have been a wand. "Can we go further back into Nathaniel's psyche? Like maybe a day or two. A week?"

Dolores cocked a brow. "Yes. I don't see why we couldn't. But why?"

My pulse rose with excitement. "It's because of something Marcus said. He told me he was going to build a case against Nathaniel. That types like him, psychopaths, have a history. He said there could be others. *Other victims*."

I saw a light-bulb moment flash in Dolores's eyes. "Yes. Yes, of course. If we can find one or more victims…"

"Then we can argue that Beverly was fighting for her life. And there's our proof. There's our case."

Her face set in determination, Dolores whipped back around the table. "Tessa?"

"Yes?" I stood, feeling good about this.

"Please put the finger back."

"Oh. Right." I laughed and dropped our only hope to save Beverly back onto the kitty plate.

"How far back should we go?" asked Ruth with a frown, but her voice sounded excited. "How will we find the other victims? Do we need to work another spell?"

"It's the same spell with just a few minor adjustments," replied Dolores. "We use the word victims. We only need to change the '*give us sight through the night you died*' part of the spell to, '*give us sight to all your victims before you died.*' It will work."

And then together once more, we uttered the spell.

"In this darkest hour," we sang, "we call upon the goddess and her sacred power. Reveal to us what can't be seen, and show us the unseen. Give us sight to all your victims before you died. Show us the faces that cannot hide."

Same as before, energy soared, and Nathaniel's finger spun around in midair, showering us with images, voices, and horrors I wasn't expecting.

I'll skip past the gruesome visuals. Trust me, you don't want to know what I saw.

There were *many* victims as we watched Nathaniel's life flash us by, literally, jumping from victim to victim as it skipped years and months. From beside me, I heard Ruth gasp a few times and a sniffle from Dolores. We were standing in our kitchen, watching the faces of many terrified female victims before their untimely deaths. I could never unsee their faces or the way the light had gone out of their eyes.

Thirty-nine victims. Thirty-nine women had died at the hands of Nathaniel. I was glad the bastard was dead. If he wasn't, I'd hunt him down and kill him myself.

Shaking, and tasting bile in my mouth, I looked at my aunts. "We need to show this to Marcus right away," I added, seeing as this was a spell that would need to be performed again. "It's enough to get Beverly off the hook. I'm sure of it."

"Call him," encouraged Ruth.

This wasn't the time to fuss over my issues with the wereape. He was the town chief after all. I had to make that call.

Yanking my phone out of my pocket, I tapped Marcus's number and waited. "It's going straight to voice mail. I'm going to text him a nine-one-one. Tell him that we have proof and to call back." I had no idea if he'd see it, but it was worth a try.

"This can't wait," Dolores said, her voice panicked as she paced around the table. "You heard Silas. He's going to find her. And then it might be too late. He'll have her shipped off to Grimway Citadel, and we'll never see her again. Once they're in, it's nearly impossible to get them out."

Ruth was shaking her head like a stubborn child. "No. Not Beverly. We have to find Marcus."

"You're right," I agreed. "We need to give Marcus the finger," I said, making Hildo chuckle. Yes, I knew how that sounded.

The sooner Marcus was made aware of Nathaniel's serial killer ways, the sooner Beverly could be back home with us.

Breathing fast, I reached out and grabbed the finger. I barely noticed the cold, rough, dead skin touching my own. I guess I was getting used to handling dead things. "Okay. I need a—"

The door to the basement burst open.
I jerked, nearly dropping Nathaniel's finger.
And my father fell out.

CHAPTER

24

"**D**ad!"

I sucked in a breath and rushed over to the fallen demon, fearing the worst.

But my father stood up and strolled into the kitchen as though he hadn't fallen over a moment ago. Straightening his light gray jacket, he said, "Sorry. Missed a step. I was coming to tell you—" He glanced at my hand. "Is that a finger?"

I glanced down at Nathaniel's finger clutched in my hand. Strange that I'd forgotten I was holding a finger from a dead guy. "It is." I moved to the kitchen, pulled open one of the bottom drawers, and yanked out a transparent ziplock bag. I dropped the finger in the bag, zipped it closed, and stuffed it in my jeans' pocket.

A smile lit my father's face and he laughed. "You witches still surprise me. And they say demons are the diabolical ones." He looked at my aunts. "Hello, Dolores. Ruth. I'm sorry to barge in like this, and at this late hour. But you seem to be…" His eyes traveled to the table. "Busy with late-night spelling with fingers, I see."

"You know you're always welcome, Obiryn," said Dolores.

"Can I get you anything?" offered Ruth. "Coffee? Tea?"

"I'm fine, thank you." He raked his fingers through his graying hair, and when his silver eyes met mine, he smiled. Only, it looked… forced.

I searched his face. "What's happened? You talked to Vorkan. Didn't you?" He looked paler than usual, drained like he hadn't slept for a while. A tightness lay in his features, and the wrinkles around his eyes creased. Was this because of the blood he gave me? Was he weaker now because of it? Because of me?

A glimmer of emotion swelled and then died in his eyes. "Vorkan knows you're alive," he said.

"I figured he would."

The lines around my father's eyes deepened. "I tried to talk him out of it, but once he's set into motion, there's no stopping him. He takes every single contract very seriously. Extremely infuriating. Very unpleasant chap. He won't even take a bribe."

"Thanks for trying." I didn't know what my father offered the demon hit man, but I was pretty sure it was something significant. Still, Vorkan had refused. The bastard still wanted to kill me. Was anything worse than having a demon hit man after you? Not really.

Despite this real threat to my very existence, it wasn't going to slow me down. The only thing that was going to stop this was if *I* killed him. It was kill or be killed. And I wasn't ready to die. Not for a very long time.

I caught sight of Hildo. The black cat was on the table, knocking down one candle at a time, as though we didn't see him. I shook my head. Cats.

My father scratched his jawline, his neatly trimmed beard making rasping sounds under his fingernails. "I might not have succeeded this time to convince him. But I'm not done with him. I won't stand around and do nothing while my only daughter's life is in danger because of me."

"Don't say that." I felt a tug on my insides at the emotion in his voice. "You didn't make up the rules. It's not your fault your demon community decided to off me because I'm not a pureblood demon."

"I can still make this right," said my father. "If I can't persuade Vorkan, I need to reach the council and find out who put a hit on you in the first place. Get them to put out a reprieve. It might take a few months, but I think I can manage to persuade them."

"A few months?" Ruth looked at me, eyes round.

My father dipped his head in thought. "More like a year."

"A year!" exclaimed Dolores.

My father's brows rose in thought. "Demon bureaucracy. It takes months to get an appointment. And these matters don't just get resolved after one meeting. It'll take time. With several different meetings. It'll be long, yes. But it's the only way."

A year of looking over my shoulder every time I wanted to leave the house at night was a real nightmare, but I couldn't think about myself right now.

"It doesn't matter." I sighed heavily. "Right now, I've got bigger problems."

My father gave me a pointed look. "Bigger than your life?"

"It's Beverly," I said. "She's in trouble."

My father glanced around the kitchen, only realizing now that one of my aunts was missing. "What happened to her? Is she all right?"

"If you think all right is being locked away in some prison, you'd be right," replied Dolores.

My father's eyes narrowed in anger. "Beverly's in prison? Why? What happened?"

"A lot happened," I answered. "She's being charged with murder she didn't commit. Her only crime was to date a serial killer witch. She's not in prison yet. The chief has her hidden somewhere safe."

"For now," added Dolores.

My father pursed his lips. "Well, I'm sorry to hear that."

"Which is why we need to leave." I patted my father on the arm, seeing as I wasn't much of a hugger, and I didn't think we were quite there yet. "Keep me posted on the Vorkan thing."

My father reached out and grabbed my arm. "You can't leave this house. Vorkan is out there… waiting for his chance to kill you. Don't make this easy for him."

I wiggled out of my father's grasp. "I get that you're worried. I really do. But I'm not just going to sit here while Beverly's life is at stake."

"What about yours?" My father's expression turned harsh. "Doesn't your life mean anything?"

I pressed my hands on my hips. "You can't keep me from going."

My father shook his head, clearly realizing that he couldn't talk me out of this. "Stubborn. Just like your mother."

Dolores snorted. "He's right about that."

My head was pounding. "I need to do this—
"

The sound of the front door crashing open interrupted my train of thought. A moment later, Iris and Ronin appeared in the kitchen.

"It's Marcus," said Iris, rushing over to me, her face flushed and her brown eyes wide.

My heart gave a jolt. "What about him?" I might not be his favorite person right now, but it didn't erase the feelings I had for him, which were rising at a faster pace than I was accustomed to.

"Silas arrested him," said Ronin.

"Cauldron help us," exclaimed Ruth, reaching out to stroke Hildo's head for comfort.

Dolores clasped her hands around the backrest of one of the kitchen chairs for support, looking like she was about to be sick.

It took a second to wrap my head around what Ronin had just said. "He can't do that." Could he?

Iris tucked a strand of black hair behind her ear. "He did. Apparently, he ranks higher than Marcus. I had no idea."

"But why did he arrest him?" I had some thoughts, but I wanted to hear it from them.

Iris was shaking her head. "Because he refused to tell Silas where Beverly was. Says Marcus was obstructing the investigation or something stupid like that."

Shit. This was much worse than I'd expected. "But… how do you know all this?"

Iris glanced at Ronin before answering. "I felt bad about losing the tail on Silas. So, we went to the morgue to see if you were still there. And that's when we saw Silas hauling Marcus down the hallway. His hands were cuffed behind him. He didn't look that upset—Marcus, I mean."

"The dude was smiling," said Ronin, with his grin twisting up his face. "Totally pissing off the other guy. Color me impressed, but I have a new appreciation for the chief."

"I bet he was." No doubt those cuffs weren't much of a constraint for the wereape. If he thought this was funny, we were going to have a serious talk later.

Ronin stuffed his hands in the front pockets of his jeans. His eyes flicked to my father, and I saw his nostrils flare, as though he'd recognized the demon scent.

Both Iris and Ronin were giving my father covert glances, which was really cute in a way. "Guys," I said and raised my hand toward my dad. "This is my father. Obiryn. Dad. These are my friends, Iris and Ronin."

My father's face transformed into a pleasant smile. "It's nice to meet you both."

Iris gave him a shy, little wave. "Hi," she said while Ronin gave my dad a nod in way of greeting.

Okay, now that the introductions were over, I still needed to find Marcus. "Where is he now?" We still had to show him what we'd discovered about Nathaniel. More importantly, we needed to bust him out.

Iris's face went stiff. "Silas put Marcus in his lockup."

"And Silas?" I said, remembering that gray door right across from Marcus's office where Dolores had pointed the holding cells were.

"He was still there when we left," answered Ronin. "He might still be there. Two witches were with him."

I nodded. "We've met."

Iris paused and looked at Ronin. Something crossed over her features that I didn't quite catch.

"What is it?" I asked, not liking the way Iris's face was pulled tight, like she had something else to tell me but wasn't sure how to break it to me.

Iris opened her mouth and closed it again.

"They're torturing him," blurted Ronin, coming to Iris's aid. "The bastard is hurting the chief to get him to talk."

"They're hurting Marcus?" Ruth's face was flushed with anger. "But they can't do that."

"Apparently, they can," said Dolores, her long face set in a hard cast.

"W-we heard…" said Iris. "We heard the chief scream right before we were out the door. It was bad, Tessa. Really bad."

Her words shocked me, and something dark and deep inside my core raged. "He's dead." I stifled the fury for just a moment. "We still need to show Marcus the evidence."

"You've found evidence?" Iris's voice was hopeful.

I nodded. "We did. It'll be enough to get Beverly off the hook."

"But how are we going to show Marcus?" asked Ruth, looking both angry and defeated. "They've got him locked up. I don't think they'll let us see him."

"Then I'll just have to break him out." I thought about it a moment. "You and Ruth will distract Silas and his buddies," I told my aunts. "He wants Beverly, right? So you tell him that she wants to come clean and that you'll take him to her. Make sure to get the witches to come too. Bring them here, to Davenport House. He'll buy it. It's the perfect place for her to hide. Right? He's so desperate that he'll follow you. I'm sure of it. And I'll set Marcus free and give him the evidence. I'll perform the spell so he'll see the evidence for himself."

"I've got an idea," said Ronin. "We can hide in Beverly's room. He'll hear someone there, but we'll keep the door closed. That should keep him busy for a while. Give you more time with the chief."

I pointed a finger at the half-vampire. "Great idea." I looked at Iris. "Just... no more great ideas in Beverly's room. Okay?"

Ronin smirked. "You give me a room with a bed, and I'll give you *loads* of great ideas."

Iris blushed, a tiny smile forming on her lips.

I let out a breath. "Okay then. Let's move." I spun around and started out the kitchen.

"I'll drive," said Dolores, grabbing her keys from the wicker basket on the kitchen island.

"Tessa."

I halted at the worry in my father's voice. He'd been watching and listening to our exchange, his posture gaining more and more tension. He looked like he was debating whether or not to body slam me to the ground to stop me from going.

"Don't worry. Nothing will happen to me," I told my father's concerned face. "Dolores and Ruth are with me."

"We'll take care of her," agreed Ruth, putting on a determined manner, though her eyes were red with fatigue.

We were all exhausted, and running on fear and adrenaline fumes. But if Marcus was locked up, our plan of saving Beverly just went up in flames.

"I'll wait for you here, then." My father grabbed a chair from the kitchen table and sat. I

274

wasn't sure that was the best idea, seeing that Silas would be coming this way, but I doubted I could change his mind.

I stared at my father, not knowing what to do with him.

"I've got this," said Hildo suddenly, seemingly having read my thoughts. He walked over to the table and lay down next to my father, his yellow eyes gleaming.

I smiled at Hildo, grateful. "Thanks. See you all later," I added. I glanced at my aunts. "Come on."

Rushing down the hallway, I grabbed my jacket from the entrance closet, pulled on my boots, and faced the door.

"What do we do if that demon's out there?" asked Ruth.

I shrugged. "We say hello." Translation—we kick his ass.

Not waiting any longer, Dolores moved forward and pulled open the door.

I was the first one out.

Thumping down the snow-covered stairs, I pulled on the elements around me as my eyes searched the darkness surrounding the street and neighboring homes. I waited for a beat longer, listening, but I couldn't see the demon anywhere.

"Guess he took the night off," said Dolores, rushing past me to the Volvo station wagon parked in the driveway.

Guess we'd been lucky. With my heart hammering, I sprinted after her and slipped into the front passenger seat.

Once Ruth was settled in the back, I glanced over toward Dolores, who had a mad gleam in her eye, and said, "Floor it."

CHAPTER

25

We got to the Hollow Cove Security Agency in less than three minutes, which involved Dolores burning through all the stop signs while Ruth screamed, "Bloody cauldron save us!"

Flattened against the right side of the agency's building, I watched as Dolores and Ruth made their way inside. I didn't know how long it would take to convince Silas to come with them, but I prayed it would work.

Once inside, I had no idea what to expect when I faced the chief. Would he even listen? Part of me feared he wouldn't, that I'd lost his trust. But this was Beverly we were talking about. And he loved my aunt. I was certain of that. If I knew one thing for a fact about the wereape, it was that he protected those he loved something fierce.

I let out a shaky breath. The clock on my phone read 1:47 a.m. I'd been waiting outside for five minutes. It wouldn't have been a big deal if this was August and not January. Despite my winter jacket, the cold was starting to settle in. The fact that I wasn't moving wasn't helping either.

But I didn't have to wait too long.

The sounds of doors closing brought my attention to the front of the building, and I peeked around the corner.

My eyes first went to Ruth and Dolores who were walking out. I held my breath. Next came Silas, followed by his two witches.

Ruth, doing her best to look inconspicuous, flicked a covert thumbs-up in my direction. Gotta love my Aunty Ruthy.

I watched as Dolores got behind the wheel and pulled the Volvo away from the curb into the street, driving at an extremely slow pace, totally out of character for her. I smiled. That would piss off Silas. And give me more time.

I waited until Silas and the two witches all got into the black SUV and drove off, tailing the Volvo.

If things went as planned, I figured I had about a half hour to break out the chief and show him the proof that would clear Beverly.

But we all knew things never went as planned. So I basically had about ten minutes.

Moving fast, I burst through the front doors and sprinted toward the steel-gray door across from his office.

I hit the door with my shoulder and barged in.

The holding cells were made up of four different blocks, stuffed in a room that appeared too small to contain them.

And the only prisoner was a wereape.

Lying on his side in a six-by-eight cell facing the wall was Marcus. Blood splattered the floor. Strings of red seeped from his shirt like he'd been flogged repeatedly. His arms were pinned behind him shackled with metal cuffs. His wrists were marred with angry red blisters, and blood oozed where the skin had split. He'd struggled. He'd struggled a lot.

Ice rolled down my spine. "Marcus?" My voice trembled. I couldn't help it.

The wereape flinched like the sound of my voice hurt him. He turned his head and I nearly lost it.

His face. Oh my God. His face!

Marcus drew in a ragged breath and blinked open one eye. "Tessa?"

Marcus's face that the goddess had blessed him with was barely recognizable. His left eye was completely swollen shut. Every inch of his face was bruised, and where it wasn't was covered in bleeding cuts.

My throat tightened at the large gashes across his shoulder to his neck. I wrapped my hands around the bars of his cell, trying to keep me from falling on my knees. "Why aren't you healing?" I wasn't an expert on the whole wereapes and shifter thing, but I knew they were blessed with advanced healing abilities. Only this wereape wasn't healing.

"It's the amulet." His body shook, and sweat formed on his brow like he had a fever. "It keeps my beast from coming out. And keeps me from healing."

My eyes found a thin string wrapped around the wereape's neck. I couldn't see the amulet. "Keys? Where are the keys?"

"On my desk." Marcus coughed. Blood dripped from the corners of his mouth. "Next to my car keys. One set opens the doors. Smaller ones for the handcuffs."

I rushed out, fighting back the tears. Silas was a dead witch. They could lock me up inside Grimway Citadel after I'd killed the sonofabitch. It'd be worth it. To think that he'd purposely put a magical amulet on the chief of this town so he couldn't heal while they beat him and cut him deserved the same fate. No. It deserved worse.

Once I found a set of long-looking keys and tiny ones that were probably for the cuffs in his office, I rushed back to the cell to find Marcus facing me and on his knees. If I thought his back was bad, his front was worse.

Peeling my eyes away from his scarred front, I stared at the keys in my hand, blurred by the wetness in my eyes and the trembling of my hands. The keys looked identical, so I used the first one, slipped it into the lock, and turned. The latch popped open.

I kicked the door out of my way and fell to my knees next to the big wereape. Fingers trembling, I grabbed the amulet, which was a diamond-shaped piece of wood carved with the same type of runes I'd seen with Silas's tattoos. Magic vibrated against my palm. It was powerful.

I yanked it off his neck and tossed it across the cell.

Marcus shuddered and fell forward. He took a few deep breaths and slowly pulled himself back.

"He shouldn't have done that." I felt my rage winding up like a miniature tornado in my gut. "I can't believe this is how the MIAD works. This is wrong. What he did to your face." I clamped my mouth shut as my emotions rose, constricting my throat.

Marcus gave me a weak smile. "Nah. You should see the other guy."

My eyes burned at the sight of him. I'd never seen anyone beaten up so badly before. It was

KIM RICHARDSON

one thing to see it on TV and quite the other to see it in real life. I crab-crawled around him and using the other keys, I removed the handcuffs. And yes, I threw them across the cell too.

I dragged back around to face the wereape. Every cell in my body wanted to touch him, to take him in my arms, to take his pain away. But I couldn't. I just kneeled next to him, staring at the man I'd lost because of my stupidity.

"How're you feeling? Better?" My lips trembled and I swallowed hard. The pain in my chest wouldn't go away so I could think.

Marcus brought his head up. "I feel like someone's in my stomach redecorating."

Blinking fast, I shook my head. "This isn't funny."

Marcus shifted. "I'll be okay. It'll take some time, but I'll heal. I'll be fine." He reached out and grabbed my hand. "Tessa..."

Oh hell, the waterworks fountained out of my eyes like Niagara Falls.

Damn it. I was an emotional wimp.

I snatched my hand back and wiped my eyes. We didn't have time for this. "Listen." I sniffed. "There's not much time before Silas figures out that Beverly's not at Davenport House."

"Your aunts were pretty convincing, especially Ruth."

"I take it that Beverly's still safe, then?"

The chief nodded. "She is."

"Good." I searched in my pocket and yanked out the ziplock bag. "This is the proof you were talking about. The proof that Nathaniel is a serial douchebag. He's killed thirty-nine other women."

Marcus blinked, and just then I noticed that his left eye was not swollen shut anymore. He was already healing. "Is that his finger?" He smiled, with blood still marring the corner of those fine lips.

I grinned back like an idiot. "It is. I cut it off."

"I thought I smelled something different on you," he said, and I remembered him staring at my pocket. "But how does this finger prove this? Fingerprints?"

"Better. Using this, we do a spell that kind of projects what the owner of the finger saw before his death."

Marcus looked confused. "So how does that help her?"

"Because we went further back. Years. To the very first victim." I swallowed, remembering the disturbing images and sound. "We saw all those victims. Saw who they were and how they were killed. It was awful."

Marcus took the ziplock bag with the finger from me. "I need to make some phone calls."

I stared at him. "Don't you want me to perform the spell?"

His gray eyes met mine, and my heart did a little dance. "No. I trust you. Plus, you and

Dolores and Ruth all saw this. Right? It's all I need."

"Okay." I nodded, a little surprised at his choice of words.

With effort, the big wereape struggled to stand. I moved to help him, but he waved me away.

"I can do this. You know, the male ego is a fragile thing." His smashed-up face creased into a smile.

He didn't want me to see him weak. He was wrong. This wasn't a weakness. Taking in the sight of his beaten face and body, he'd endured an insurmountable amount of pain and suffering, all without giving up Beverly. To me, that was real strength.

I watched as the big chief opened the door, his motions stiff. I started to follow him but halted, my eyes going to the amulet on the floor across from me. The idea that Silas might use it again on someone else didn't sit well with me. Not knowing what else to do, I rushed over, jammed it in my pocket, and hurried after the chief.

I followed him back to his office where he disposed of the finger in a safe and locked it.

Next, he picked up his cell phone from his desk, and I watched in silence as he punched in a number.

"Yeah, it's me," said Marcus to whoever was on the other line. "Got the proof I told you about. I think we can match it to those unsolved cases I mentioned. Exactly. All thirty-nine."

I raised my brows. Now I was interested.

"You can call off your dog." Marcus paused, listening. "He used an obscura amulet on me. If he oversteps again, you know what will happen."

"Please, please let it happen," I muttered to myself. The thought of Silas getting his head pounded in made me all giddy inside.

Marcus looked at me, and his face spread into a wide grin. It was less bruised, and his cuts had stopped bleeding; some were already healing into fine lines. Guess those were the perks of being a wereape.

"Yeah. I'll be here." He hung up and stuffed his phone in his back pocket.

"Who was that?"

The chief grabbed his winter jacket from a standing coatrack in the corner. "The head of the MIAD."

"And you guys are chummy chummy?" Good to know.

The chief shrugged. "Something like that." He reached over and snatched his car keys from his desk. "Come. I'll take you home. It's been a long day. You must be tired."

A knot formed in my stomach. The idea of me and the chief alone in his Jeep made me nervous. I didn't know if he was going to bring up the fight we had earlier today. Maybe he wouldn't. Maybe he was going to bring up the "let's be friends" conversation.

But as we left his office, I realized then how tired I was. As though all of the day's events just hit me now that all my adrenaline was spent.

We reached the front doors and headed out. Despite the warmth of my coat, I was shaking, and a cold feeling sprouted from the pit of my stomach.

The thought of a warm bed was almost as good as sex with Marcus. Almost. Better if he was in the warm bed with me.

But it didn't look like I'd get my warm bed anytime soon.

Resting lazily against Marcus's Jeep was Vor-kan.

CHAPTER
26

I stared for a few beats at the demon, shaking my head. "Seriously?"

A groan escaped me, and I might have whispered a few prayers to the goddess. Probably not the best response when facing the hired demon hit man, when showing any traces of fear would surely get me killed.

Vorkan pushed off the Jeep slowly. His red eye fixed me with such intensity, it was as though nothing else mattered in the world at this very moment. It was all about me. Me. Me. Me.

Under other circumstances, I would have been flattered.

But not when my ass was on the line.

He looked like he hadn't showered in months, his mess of black hair lay in clumps around his shoulders. The streetlight hit his face, making the scar across the other side more gruesome and angry.

Every fiber of my attention went to Vorkan. His lips moved in a chant, his voice low and steady and strong. A ripple of cold energy stirred the air, swirling around and forming a constant, intimidating pressure over me. Pin-pricks of power rolled over my skin. I knew what that was. I tapped into the nearest ley line's power, and all I got was a big fat nothing. He was doing it again, preventing me from using the ley line's power.

"Is that the demon after you?" Marcus's voice rumbled with the beginnings of a growl.

"Unfortunately. And he just ruined my night." Ruined because Marcus and I needed to have *that* conversation. Needed to have some alone time to work out our problems. And the demon had just taken that away from me.

Yes, I was exhausted. But I was also pissed that he'd taken those precious moments with Marcus away from me.

"And he's here to kill you." A fierce light backlit Marcus's gray eyes. His posture shifted to predatory, and the hair on the back of my neck prickled. It was scary, and if I didn't know the chief, I would have bolted.

"My money's on a very big yes," I answered instead. "I doubt he's here to ask me out on a date or exchange makeup tips."

Marcus swore, and a snarl emanated from somewhere deep in his throat. "Go. Jump a ley line. I'll take care of him."

I glanced at the wereape. "First… he's got some sort of demonic magic that keeps me from using a ley line… and second… you're hurt. You're not fighting him. End of story." His face was nearly free of the evidence from the beating he took. But that didn't mean he was healed. Not when the injuries I couldn't see, the internal ones, were most probably a lot worse.

When Marcus spoke next, his eyes were on the demon who'd positioned himself about twenty feet from us. A wicked smile was spread on his gaunt face as he waited, and anticipation brightened his expression as though he wanted to fight the chief too.

"Wereapes are predators by nature, Tessa," said Marcus, his voice holding an incredible amount of ferocity. "But I also protect what's *mine*."

Hmm. Not sure how I was supposed to react to be called someone's *mine*. Okay, I liked it. I liked it *a lot*.

Heat rose from my core. Passion intensified to new levels. Damn. Talk about being distracted before a fight.

And what came next was even *more* distracting.

In a blur, Marcus stood there, jacketless and shirtless as he yanked off his jeans, and kicked away his boots. I glimpsed a very fit, golden-brown body, rippling in muscles that bulged in places I never knew could *have* muscles. Despite his smooth skin, dark, angry bruises also marred his back. Not to mention the myriad of dark and light, thin scars over his skin, evidence of where he'd been cut. Jesus. It was a web of scars. It was horrible. And a hell of a lot worse than I'd thought.

Before I could stop him, his features rippled, his skin swelling and stretching his body to impossible proportions. There was a flash of black fur, and a horrible, tearing flesh sound accompanied by the breaking of bones.

And then, instead of a man, stood a four-hundred-pound silverback gorilla.

I couldn't help but stare at this magnificent and yet terrifying beast. The muscles on his chest flexed as he stood on all fours, his front hands resting on his knuckles.

The gorilla opened its mouth and let out a terrifying growl, flashing carnivorous teeth the size of kitchen knives.

The two of us at our best, we'd have a fighting chance against the demon. But with me nearly overspent and Marcus still recovering, I wasn't so sure.

Still, I put on a brave face as I flicked my gaze over to Vorkan. "That's twice in two days, Vorky. I'm flattered. But it's also stalkerish and really pervy." I raised my arms. "As you can see, I'm still alive."

"Not for long," answered the demon. A dark blade slipped down to his right hand from inside his sleeve. He twisted it in a carving motion, anxious to be slicing up our flesh with it. "That goes for both of you." He pointed the blade at me and then at Marcus. "My business's not with the monkey. But if he fights me, he's fair game. His head will look great over my mantel. And his fur, well, I needed a new rug."

The gorilla pounded his fists on the ground, agreeing to the terms and acknowledging that he was indeed going to fight.

"Watch out for that dark blade," I told the gorilla, my voice low. "It's poisoned. If you're cut, you might die." I knew Marcus was somewhat resistant to magic, but I had no idea what would happen to him if he was nicked by that poisonous blade.

Guttural words spilled from Vorkan, and I felt a cold pulse of magic rippling in the air, dark and powerful as it wove around us. He snarled, and tendrils of black energy dripped from his left hand. Demonic magic.

The gorilla exploded into motion.

With a fierce thrust of his back legs, he shot forward and rushed to meet the demon. Vorkan flicked his wrist, and a coil of darkness hit the gorilla in the chest. The gorilla staggered, his balance off to one side, and I hissed through my teeth. But then he was shaking his head like he was shaking the demonic spell off. A second later, he pulled back his lips and roared, flinging himself at the demon again.

A cry echoed along with the sound of the tearing of flesh. Marcus the gorilla tore at the demon with an insatiable speed, his mighty body a killing machine on steroids.

The demon howled, and twisted around, shuddering under the gorilla's onslaught with the wereape tearing into his back.

Unrecognizable words came from Vorkan. A blast of black tendrils exploded, and the wereape went spinning in the air, end over end before smashing against a parked car across the street. He slumped to the pavement and didn't move.

I froze, but my eyes were pinned on the wereape until I saw his chest rise and fall. Slowly he raised his head, and his eyes met mine. He was hurt. But with that insatiable fury that burned in his eyes, I knew he'd be back before too long.

I turned my attention back to the demon. "You shouldn't have done that."

Vorkan scoffed. "He attacked first. I'm here for you, but if he gets in my way… this is a fortunate night."

292

"How about you take off your cloak and make this a fair fight?"

Vorkan gave me a wicked smile, his dark magic pulsing in the cold air around me. "It is a fair fight. You're just weaker than me. The bastards always are. I'm here to remedy that. Blood will be spilled. Yours, not mine. Your death is inevitable, and balance will be restored."

A sudden wash of cold in the air set my skin riddling in goose bumps. He was about to curse me with his demonic magic.

I took a step forward, challenging him while spindling my magic from the elements around me. "Since we're having this lovely chat, I've got to ask, who hired you?" My father might not have convinced him, but maybe I could.

He watched me, and his smile became wider, more ghoulish.

"There's always a better offer," I pressed, seeing Marcus from the corner of my eye, using the car to pull himself up. "Name your price." I also wanted to keep the demon talking. The longer he talked and was distracted, the more time Marcus had to heal, so he could pound *this* bastard's head in.

A dark laugh rumbled in Vorkan's chest. "It's not about money."

"No. Looking at you, I guess it's not. Then what's this about?"

"That's hardly your concern," said Vorkan.

I snorted. "I kinda think it is. You *are* trying to kill me."

The demon let out a low chuckle and said, "It's about keeping the bloodlines pure." With a flick of his wrist, Vorkan sent a shoot of his dark magic at me.

Shit.

I tapped into my will and shouted, "Protego!"

A sphere-shaped shield of golden energy expanded over me just as his tendril of darkness hit.

It struck my sphere and then spread over it, like black electrical currents, leaving me in total and utter darkness. The air tightened around me and pressed against my chest. Gasping, I gagged at the choking smell of rot and sulfur.

And then my protection sphere fell.

CHAPTER
27

A searing blast of demonic magic smashed into me, pushing me nearly to my knees. Oh God, it hurt. I clenched my teeth as waves of pain hit and then subsided.

I looked up at Vorkan. His smile said it all. This was just a fraction of what was coming. He was just teasing me. Playing with me, like a cat plays with a mouse, tearing out its guts before it finally kills it.

Nausea hit, and my magic took its payment. On top of the pain, my magic reserves were draining quickly.

The demon was very powerful. But I wasn't done yet. I too had some skill with magic.

"Accendo!" I shouted and flung out my hand, sending a fireball straight for the demon, like a miniature comet.

With a simple flick of his wrist, Vorkan pulled his cloak over his body. My fireball hit and burst into a cloud of smoke.

"This is going well," I mumbled as fear pounded in my chest. Damn that cloak. If I could get my hands on it, pull it off him, I might have a fighting chance. I needed to get closer.

Heart thrashing, I pulled on the elements again and cried, "Inspiratione!" Fractures of red energy shot from my extended hand.

Again, the demon flicked his cloak up and around his body, like a magician performing a trick, and my red energy hit the cloak, fizzled into tiny sparks, and went out.

"Worth a try," I said, not sure if I was telling myself or him.

Drawing himself up, Vorkan whispered in his demonic tongue, his hands taking on a sinister mien. He gestured with a flick of his wrist.

I flung myself to the side, but searing pain flared up my back. Doubling over, I crashed onto the pavement, convulsing. The demonic curse hit, and I curled into a ball as it spread through my bloodstream, burning. My head felt like it was splitting in two. The scent of burnt flesh filled my nose. My flesh. I was burning from the inside.

And then the pain subsided.

296

I sucked in a ragged breath of air, and then another. My muscles relaxed, leaving only my pounding head and the taste of blood in my mouth.

"Okay. Ow." I spat on the ground. The snow turned red where it landed.

Vorkan laughed. "I like you. You've got spunk. But it's not up to me who lives and who I kill." A smug grin split his face as tendrils of darkness spilled from his outstretched hands. "I've been fantasizing about this very moment. Planning how I was going to do it." He laughed. "I'm going to take my sweet time killing you, an abomination."

I blew out a breath. "I've been called lots of things, but *abomination*? That one's the clear winner." My arms were shaking, and my legs trembled as I rose to my feet, barely supporting my weight. My stomach rolled, and I grimaced as nausea set in again.

Vorkan snarled, not in a frustrating way but more like he was enjoying this. Like he was going to win. His red eye shone with magic.

And then he flung his hand at me.

It was a killing shot. I knew it. He knew it.

I also knew I'd never have time to pull on my magic to save my own ass.

Fear hit me in a cold wave. "Oh. Sh—"

A flash of black and gray fur appeared from the corner of my eye.

The gorilla's body slammed into my side, pushing me out of the way, and getting the full brunt of the demon's magic right in the chest.

Marcus fell to the ground. It was that fast. He lay in a fetal position, smoke rising from his body like he'd been cooked from the inside. He was still. Too still. And I couldn't tell if he was breathing.

He'd done what he'd said. He'd protected me.

But now he was on the ground. Wounded, or maybe even dead...

A rage like I'd never known welled in me. I saw darkness. I saw death. I wanted to kill the demon.

Gathering my anger, I turned toward Vorkan and shouted, "He called me his *mine*!"

Yeah. I'd totally lost it.

"Mine!" I repeated, raging like a crazy person. It's official. My mother dropped me on my head as a child.

Marcus had just acknowledged that I was his. I'd never truly belonged to anyone before. Like hell was I going to let him die on me.

Vorkan stared at me like I was nuts. Guess I was. But it worked. He was so surprised at my crazy-ass outburst that it had him immobilized.

And then, I let *my* magic rip.

Gathering my will, and using my rage to fuel my magic, I threw everything I had at the demon. And then some.

Elemental magic throbbed through me like adrenaline, only a thousand times stronger. I planted my feet and really let loose as I shouted, "Fulgur!" at the top of my lungs. The word thundered from my lips.

I unleashed everything I had into it. A bolt of white-purple lightning shot through me, and I staggered.

It hit the demon. Not in the chest where I was aiming, but part of his thigh. Still, it worked.

Vorkan went sprawling back in a blur of limbs and dark cloak, crying out in pain as my magic burned through him.

I'll admit, Vorkan had been at this magic thing a lot longer than me. He was bigger, faster, and more powerful. I didn't think I could destroy his magic-countering cloak either. But if I could *remove* it from him, I might have a chance.

While he was still down, I rushed over, grabbed a fistful of his cloak, and with more strength than I knew I possessed, I yanked it off.

I tossed it away. "Ah-ha!" I said, thrilled at my astonishing skill and strength. I even made a little dance.

But my dance was premature.

He moved so fast, I never had time to react.

A cold, icy pain seared along my left arm. I knew what that was. I'd felt it before.

I stared at the blade in Vorkan's hands, stained with red at the tip and along the side. My blood.

The bastard demon had cut me—*again*.

And this time, I didn't think my father had enough blood to do another transfusion.

"Your father can't help you now," said Vorkan, as though he'd just read my thoughts. "He might have saved you once, but he can't this time. This time, you will die, bastard."

I glowered at the demon, frustrated that he'd gotten me. Fear settled deep inside my gut, fear that I was about to die a slow and painful death. I knew what was next. The nausea. The feeling as though my blood was molten lava, scorching me from the inside.

I took a deep breath and waited.

And waited some more.

I should have fallen over in excruciating pain by now, or at least vomited, or felt something.

But I didn't.

I felt fine. More than fine, although a little tired from the day's events and now from using a couple of power words.

I blinked and watched Vorkan's face. It mirrored the same shock and bafflement as I felt at the moment.

A puzzled expression formed on the demon's face. And the next thing he did was even more puzzling.

He grabbed my arm and lifted my sleeve, his red eye fixed on the long cut along my skin.

"Hey! What are you doing?" I asked, my heart racing, yet I let him.

He let go of my arm, his red eye fixed on me. "Your contract is voided." And just like that, with nothing else to say, Vorkan spun around and grabbed his cloak from the ground.

The demon's lips moved, and a haze of darkness rose around him, coiling like rings of smoke until he disappeared under it. The swirling mist of darkness swayed and wavered. The air shifted, and then the haze lifted.

Vorkan was gone.

"Did he just leave?"

I turned to the sound of Marcus's voice and found him standing behind me. He'd changed back into his human form in all his naked, exposed glory. Not that I minded. No, I really didn't.

"He did," I answered, pulling my eyes away from his perfect abs.

Marcus's breathing was coming fast, but he seemed to be doing rather well for someone who just took his share of beatings in the space of a couple of hours. His eyes fell to my arm where Vorkan's blade had sliced me. The wound was still very visible, even in the night.

The chief's posture stiffened. "He cut you with one of those blades. You said they were poisoned."

"They are."

"But you don't look sick." The chief took my injured arm, turning it over gently as he examined it. His brow wrinkled. "The cut's not deep. You won't need stitches. But you'll need to bandage it up. I've got a first-aid kit in my Jeep."

"Okay, thanks."

His gaze traveled over my face. "The poison's not affecting you this time. I saw him take your arm and look at your wound. He saw it too."

"I think it's because of my father's blood. Maybe the amount of blood he transferred to me was enough to kill whatever poison was used on that blade." There was also the possibility that the volume of demon blood my father gave me made me more demon than witch. But I decided to keep that to myself for now.

"Is that it?" asked the very naked chief. "Does this mean he won't be back?"

"Honestly… I'm not sure." I wasn't sure, but I had an idea. "I think it means… *he* won't be back."

Brow furrowed in concern, Marcus hesitated. "You think there'll be others? Other hit-man demons?"

My gaze flicked back to where I'd last seen Vorkan. "I don't know. But I wouldn't rule it out."

I might have won this battle with Vorkan. But that didn't mean the war was over.

The council of demons was still out there.

But tonight, I'd take this as a win.

CHAPTER
28

I sat on a hard plastic chair, my back to the wall, staring at the large black door to the conference room, where'd I'd been waiting for the past half hour.

To my right sat Dolores and then Ruth, and to my left was Iris. Sitting next to her was Ronin. I was having a serious déjà vu moment of the time when we were waiting outside the Hollow Cove Security Agency's conference room to hear the verdict from the Gray Council regarding Ruth's hearing. Only this time it was about Beverly.

The chief had called me around seven this morning to tell me that there was a meeting with the heads of the MIAD to discuss the case against Beverly.

"You and your aunts should be there," the chief had said. "In case you're called as witnesses. But I'll need one of you to perform that spell that'll show Nathaniel killing all those other women."

"Okay. We'll be there," I'd told him and rushed to wake up my aunts, Iris, and Ronin in the process since he'd slept at Davenport House.

Marcus had driven me home last night. We barely spoke in the seven-minute Jeep ride. We were both too exhausted to have *that* conversation. Still, it wasn't an uncomfortable ride, quite the opposite. We sat in comfortable silence, both lost in our thoughts and both glad this night was finally over.

I was surprised to hear from him so early in the morning. I had to peel my eyes open to search for my phone. Despite the night I had, and only four hours of sleep, I felt good. More than good.

After Marcus had dropped me off at home last night, I hurried back into the house, thinking Silas was probably still there and was now harassing my aunts, or worse. Only he wasn't there when I came barreling into the kitchen. According to Dolores, he'd just left a few minutes before I got there, thankfully. For him, not for me. I wasn't sure I could have controlled my temper, not after what he did to Marcus.

My father also was a no-show, which I thought strange since he was clearly distraught with the idea of me outside of Davenport House at night. But I'd get my chance to speak to dear ol' Dad later.

"How did it go with my dad?" I asked the cat.

The black cat's eyes shifted lazily toward me. "As exciting as watching paint dry."

Okay then.

So far, the meeting hadn't called for any witnesses—said witnesses being us. I'd watched Silas enter the conference room about a half hour ago, followed by Tweedledee and Tweedledum, his homeys. When Silas caught sight of me, his face twisted in a snarl, and his eyes darkened with hate.

So I did the only thing I could. I plastered a grin on my face and flipped him off.

A group of important-looking witches went in next, three females and one male, which I pegged as the heads of the MIAD, followed by Marcus, then Cameron and Jeff, his deputies, who had enough muscles to put Arnold Schwarzenegger to shame.

I glanced down the hallway at Grace, the chief's administrative assistant, but she was busy typing away at something. She barely paid us any attention.

The door to the conference room swung open and I flinched. "Would one of you like to perform the spell?" The chief's eyes went from me to my aunts. "I have Nathaniel's finger ready," he added with a tight smile.

"I'll do it." Dolores jumped to her feet before I even had a chance to open my mouth. "I've already packed some candles and all other elements necessary to perform the see-beyond spell, in my bag. A Davenport witch always comes prepared." She tapped the large, brown leather tote bag on her shoulder.

I glanced over to Ruth who had a smile on her face. She caught me looking and burst out in tiny giggles. We both knew how much Dolores wanted to be *the one* to do the spell. She hadn't shut up about it since I woke her this morning and told her.

"It's our chance for Davenport witches to shine," she'd said at breakfast, sipping her coffee. "Only the truly proficient in the arts can conjure such a difficult and taxing spell." Her eyes had shone with something weird. "I'll show these MIADs never to mess with a Davenport witch, ever again. We are true Merlins. Investigating us was a huge mistake. And I'll prove it to them."

It didn't make a difference to me who did the spell as long as it showed Nathaniel's long line of victims. Dolores was the right choice. She excelled under pressure. She had this.

Marcus held the door open for Dolores. He caught me staring. Our eyes met for a moment, and my heart skipped a bit, and then he and Dolores disappeared behind the closed door.

Iris leaned into me. "Did you guys talk yet?"

I let out a sigh, knowing exactly what *talk* she meant. "No. It's been a crazy morning and crazy night. I'm not exactly sure where we stand now."

He had called me his—*mine*, was his choice of a word. That had to mean he hadn't given up on us. Hopefully…

"I wouldn't worry too much, Tess," said Ronin as he leaned back against the wall and stretched out his long legs. "The guy's into you. Totally whipped."

"How do you know that?"

"It's a guy thing." Ronin dipped his head and blinked at me through his eyelashes. "Yeah, the guy can be an overprotective jerk, and he has really great hair, but he's loyal. And he cares for you."

Gasps and shouts came from somewhere behind the conference door.

"It's happening," said Ruth, her face grim. "They're seeing those poor women. Seeing what that miserable witch did to them."

The memory of all those victims and the way they died was still very clear in my mind. I knew I'd never forget it or forget any of their faces.

Iris reached over and squeezed my hand. She didn't say anything, and neither did I. I'm not sure how long we all sat there in silence, lost in our thoughts, when the door to the conference room suddenly swung open again to reveal a very proud Dolores.

Her face was flushed, but she looked pleased. "It's done," she told us, straightening to her full height of five ten. "Despite the hurried nature of this case, my spell work was exemplary. I performed the see beyond flawlessly. Given my status as a Merlin, and my perfect record in recent years, let me tell you, the Davenport witches will be remembered. Mark my words."

Oh boy. I stood up. "That's great, Dolores. But… what about Beverly? What did they say?"

"Beverly has been exonerated of all charges," answered Dolores. "They ruled self-defense."

"As it should have been," commented Ruth, her eyes rimmed with tears.

I let my head fall back. "Thank the goddess."

"And me," said Dolores, who was still glowing from her performance. I would not interrupt that.

Though Dolores was still on her high of showing off her skills, her eyes were wet, just like her sister's.

As I've mentioned before, I wasn't much of a hugger, but this called for one.

Arms out, I grabbed both aunts and pulled them into a hug. Ruth's tiny shoulders bounced as she sobbed into my armpit while Dolores sniffed on my other side, and I felt her posture lose some of that tension.

I released my hold on my aunts as the door to the conference room opened again. This time, Silas came out first. With his face darkened with emotion, he rushed out and made for the exit but not before giving me one of his truly ugly scowls. I scowled right back at him.

His two cronies followed behind him, but I barely took notice of them. My eyes were on the four witches who came out after with Marcus coming out last.

"This way to my office," instructed the chief as he led the heads of the MIAD around the corner to his office. One of the females was taller than Marcus. I hadn't noticed before. They were all different, some petite, some heavy, but what they shared was age. They were all easily into their seventies.

The chief caught sight of me and gave me a nod of his head. In his right hand was a transparent ziplock bag, Nathaniel's finger resting in the bottom. His eyes gleamed with some primal power. I held his gaze, my stomach doing a few backflips when he smiled.

"So, when do we see Beverly? And who's going to tell her? Where is she?"

I pulled my eyes away from Marcus as he entered his office to find a very distraught Ruth. "I'm sure wherever she is, the chief will make the necessary arrangements. We'll see her soon. I promise."

"Let's go home," said Dolores.

Ruth found her smile again. "Oh, I know. I'm going to make a surprise party for Beverly. Oh! And I'll make her favorite dish—vegetarian meatballs."

Ronin nodded. "She does love balls."

"She probably hasn't eaten, locked up in a dungeon somewhere," Ruth was saying. "We'll invite all of her friends."

Dolores placed a hand on her hip. "You mean all her *male* friends?"

Ruth giggled. "That's true. Doesn't matter that they're all male." And then she added happily, "As long as they come."

Dolores choked on her air.

Ronin opened his mouth to comment, but Iris smacked his arm, hard.

"What?" He laughed as he rubbed his arm. "That was way too easy."

Laughing, we all exited the Hollow Cove Security Agency. I felt like we'd made a difference today. Not only was Beverly off the hook for murder, but all the families of the victims could finally get some closure, knowing the man who was responsible for their deaths could never hurt anyone ever again.

First to reach the exit, I pushed open the doors and froze.

Beverly stood on the concrete entrance walk-way. Her face was fresh, her makeup flawless. Hell, she looked like she'd just stepped out of Martha's beauty salon. Her pretty green eyes were fixed on Silas, who was standing next to his black SUV, which happened to be parked behind my family's Volvo.

I wasn't sure if Beverly was smiling at him because she was contemplating whether he was good in bed or if she wanted to slice off his manly parts. I opted for the latter. Maybe a bit of both.

I walked over. "Beverly?" Where the hell did she come from?

Beverly turned around, her red winter coat accentuating her eyes and perfect complexion. "Oh, there you all are. I've been waiting for you."

Dolores pushed her way next to me, her gaze calculating. "Where were you all this time? You weren't locked up in some dingy cell or safe house. Not by looking at you. And you got here fast, too fast. I don't remember you being *gifted* with ley lines."

Beverly beamed as Ruth, Iris, and Ronin joined our little group. "Me? Locked up?" she giggled. "Darling, the only time a man locks me up is because we're locked in *together*," she added in a sultry voice. She stared at our confused expressions and let out a puff of frustrated air. She pointed above our heads. "I've been upstairs in Marcus's apartment this whole time. And having a *marvelous* time." She looked at me. "Did you know he has the entire *Rambo* collection? I couldn't take my eyes off Sylvester Stallone's oiled, hot, nearly naked body."

Dolores shook her head at her sister. "Are you telling me… that you've been safe and cozy in the chief's apartment while we've been killing ourselves trying to clear your name?"

Beverly rubbed her curves with her hands. "This petite body doesn't belong in a cell. Not unless it's to play Prison Break again," she laughed. "I look stunning in anything orange."

I laughed hard. Maybe too much. But then so did Iris and Ronin, which made me feel like I wasn't losing my mind. It was nice to have Beverly back to her old self again. Good to be a family again.

Beverly pulled out her compact from her purse and started to dab powder on her nose. She then applied a taupe-colored lipstick and smacked her lips together.

"Going somewhere?" asked Dolores.

Beverly snapped her compact shut and stuffed it in her purse. "I've got a lunch date with Gino Costa. He owns the Costa vineyards, and he's recently divorced," she added with a twinkle in her eye.

"You can't be serious?" argued Dolores.

Beverly raised a brow. "Of course I'm serious. I've been waiting for five years for Gino to dump that thirty-something gold digger. It's time to show him what he's been missing all those years."

"Don't you want to take it easy for a while?" said Dolores.

Beverly flashed her teeth at her sister. "*Easy* is my middle name."

This time Ronin burst out laughing. "Sorry," he said, catching one of Dolores's glares. "You guys are killing me."

"What Dolores is trying to say is," interjected Ruth, "that we wanted to throw a party in your honor. Can't you cancel? It would be nice to be all together again."

"Without a murder charge pending," added Dolores.

Beverly shrugged. "Oh, all, right. I'll can put off Gino till later tonight. I'm a little restless after all this. A girl needs a little release from time to time. Otherwise, I'll get wrinkles."

"Obviously," noted Dolores. "Sluts are wrinkle free."

Beverly ignored her sister. She lost some of her smile as she eyed Silas again. "That miserable witch should lose his license as an agent for the MIAD. I can't believe he nearly ruined my life." She looked at me and said, "I can't imagine they'll let him off the hook so easily. Marcus told me a bit about what he did to him. He can't get away with this. Not after what he did to Marcus."

"Oh, he won't. I promise."

Beverly eyed me. "What do you mean?"

My mouth twitched. "Just watch."

Catching both Iris and Ronin smiling at me, I moved toward the Volvo, but I was really going toward Silas.

The tattooed witch narrowed his eyes at my approach. "Your aunt might have gotten off easy, but it won't be the same for you."

"You call charging her for murder easy?"

His smile was wicked. "I'm not finished with you. You won't be a Merlin for long."

"What's he talking about?" Beverly was next to me.

I shrugged. "Don't worry. It's nothing." At that, Silas's accomplices both started to laugh, like I was the butt of the joke. We'll see about that.

Dolores smiled at me before she disappeared behind the wheel of the Volvo. Ruth gave me a thumbs-up and bumped her head against the door before she slipped through the passenger side.

Silas's face practically glowed with glee. "It's not nothing. You're finished."

"Right." I stood facing him. The air hummed with current, his homeys pulling on their magic trying to intimidate me. It wasn't working. "So, that's it, then. You're not going to be repri- manded for what you did to Marcus? I'm pretty sure that was illegal."

Silas raised his chin, his face composed in arrogance, but something like fear slipped behind his eyes. "Don't know what you're talking about."

"Sure. What do I know, right? I'm practically a witchling. And a cheating one too, according to you." I met his dark gaze with my own and felt a little crazy smile turn the sides of my mouth. I dug into my pocket. "Here. You forgot something," I said and tossed a flat piece of carved wood with a string of leather at him.

Silas caught the diamond-shaped amulet carved with runes that matched his tatts easily, with his right hand. Its leather string hung on the side.

He frowned at me. "So?"

The next thing that happened had my gut filling up with joy.

Silas's eyes widened as he howled in pain. The amulet in his hand burned a bright red like glowing coal until it flashed a brilliant hot white. He let it go, screaming, just as it exploded into a cloud of dust and the particles disappeared into a gust of wind.

An angry, deep burn in the diamond shape of the amulet branded the inside of his palm, where his smooth flesh used to be. It looked painful. Good. Very good.

Silas cradled his injured hand. "You bitch! What the hell did you do?"

I smiled. "We," I said, gesturing to my Aunts Dolores and Ruth, "put a curse on your amulet this morning. Now you're marked. See, you'll never be able to use that kind of magic ever again." I clenched my teeth, rage filling me at the memories of what he'd done to Marcus. "Not on shifters, paranormals, or humans. No one. Because if you do, well, the pain will revert back to you. And well, if you think it hurts now… wait till you try that spell again."

Silas's face darkened three shades of red. "You whore! You fucking bitch!" he spat, spit flying out of his mouth as his dark eyes glittered with rage and hate.

I shivered in mock fright. "Yikes. Those are some big words for a not-so-big man. Sucks, doesn't it? When you're the one who's hurting. Not getting the same thrills when you inflict the pain. It hurts. Doesn't it? And it really stinks."

"Yeah, who knew skin smelled that bad when it burned," said Ronin.

"I did," replied Iris, and I really didn't want to know.

The look Silas gave me was pure liquid venom. "You'll pay for this. You're gonna pay. Bitch."

And with that, still clutching his hand, the witch slipped inside the front passenger door the female witch was holding for him. And a moment later, I watched as his SUV drove off, made a left turn, and disappeared down the street.

I grinned, feeling my mood lifting, and said, "Yeah. I usually do."

CHAPTER
29

"I'll get it!" I called out, my stride quick to match my beating heart, as I rushed down the hallway to the front door. My bare feet slapped on the wood floors, and the sound of music echoed around me as I picked up the pace.

When I reached the door, I halted, taking a moment to calm myself. Marcus was the only one who hadn't shown up yet. Not that he'd received a formal invitation. I just assumed he'd be here and would want to see me.

Beverly's case had been dropped three hours ago, and I still hadn't gotten a word from him. No calls. No texts. Nothing.

I wasn't sure what to expect when I saw him again. We needed to talk; that was certain. The thought of how that conversation would go both terrified and excited me. I still wasn't sure if he wanted to be with me.

What am I saying? *Of course,* he did. He said *I* was *his*—mine. Mine. *Mine. Mine.*

To me, that sounded like a mate thing. Being someone's mate was a permanent bond that connected two paranormals together, that depth of feeling that grew every day, an inseparable union. He might have said that this mating thing was passé, an old tradition he didn't believe in. But it sure as hell felt like it.

Marcus had publicly claimed me as his property. Okay, it had been before a demon, but it still counted. No doubt this was a primal, wereape thing and very caveman-esque if you ask me. And I *liked* it.

Sure, I'd made mistakes along the way, but I'd learned from them. I had trust issues. Major ones. With an inattentive mother and absent father, and a string of not-so-great relationships, who could blame me? I'd built a wall to protect myself, to protect the girl. But I was a grown-ass woman now with some serious lady balls, and it was time to smash the wall down. It was time to share everything with Marcus, to share myself, and to trust in him. I wouldn't keep anything from him again.

My stomach tightened as I reached for the handle.

"Gilbert?" I exclaimed, opening the door to find him standing on the snow-covered front porch, wearing a brown jacket, a gray newsboys cap, and his usual sour expression.

"I take it I'm not who you expected?" grumbled Gilbert. "Typical. Witches never..." The rest of his mumbling was lost on me as he lowered his voice. Probably insults, as usual.

"Um…" What was I supposed to say? I thought you were Marcus? No. I was *hoping* you were Marcus?

The goddess only knew why Dolores thought it necessary to invite Gilbert. Yes, he was the town mayor, but I never thought of him as a friend to my aunts. The only reason she'd invite him was that she loved a good argument.

A frown creased his forehead, his brown eyes obscured by his thick brows. "Are you going to invite me in, or do I have to stand here in the freezing cold like a shmuck?"

"Right." I held the door open for him and stepped aside.

Gilbert glowered at me. "You need to work on your manners, young lady. Your aunts, clearly, have neglected your education. I'll have a word with Dolores to remedy this problem."

Right. Because Dolores was the boss of me. But even Gilbert couldn't dampen my spirit. Beverly was a free witch. We had lots to be thankful for. I would *not* strangle the tiny shifter today.

He shrugged out of his coat, grabbed his hat and scarf, and tossed them at me like I was the coatrack.

Maybe just a tiny strangle.

"Really?" I brushed his scarf from my face, but our town mayor ignored me as he strutted into the living room with his head held high.

The living room furniture was pushed back against the walls to make room for a dance floor. An old record player blasted Harry Belafonte classics while Beverly took turns dancing with all of her friends—all her *male* friends. She was positively glorious, with that classic Hollywood star look of Jayne Mansfield. The tall, dark, and handsome man she danced with made her twirl, her white, off-the-shoulder dress with knee-length, flowing skirt lifting to reveal her trim thighs.

Ruth had come through with inviting Beverly's friends. More men were in the house than at the local sports bar watching the football game.

Still, a few female friends had come as well. I recognized Maddalena, the alpaca shifter who owned the Boutique Maddalena, and the two female witches who owned the Hocusses and Pocusses shop, Tilly and Fionna.

Martha was there, her long black-and-burgundy dress swinging as she moved her hands excitedly. Her face was flushed as she barely came up for air while she talked to a small woman whose head was slightly back like she was trying to avoid the spit coming from Martha's mouth, or she was about to pass out.

My eyes found Gilbert again. He'd been here barely a full two minutes, and he was already in a heated discussion with Dolores where the words "gazebo" and "council" could be heard.

Little shit. I dropped his coat, hat, and scarf on the floor and made my way back to the kitchen.

"Hildo, can you get me some ground mushroom wort from my special shelf in the potions room?" asked Ruth as I entered. "I need some for my veggie meatball sauce."

"You bet." The cat jumped off the counter and trotted past me with his tail in the air and made a left to the potions room.

I leaned my elbows on the counter next to Ruth, who was stirring an orange-colored sauce in an iron pot on the stove. "You and Hildo are getting pretty close," I said with a smile.

Ruth's eyes widened in joy. "He's such a treat. Really helpful in the kitchen and with potions too." She let go of her pink spoon and checked her recipe book next to her on the counter, though the spoon kept on stirring.

"I don't get it," I told her, eyeing the spoon and wondering how long it would take me to learn that skill. "If you love having a familiar around, how come you never called one up for you?"

Ruth's smile faded, and her expression took on a sad cast. She sighed and said, "Leo."

"Leo? Who's Leo?"

"He was my familiar. A cat too. A big orange tabby... lovely creature..." She clamped her mouth shut, as the last word came out a little strangled.

I felt a pang in my chest as I exhaled. "And something happened to him?"

She nodded. "He passed away. He was sick. It happens sometimes with the old ones. I tried to save him... but nothing I did worked. I was devastated. I never wanted to feel that kind of loss again. It was just too painful, you know. He was my best friend." Big fat tears fell from her eyes, and it tore a little hole in my heart.

I blinked fast. "I'm sorry about Leo."

Ruth sniffed and went back to her mixing. "It's okay. It was a long time ago." She cleared her throat. "We love our furry babies. Don't we?"

We stood there in silence, and I felt like a giant asshole for bringing that up, seeing that real pain on her face. We were supposed to be celebrating, and now I made Ruth cry.

Something brushed up against my shoulder, and I turned to see Hildo walking past my face with a small leather pouch in his mouth.

The cat dropped it next to the stove. "Here you go, Ruthy," said Hildo proudly.

Ruth's solemn face transformed into a bright delight. She was the only person I knew who had that special kindness that shone when she smiled, the kind of face that was best suited for smiling.

She rubbed under his chin. "Good boy, Hildo. Now. Here we go. Stand back!"

I stayed where I was. So did Hildo.

Ruth snatched up the pouch and sprinkled some brown powder into the mix. There was a loud popping sound, like a crack of thunder, and a cloud of brown smoke rose to hit Ruth in the face.

She batted it away with her hand, laughing. "My favorite part," she giggled. "It'll smell like rotten eggs for a while, but I promise it'll taste much better."

I wrinkled my nose at the rising stench of rotten eggs. "Can't wait."

Hildo lay on his side next to the stove, his eyes full of admiration and love for Ruth. That was a beautiful thing.

A knock from the kitchen back door pulled my attention away from Ruth's cooking. I pushed off the counter in time to see Marcus and his mother standing in the doorway.

Now, I was not expecting that.

Mrs. Durand stood in the kitchen, all graceful curves and poised reserve. She looked just as elegant and imposing as I remembered, though she wore her hair down, which softened her features and made her look years younger. Her gray eyes stood out against her flawless complexion, which was tastefully graced with cosmetics.

And Marcus? Well, he looked like his hot self—a broad-shouldered man with an incredible physique, who stood out no matter where he was. His hair was still wet, which told me he'd just stepped out of the shower.

He caught me staring, and the slow-burn smile he gave me had fireworks set off in my lady parts.

"Oh, hi, Katherine. Marcus," said Ruth happily, snapping me out of my carnal thoughts. "Come in. Come in. Everyone's in the living room. Tessa, can you take their coats?"

"No need." Marcus took his coat and his mother's and hung them on the wooden peg rack on the wall next to the back door.

My blood pressure rose. What was Marcus's mother doing here? She was the last person I'd expected to see, especially after my rude behavior at her dinner party.

"So..." Hildo jumped off the counter and walked over to Marcus to sniff his leg. "This is the guy, eh?" He proceeded to smell his other leg. "This is *the* Marcus? The one who occupies your thoughts day and night. The one you had sex with?"

Shoot. Me. Now.

"Smells decent enough," said the cat. "But smells can be deceiving. I can help." Hildo proceeded to rub his face all over Marcus's pants, adding his scent. "Much better." The cat sat back on his haunches. "Unfortunately, we're in the middle of hosting a party, so I don't have time to do a thorough inspection of this specimen right now. But don't you worry. I'll be all over you later," warned the cat, his yellow eyes squinting into slits.

The chief laughed. "Who's this?"

My mouth twitched into a smile. "This is Hildo. My—Ruth's familiar."

Ruth spun around, her eyes wide, and then she burst into tears before whipping back around with her back to us, her shoulders shaking.

Oh dear.

Hildo blinked at me. Whether he was surprised or not at my declaration, I couldn't tell. Sensing Ruth's emotions, the cat leaped onto the counter and rushed over, rubbing his face all over Ruth's. She laughed, sobbed, and stroked his gleaming black fur, and it warmed my heart to see her joy.

Mrs. Durand stepped forward, and I pulled my attention away from Ruth. She looked chic in her red cashmere sweater and black pants. She smiled and said, "This is for you." She handed me a large, flat package wrapped in red-

and-green paper, no doubt leftovers from Christmas.

My face flamed. "For me?" I took it because that's what you do when people offer you a gift. You take it.

"Open it," encouraged Marcus, seeing my indecision.

Nodding, I tore the wrapping paper away and stared at an exquisite painting of a black horse in a meadow. My breath caught. This was the same painting I'd seen hanging on Mrs. Durand's wall.

"Audrey told me you liked it," said Mrs. Durand, searching my face. "I wanted you to have it."

She wanted *me* to have it? "It's beautiful," I stammered. This woman was full of surprises. "Thank you." I didn't know what else to say. She'd clearly just given me something that meant a great deal to her.

Apparently it was the right thing to say, as Mrs. Durand's face blossomed into a stunning smile. "I'm glad you like it."

"I do." I smiled back, feeling nervous suddenly. "And I have the perfect spot to hang it in my room."

"I can help you with that," said Marcus, and I could hear the intent behind his words. He wanted to talk.

Mrs. Durand seemingly sensed this as well and moved to the stove. "What can I do to help, Ruth?" She folded back her sleeves.

Ruth smiled, a sparkle in her blue eyes. "Are you good with balls?"

I did not want to hear the answer to that.

With my new painting in my hands, Marcus and I left the kitchen and started up the stairs, me first, which was a little unnerving.

My pulse hammered at his closeness, and it sent a spike of desire through me. Plus, I knew he was staring at my butt.

"What happens with Nathaniel's body?" I asked, trying to think of something to say.

"The family sent a team to pick it up. They arrived just before I came here. It was all very hush hush, all very neat and quick. Now that we were able to link those thirty-nine victims to him, Nathaniel's family didn't want a scandal on their hands. They were gone in less than five minutes. No trace that Nathaniel was ever here."

"Basically, they're covering it up?"

"Yes. They just want to put him in their family grave and forget this ever happened."

"I bet they do."

We reached the landing and I entered my bedroom. Crossing the room, I moved to the bare wall between two bookshelves and held up the painting.

"House? Could you help me out here and put a nail to hang this painting?"

In answer, there was a sudden rush of energy, and I felt tiny electrical prickling over my skin as a nail pushed out of the wall where I'd specified.

Since the cold shower and door-slamming incidents, House hadn't hit me with any hostile magic. It seemed Davenport House had finally accepted me back again, though you could never really be sure with magical houses. Only time would tell.

"Thanks, House." I hung the painting and then stepped back, admiring it again. "It's beautiful. I can't believe your mother would give me this. I mean, why would she?"

"Because she likes you."

"I doubt that."

"She does. And she knows how important you are to me. This is her way of acknowledging that and welcoming you to the family."

I turned from the painting and looked at him. A smile hovered over his features, and his gaze became more intent. A thick stubble coated his face, jet black and sexy. My gaze slid down to his wide chest, muscles bulging from his fitted black sweater.

Holy hot cauldron. The man was smokin'.

He reached out and pulled me against him, his big manly hands back at work again as they stroked my back slowly. "I'm sorry for how I behaved the other night. I overreacted." He dipped his head and kissed me, sucking on my bottom lip and sending bolts of energy across my skin until heat pooled into my core. He pulled back, tracing his lips down my jaw and grazing my throat. "It's in my nature to want to keep you safe… to protect what's dear to me."

"I know." A flush of desire rolled through me and I swallowed hard.

"Those words I said… can you forgive me?" he said, his voice tingling through me.

My heart just about melted and oozed out of my belly button. I looked into those fine gray eyes. "Of course. But I'm sorry too. I'm to blame for this just as much as you. I was wrong. I should have trusted you. I should have told you everything. And I'm sorry for that. You're a good man, Marcus. You didn't deserve that."

The chief's smile was sly, and it went right to my gut and tightened. "Keep talking like that and it's going to get you into trouble."

I cocked a brow, though my heart was racing. "Oh yeah? What kind of trouble?"

Marcus's gaze was fierce. "The naked kind."

I grinned. "It's my favorite."

I'd barely finished my sentence as the chief had already crossed the room and shut the door. Then he strode over to me, scooped me up, and threw me over his shoulder as I screamed and kicked out in excited delight.

I bounced on his shoulder as he walked across the room and lowered me on the bed. I didn't care that we had guests or that his mother was downstairs. I needed this. We needed this.

He slid himself over me. "Tonight," he purred "you're in trouble… big, big trouble."

Yay for me.

Don't miss the next book in The Witches of Hollow Cove series!

ABOUT THE AUTHOR

Kim Richardson is a USA Today bestselling and award-winning author of urban fantasy, fantasy, and young adult books. She lives in the eastern part of Canada with her husband, two dogs and a very old cat. Kim's books are available in print editions, and translations are available in over 7 languages.

To learn more about the author, please visit:

www.kimrichardsonbooks.com

Printed in Great Britain
by Amazon

81286248R00202